A Hearse at Midnight

An Abbot Peter mystery

Simon Parke

www.whitecrowbooks.com

This book is dedicated to the magnificent Nicky Auster and
Chris Hesketh – and the rest of the Crypt Gallery trustees.
I do their hard work and creativity no justice in this book.
And as one who's had the honour of speaking there,
I can confirm it was wonderfully warm.
And no one died.

My deep thanks, as ever, to Karl French, for his kind yet incisive editing. Both prose and structure are better for his attentions.

Prologue

Daffodils freeze and shrubs cry. The temperature is unholy, it crucifies all with nails of ice. And there will be a further killing tonight, human not plant.

The good folk of Stormhaven do their best in bitter circumstances. They were bitter before but more bitter now by far, walking hatted, gloved, scarved and hunched. How they long for spring! They long for spring like the watchman longs for morning. They long for the brief hope it brings; for the light, colour and warmth, as if life will now be better; as if from here on, their lives will be fine. But when were their lives last fine?

'I'm ready for spring', they say in a supermarket queue made pale and gaunt by sharp winds and disappointing families, who made such a mess of Christmas. 'Why can't they all just get on? Is it really too much to ask?'

Stormhaven is a littoral town – which, as the clever girl in the tourist office explains, means existing, or taking place on the shoreline, at the edge of things. And the residents are right on the edge tonight. They are ready for spring a hundred times over, ready for change; but neither appear, hope murdered in cold blood – cut to shreds, frozen out, small buds stabbed in infancy, the massacre of the innocents. They call it *The Beast from the East* and sea gulls shiver, rooks cower, flower beds harden and beneath a clear cold sky, ice glistens on the rail tracks to Newhaven. We'll not trust any timetable; no one will escape the town tonight by train.

And the boy – no, he's a young man, finding his way, earning a little, some money in his pocket at last! But he's aware of the sudden cold and it's hurting, like being attacked with knives, like being slashed and cut. Why does he have no coat? Is this a dream? Have they forgotten the coat?

Memories arise. He had been in a car, it's coming to him now, returning slowly. A misty mind is clearing, shocked by the wind which drills through his ears – he had been in a car, he could feel the road beneath him, the bumps and the holes, lying there on the seat; he'd been lying not sitting. Why had he been lying and not sitting? But now he's outside in hell's freezer and he doesn't know where, and he doesn't know how, because he'd been at the funeral, carrying the coffin – he remembers carrying the coffin, steady steps to honour the dead. Yet now, he himself is carried – heaved, lifted and carried, the warmth of another body, he feels the warmth and he can hear the sea and he wants to move but cannot move, this could be a dream and he's laid down – no, dropped down – *aagghhh!* – pain all over, this must be a dream but he can't open his eyes, his eyes are closed and the stone is ice and he wants to wake up. The ice hurts, quite terribly; his leg is tied, someone's tying his leg and the water's cold, the freezing spray, he will wake up and his mother will psychoanalysise everything, like she does; he won't mention the dream, it's too wet.

And he's lying on stone, though it feels like ice and he can hear the sea and he's hurting again, and he wants to wake up, the cold splitting his joints, the water smashing his face, salt in his throat, gusts of frozen air, ice-spray needling his eyes and he wants to wake up. How he longs to wake up.

He longs for that more than anything.

Part One

1

The Crypt Gallery have mended their boiler, which is a huge relief to all.

It had been touch-and-go for a while: always there in the trustees' 'matters arising' – but a decision never quite made as they, like every committee since the beginning of time, weighed cost against life, life against cost. Though in the end, and it was a surprise, they opted for life; Maureen, the chair, is particularly surprised.

'I do believe we can afford it,' she says, though she doesn't believe it at all and is still in shock at the decision. Her jaw is locked in fury and dismay. 'So it's agreed! We'll pay to have the boiler mended and let the minutes record my full support for this decision.' How does she force these words from her mouth? She'll never know; it is a super-human effort. She protects the Crypt's bank balance with the diligence of the Swiss Guard: no one shall pass. There is no 'legitimate expense' for the Crypt – all expense is illegitimate, a bastard's claim. She ran school finances for thirty years, knows all about a 'tight ship' and the sad and wretched end for spendthrifts.

But recent events at the Crypt could no longer be ignored; and those gathered round the fold-away tables tonight know this.

'The recent case of hypothermia?' This was how the revolution had started.

'Hypothermia?'

'During the "African Safari" lecture.'

'Oh that. Well, what about it?' says Maureen. She has more pressing issues to discuss.

'Is it perhaps problematic for us?'

'It happens,' says Maureen wearily, running her hands through her short grey hair. 'Or "Shit happens," the technical phrase, I believe.' She looks around the table; but the revolt is not quashed; they need more. 'Look, we all know it's dangerous to get out of bed in the morning. People are knocked down by cars, they're hit by trees, they fall off bikes...'

'...and suffer hypothermia at the Crypt.' A trustee checks this is also considered part of the accidental universe.

'I'm just saying these things *happen.*' And then more quietly, 'They happen.' Maureen is at her wit's end; the last Swiss Guard left standing.

'I agree it's a dangerous world, Maureen; I think we all do.' There are nods around the table: it's a dangerous world, the revolutionaries do agree. Shit does happen. 'I suppose we just want to avoid hypothermia, *if we can.*'

'If we *can,* certainly.'

'And maybe mending the boiler...' adds another, almost whimsically.

And the whimsy does it. Maureen finally backs down, she falls on her sword, the revolutionaries have the day. Leadership is following opinion whilst appearing to shape it; and there's no question, the incident had been awkward, the whole hypothermia thing. The *Facebook* comments weren't favourable, re-naming the Crypt as 'The Fridge – The Stormhaven branch of Iceland'. But the woman shouldn't have come that night, she obviously wasn't well. What was she even doing out? Yet somehow – and this really gets on Maureen's nerves – *somehow,* she manages to blame the Crypt for the cold, with her hysterical health and safety claims!

The other trustees lack backbone, however; she knows this – two of them are writers. And so the bank account was savaged, (Maureen's view), the boiler mended, warmth restored – and all guests at this evening's historical lecture sit cosy as toast in the ancient arms of the Crypt's vaulted Undercroft; while up at the front, Melvyn Strutt, the eminent historian, does his best with the topic: 'The single witness – should they ever be trusted?'

~

Chief Inspector Wonder knows a car crash when he sees one; and he has seen a few in East Sussex.

Sometimes investigations go wrong. They start off on the wrong foot and never recover, hobbling towards ridicule and disaster. Egos intrude, small empires appear, personal fiefdoms form, lines of inquiry become totems, 'us' and 'them' in charge, information unshared and a fight against crime becomes a fight between colleagues, with truth and the Chief Inspector as casualties. *Particularly* the Chief Inspector – he has to sort it all out and it's a bloody nuisance and the last thing he needs.

And Shoreham *had* been a car crash, with debris still being cleared from the metaphorical road. It even had Wonder looking up the collective noun for egos. There isn't one, more's the shame; though of the suggestions available, he liked 'A scrotum of egos' the best.

DI Shah had made mistakes, there was no question of that. But sitting here now, taking the big view, he doesn't much like Sitwell's performance either. His recent arrival from Kent had been in the cause of 'new policing', whatever that is. He came with a big reputation for 'Face-off Management'. 'Geoffrey Sitwell's your man,' said one head- hunter. 'He's cleaned that place out, top to bottom.' And now he *is* their man, six months into the job at Lewes; but a man with a weasel heart, that's Wonder's take, who seems to like nothing better than to undermine; to kick ladders from beneath his colleagues' feet, imagining that he rises as they fall. And perhaps it had worked for him in Kent, where the sense of bereavement at his departure was minimal. As one delighted emailer said, 'Thank God we've got rid of that shit-shower! Cock-a-hoop here! Best thing that's happened to Kent since Dickens. He's all yours, Wonder!'

He needed to speak with Shah; and he needed to watch Sitwell.

~

'"Testis unus, testis nullus!"' declared Melvyn Strutt at the start of his talk. 'But do you agree, my friends? Well, do you?'

No one in the Crypt knows if they agree, because he isn't speaking in English, and you need to speak English in Stormhaven. (The town welcomes visitors from abroad, no racism here; but they will need to speak the language. The French ransacked the town in the 14th century and some still remember.) There are also some male giggles at the question because it sounds a bit rude, the *testis* bit, which is perhaps Melvyn's intention. He likes the 'controversial' epithet he has acquired; it has some swagger about it, the scent of fearlessness, and when you are small and bald, you need whatever scent you can get.

But Melvyn Strutt, a lecturer at Brighton University, mostly wants applause as he addresses the Stormhaven Historical Society. Round, shiny and bow-tied, he is a man in search of praise, the warming sun of affirmation – though he should be warned, and it's not clear he has been, these things will be hard-won here. The residents do not wish applause to go to anyone's head; so it is usually witheld on health grounds.

And only slowly, as the talk proceeds, and his arm pits moisten, does Strutt become aware of the strangely-shaped man in the second row, lurking in the shadows. He is a man in a habit, some religious throw-back, quaint in his way. Are there really monks in the 21st century? Ye Gods! So he might need to tone down some of the adult humour tonight. Though really, and a different thought now kicks in – what the hell?

What the actual hell? This *is* the 21st century, for God's sake! It can't all be fish on Fridays and Gregorian chant.

Though the monk in the second row sees right through him, this is Melvyn's uncomfortable sense; as if his performance, like wet cloth, is suddenly see-through and exposed in some manner, all artifice removed. And were we to know these things, it's true: the monk does see through him, as he sees through everyone and out the other side. He sees people like we see a filleted rat in the science lab, spread bleak, boneless and bare – though he'd later suggest that on this particular evening, beyond insecurity and pretension, there was not a great deal to view.

The monk, in his sixties, is called Peter and the sixties are the happiest age, according to a survey he read. (Headline: 'When I'm 64 – I'll be happy at last!') But really, what is age? Whatever one's decade, for those who look hard enough, there are ever fresh ways to be unhappy; always good reasons to be cheerless. Like the punishing cold, for instance. His hands still hurt from the freezing walk along the sea front; though he's hardly new to inhospitable climes.

The monk in Strutt's eye line – a former abbot, if anyone asks – is a recent arrival on these shores, dumped here by odd circumstance, after twenty-five years in Middle-Egypt. So he is familiar with the clear-skied freeze of the desert night, when heat escapes the dry air with indecent haste, like a school emptying at the end of a day. It can neither be held nor trapped and 40 degrees of sweltering sun is quickly dissolved to minus 4. It's not the antarctic; but it's certainly coat weather for any night vigil in the chapel or starlit trek in the sands.

But what he is *not* familiar with, or happy about, is this unrelenting drift, this utter endlessness. The desert cold had an end; a proper start and finish. It arrived and then left; it knew its place. Dawn arrived like matron in the Sahara, with a brisk dismissal of the chill. In the desert, the sun rose heavy and hot, pushing the cold aside like a weedy trespasser. But it forgets to do so here on the south coast of England, where the freeze has no end – and the same might be said of the talk, indeed some would say so later; though Melvyn Strutt is doing his best, and John, the organiser, sits happy with his booking.

'I think we can expect him to "Strutt his stuff"!' he'd said a few weeks ago in the society's mail out, which now has twenty-three names on the list – no, twenty-four including his own. *'His subject will be witnesses in court – "Why the single witness is no witness." Controversial, eh?! He'll make special reference to a remarkable court case in the 1800's. It should be great, fellow Historicos! So I hope you can all make it to the Crypt, where I am told they are mending their boiler at last! And it's also really great that he wanted to join us. Maybe the Stormhaven Historical Society is building a reputation for itself!'*

Or maybe John is deluded, think some, and Melvyn Strutt would be among them, for – whisper it quietly – he did not want to come at all. The Crypt is his last resort, not his first.

His reply had been positive. *'I'd be absolutely delighted to come and speak to the Stormhaven Historical Society, John. Sounds like you're doing a great work there.'*

But he's not absolutely delighted; and the scant audience before him is no great work. The Crypt is not where he wants to be – though maybe better than the bathroom mirror. In front of the mirror, he can gaze on himself in full oratorical flight, delight in his mimed performance, a latter-day Cicero; but there's no applause from the glass, no appreciative murmurs, which is a downside, and a significant one; for applause is surely the purpose of life? Without it we wither and die; or Melvyn does anyway.

So here he is at the bottom of Church Street, trying out his talk in the Undercroft at the Crypt – not the real thing, of course, but a dress rehearsal for more prestigous venues, with more seats and deeper pockets. There has been some interest from hotels in Brighton, which is absolutely where he needs to be – Brighton or Lewes. They are going to get back to him, including *The Grand*, which is obviously the pick of the crop. And the *Hydro* in Eastbourne had been in contact today, an email enquiry, which could be interesting. Such a nice young girl at the bar there – *be calm, Melvyn, be calm! And* a free dessert from the restaurant afterwards; they usually did that, fresh profiteroles from the freezer.

But nothing's free here, apart from weak coffee and biscuits; and that's Stormhaven for you in a nutshell. Of course, the cruise ship gig is the Holy Grail for the 'history whores', as he was once described – the 11.00am lecture slot in the Caribbean, with an ocean between him and his family. The feelers are out for that; Melvyn's learning to network. But imagine it! Well, he hardly dares. Appreciation in the Caribbean! Attention in the South Pacific! The perfect circle! And why not dream, everyone has to dream; though nightmares are more common – and there'll be one at Splash Point tonight, a nightmare in the icy spray; some way from applause.

~

'It could be good,' says the abbot casually, after reading John's mail-out.

'The endlessly controversial Melvyn Strutt, of Brighton University, on "The Single Witness – Can they be trusted?"'

He looks out his window, with the smash and shudder of the salty wind hitting it from the sea; it isn't the desert. And he has wondered – casually, of course – if Tamsin would like to attend. 'So would you like to come? I'm going. Think about it anyway.'

'No.' Tamsin doesn't need to think about it.

'I don't know Melvyn Strutt, but John, the organiser – he regards his presence as something of a coup.' And then as background – because Tamsin lives in Hove and wouldn't know John or anyone like John – 'He's a nice man, does his chaotic best. He used to be in Higher Education but lost his job, I think – and he's been a bit lost ever since; always reminds me of a ghost – trying to get back to something, some former time, that I'm not sure ever existed. But he was as happy as I've seen him on discovering the great Melvyn Strutt had agreed to come and speak.'

Simon Parke

'Small fish, miniscule pond.'

'He's a Professor at Brighton University.'

'And that's a waste of space.' There's no room for Brighton University on Tamsin's cultural map.

'But it's his *topic* rather than his position which I thought might...'

'I'm doing something else.' She speaks sadly but firmly; as if this is a great disappointment and one from which it will take a while to recover. But truly, Tamsin can imagine nothing duller than an evening in Stormhaven with the 'great' Melvyn Strutt, however controversial – and anyway, isn't that just another word for 'needy'? Beyond the odd murder – and there had been some odd murders – Tamsin sees only charity shops in Stormhaven: and when did she last go in one of those? 'Pre-loved' may be the new name for 'second-hand' – but it still smells of urine.

'It could at least be professionally interesting,' says the abbot, who, like the Good Samaritan, is still trying to heal her, however foolish the venture. 'It's about the validity of the single witness. That is, can you ever build a case on the word of one person? It's next Tuesday.'

'Yes – such a shame.'

'What's a shame?'

'That I can't be there; still, another time, abbot.'

'I doubt he'll be back.'

Small mercies. They'd both then sat with their wine for a while, with a question in the air.

'So what is it you're doing next Tuesday?' he asks; though nothing so simple should need to be explained.

'I'm standing in my kitchen. What do you think I'm doing?' Peter laughs. 'I just don't want to come. Why would I want to come to some dull meeting in Stormhaven?'

'You don't know it's going to be dull.'

'I do know it's going to be dull.'

'It's in the Crypt. Have you seen the Crypt?' Tamsin shrugs. 'Bottom of Church Street. The Undercroft is wonderful...usually better than the talk, actually. Fourteenth century arches; they think it may have been a wine cellar in its day. And they have a new heating system...'

'I still don't want to come.'

Peter does not press further; his intention is only kindness towards this lonely soul. Tamsin is an early Detective Inspector, almost indecently fast-tracked, with the rails of promotion well-oiled. Attractive and successful, she is also a solitary figure; a detached cottage with a high fence around – and perhaps the abbot is simply trying to save her from herself, encouraging her to join in, like a nervous child taken to parties. But Tamsin likes goals; she likes clear and obvious outcomes – or what is the point? So her colleagues have given up asking her along to post-job drinks. The excuses will vary, but the result is the same – she will not be joining them, with the benefits unclear to her. And this pisses them off, frankly; and they call her a snooty bitch and worse.

'Why do they keep asking me out for a drink?'

'Because they want you to be there?'

'But why would I want to be there?'

'Solidarity?'

'I don't know what you mean.'

'Perhaps sometimes you could just go with the flow, Tamsin. You might find you like it.'

Her laughter is mocking. 'And when exactly did you last go with the flow, abbot? You never go with the flow. You're like a rock in the stream. The flow is around you or against you...but you're not travelling with it.'

Attack is the best form of defence, Tamsin knows this, learned from her father and his occasional unpleasant visits. Give your opponent something to think about, distract them – *unsettle* them.

'When everything has to have a point, Tamsin, and everything has to have a reason and be logical, and nothing can just *be* – well, life is quite exhausting. Can you ever just *be*?'

More chance of Stormhaven twinning with Paris and so she returns to her issue: what exactly would be the point of attending a talk? What would be gained? Was Melvyn Strutt – and really, what sort of a name was that? – was he *honestly* going to tell her anything she didn't already know about witnesses? She'd spent half her life in court rooms! She was a Detective Inspector, for God's sake! And if he didn't tell her anything she didn't know already, then she'd simply have said 'yes' to a dull waste of time, hours of her life she could never reclaim, lost forever in Church Street. For a moment, the thought leaves her paralysed.

'It's bound to be appalling, Peter, you know that.' Peter sighs. 'You *do* know it.'

'I don't know it.'

'You do know it.'

'This feels a little like the playground.'

'You've got a good memory.'

'I don't know it.'

'You do know it.'

'The future doesn't exist, Tamsin.' It is delivered as an announcement; like breaking news. 'Nothing is written – so no one can know. You can speculate the talk *might* be appalling, but your speculation is worth nothing beyond the expulsion of air. Future declarations are for fools....no offence.'

'None taken, I wasn't listening.'

'Such fear of the untutored moment.'

'"The untutored moment?!" Tamsin explodes, Peter shrugs, though not in apology. 'The talk *will* be appalling, I'm just confirming that,' says Tamsin, 'and I know you agree – I absolutely *know* you agree, if you weren't being so pompous. I mean, when did you last hear a talk which didn't disappoint you, abbot? *Well?*' To be fair, Peter couldn't immediately think of one. 'And, I mean – the Stormhaven Historical Society?!'

'Local history mainly...very interesting talk on Blatchington Hill last year.'

She's shaking her head in silent derision. 'Welcome to the *End of the Pier* show.'

'Well, funnily enough, there was a talk on the end of the pier; or rather, the end of the pier *project*. Stormhaven was going to have its own pier – you may not have known that.'

'Yet somehow I've survived.'

'Back in the 19th century, it was going to have a pier like Brighton and Eastbourne. Stormhaven was going to matter to the world, become a source of huge local pride and a generous cash cow to its increasingly rich residents.'

'There must be a "but"'

'Funding got withdrawn.'

'It's a town of "if onlys", abbot – the saddest words on earth; an exercise in managed decline. And who in God's universe calls themselves Melvyn Strutt?'

~

And so the abbot is here alone, Tamsin in her kitchen and maybe others agree with her; maybe she's ahead of the curve, as they say. The Undercroft holds forty if pressed, but no one's pressing it tonight. Whether it's the speaker, the subject or the cold, there are too many empty seats – dark holes in the lecturer's sight lines; though the abbot is gripped as the waist-coated Strutt, with his over-long sideburns, continues with sweat and verve. He's a lecturer, after all. This is what he does. He lectures. He performs.

'So, the question is, dear people: should we reject all information based on one single source? Or to put it another way, can we believe one person's version of events? This is our dilemma tonight. For with only one source, we have no information control, no checks on the information offered. So can one source ever be trusted? Should one witness ever carry weight in a court of law? The world is full of liars, after all – quite apart from you and me. So, the place of the single witness is an issue with a long history – a discussion lasting thousands of years, in fact.'

'Then let us hope for some editing,' whispers James Fairburn, a surgeon at the *Royal Sussex* hospital. 'No talk should be more than two centuries long.'

Strutt continues: 'And the impact of the single witness was never more clearly shown than in the famous case of Elizabeth Canning vs Mary Squires. Anyone familiar with this titanic legal battle?' There is awkward silence. No one in the Stormhaven Historical Society seems to know anything about it; and Strutt is delighted. 'No?' He tries to sound unmoved but truly, he has no wish for knowledgeable competition. The lecturer must be king and his subjects bowed in awe. 'It was the most remarkable case – the subject of much gossip in 18ᵗʰ century London and not a little tabloid fury! Plus ca change, plus c'est la meme chose!'

'Is anyone providing translation?' asks Nick Hallington, Stormhaven's only youth worker. 'Or do we need to put another coin in the slot?' Next to him, the Reverend Ernest Hand, leans over to explain.

'"The more things change, the more they stay the same," he says before realising Nick already knew. He blushes at his needless intervention; but there's also some anger. Youth workers did sometimes play up their lack of education, the reverend had noticed this – as if ignorance was a badge of honour, drawing them closer to 'the kids', when really – why not give the young something to aspire to? Why stoop down to their level when he might invite them to climb up to his? Or was that altogether *too* 19th century – the idea that there's a hierarchy of attainment, that we are not all equal in our opinions, that there actually *is* such a thing as wisdom? In certain circles, the reverend does stand accused of being more *then* than *now*.

'So would you like to hear the story?' says Strutt, bringing the reverend back to the Crypt. There are some embarrassed grunts, indicating that yes, they probably would like to hear the story, though it's so hard to know before it's been told; whilst not entirely happy, the grunts contain this also, at being treated like five-year-olds.

'I was last spoken to like this at Sunday School,' complains Ephraim Fenning, the local undertaker. 'I did not like it then and do not like it now – not in the least little bit.' He speaks to no one in particular, staring into middle distance; though the reverend, to his left, concurs.

'I'm told one can actually die from being patronised.'

'Then hush, friends, please, as outside they freeze!' says Mr Strutt, 'and if you are all sitting comfortably – and more important, *warmly* – the story starts in London on New Year's Day 1753.

~

He's thinking about the tea; he drank the tea – but what then? Though mainly he's trying to wake up, trying to move, but remembering the tea, as if everything started there, as if that was the door through which he tumbled, like Alice in Wonderland, tumbling through a cup, tumbling down, and now he can't tumble back – back to the light and the warmth, he can't get back and the water's beside him, smacking and slurping, like in the bath, the water's beside him and rising, though the wind is worse, and he thinks it's ice, it feels like ice, an arctic swim, slurping and lapping around him, a freezing headache, his head is a–freeze, though he can't think now, and he can't get back, can't get back through the door to the warmth and the light, with salt in his mouth, coughing it out but the salt comes back, a bigger dose and he would love to tumble back through the door, out of the cup, but there is no door, just the cold Splash Point sky, no friend to hand, but a crucifying wind of whistling spite; an avoidant moon that shines but can't bear to look.

~

'So, it is New Year's Day, my friends, 1753 when Elizabeth Canning, an 18-year-old maidservant sets out for a walk. But before she has gone far, she is attacked and abducted by two men.' Strutt has them now, easy in the palm of his hand. 'They are ruffians and robbers, rogues of the first order, an affront to the Tax Payers Alliance, and these wretched men half-strip her, rob her of her meagre possessions and then carry the poor girl off in a carriage to a brothel in Enfield, eleven miles out of London. Could you imagine a worse fate?' Some can. 'But it is here the darkness deepens as Mother Wells, the madam of the establishment, tries to force the girl to become a prostitute, a woman of the night! A sorry tale indeed, ladies and gentlemen!'

Though he doesn't sound sorry, and isn't; for every story benefits from the early arrival of a whore – particularly with the middle-aged men. Lead them to a brothel, and the history just melts in their mouth – it's certainly melting in the reverend's mouth, he adores such tales, all mention of prostitutes who he both wants to save and screw, though mostly the latter. He did have desires, many in the past; and while they lessen with the years as his belly expands, they have not quite died; they still have breath and call out to him in the darkness.

'But Elizabeth Canning,' continues Strutt, 'refuses to be part of such base ignominy.'

Shame.

'She will not lower herself in this manner, not at all! She still has her pride. But then Mary Squires appears. Ah, Mary Squires! She is a hideous gypsy woman, staying in the house – with 'hideous' and 'gypsy' almost interchangeable at the time. She slaps her about, cuts lace off her stays worth 10 shillings and pushes her up the creaking stairs. With a screeching tone, she forces her into the room at the top and locks the door after her. Poor Elizabeth, this innocent, is now imprisoned in an attic with only a few crusts of bread and a jug of water to live on.'

'Another story about my boarding school,' mutters the Reverend. 'At least she didn't have to play rugby on cold afternoons in February and bend over for the maths teacher, as he worked on his angles.'

Ephraim Fenning, undertaker, sniffs a little; the reverend could perhaps learn some discretion. For the undertaker, discretion must be one's middle name.

'However,' says Strutt, 'Elizabeth is a resourceful young woman, so three merry cheers! And on January 29th, after almost a month in captivity in Enfield she bravely escapes through a window and walks all the way back to her mother's house in the City. Such relief! She then reports everything to the police, recounting her terrible experience. Mother Wells, the Enfield madam, and the 'hideous gypsy' Mary Squires are promptly arrested and brought before a magistrate; and not just any magistrate, but none other than the soon-to-be novelist Henry Fielding. It is he who is asked to interrogate a witness to these events – a working girl in Wells' brothel, un-aptly named Virtue Hall.'

There is knowing laughter in the Crypt. 'But now a twist in the plot, my friends, a pulling of the rug from beneath our feet: for Virtue maintains she has *never set eyes on Canning* – 'never seen 'er before, on my life!" she says. So just who is telling the truth? Elizabeth or Virtue?

'Yet Fielding smells a rat, and under pressure, Virtue changes her statement and supports Elizabeth's story. "Yeh, she were there," she says. "Locked upstairs, she were." And suddenly the case acquires legs, Elizabeth is believed and Squires and Wells are duly tried at the Old Bailey later that year.

'Wells is sentenced to be branded on the thumb for keeping a disorderly house – a most painful punishment and carried out straightaway amid a jeering, cheering crowd. But Mary Squires, the hideous gypsy, also found guilty, is to be punished more severely. She is sentenced to be hanged for stealing Canning's stays.'

'I'm sorry!' A voice interrupts from the audience. It is the surgeon again, James Fairburn. He has a loud voice, one used to being heard. 'But is it just me who doesn't know what a "stay" is?'

'Be not ashamed, sir – rather, be proud of yourself!' says Strutt, tucking his hands in his braces. 'You display only a reassuring ignorance of women's underwear!' He enjoys the chuckles. 'But a 'stay', just so we're clear, was the lace bodice worn under the woman's clothes in the 17th and 18th centuries.'

'Thank you,' says the surgeon, boldly. 'I believe I can continue my own research from here.' More laughter, though slightly nervous, which Fairburn picks up on. 'I joke, of course,' he says. 'Let no one imagine the Stormhaven Historical Society is some seedy gathering of inadequate men like the Spearmint Rhino club in London!'

An unlikely confusion, thinks the abbot – though one of the two women present, in the row behind, walks out in protest at the allusion, at the mere mention of the place; she leaves her husband behind. 'It *was* just a joke, I think,' says the abbot, turning round.

'Nothing men say is *just* a joke, not according to her; everything's a strand in the fabric of oppression.' The abbot nods. 'And now she's gone home and taken the car.' He seems more concerned about the car than the offence. 'Do you have a car?'

'I'm afraid not.'

'I'm going to freeze.'

But now Melvyn Strutt approaches the crux of his 18th century drama. 'So, Mary Squires has been sentenced to hang on the testimony of Elizabeth Canning. But Sir Crispin Gascoyne has other ideas. Sir Crispin is Lord Mayor of London. He has sat in on the trial and is dissatisfied with the verdict on the grounds that Squires, condemned to hang, apparently has a watertight alibi – an alibi that places her in Dorset at the time of the alleged crime, and therefore many miles from Enfield and the brothel in question. The court heard from many witnesses to her presence in that county, casting serious doubt on whether this gypsy woman could have stolen any lace from Elizabeth Canning, the present darling of the London crowds.

So who's telling the truth, my friends? Is Elizabeth a childlike innocent, horribly skewered by false testimony? Or is she herself a wily and dark manipulator of events, trying to escape the consequences of secret deeds of her own – falsely claiming abduction to cover herself? A show of hands, please from those who believe her story? Yes, we become our own court here in Newhaven!'

'Stormhaven.'

'*Stormhaven*, precisely – still awake at the back there, extra marks for you! So who believes her innocent? Hands up!' Strutt peers into the gloom. About ten hands are slowly raised, some only to half-way; no one wishes to appear stupid, they could be scratching their ears and the abbot is among them. He is mainly wondering why she would lie, what was to be gained? There doesn't appear a good reason, for this was one almighty pickle she was landing herself in. Why not stay quiet – unless there really was a story to tell? And he'd like to know more about the witnesses for the presence of Mary Squires in Dorset. Were they reliable, salt-of-the-earth locals? Or country low-life in the pay of some landowner, with his own dark reasons for keeping Mary alive?

The abbot starts with belief; especially in the young.

'Truth and lie are such difficult strands to unravel,' continues Melvyn, with a quick fiddle of his bow tie. 'Such untidy threads. The public were strongly behind young Elizabeth. They even stopped defence witnesses physically getting to court. Imagine that! They wouldn't let defence witnesses through to give evidence! But Gascoyne, the Lord Mayor of London, felt differently. Indeed, so convinced was he of Squires' innocence that he appealed to King George II, the inadequate monarch at the time. In those days one could do that; one could appeal to the king, they had no difficult grand children to consider; and the king was clearly in a good mood that day for he granted gypsy Mary first a stay of execution and then, would you believe it? – a free pardon! There were just too many voices placing her away from Enfield and therefore away from the scene of the crime – if crime there was.'

'And what of Canning?' asks the abbot. 'What happened to her?'

'We seem to have a monk in our midst,' mutters the Reverend Hand, with disapproval. It feels like competition and the habit comes across as superior; silently and humbly holier-than-thou. 'Is he unaware of the Reformation? And, more pressing still, is he unaware that the Pope is *burned* every year without fail on bonfire night in Lewes?' Ephraim Fenning, the undertaker, fills him in, briefly.

'He's not a Roman Catholic, Ernest – God be praised. That's Abbot Peter, lives in Stormhaven. I don't think he could afford Lewes. Used to be in the desert, ran some down-at-heel monastery...but a perfectly decent fellow. Odd, obviously – how could it not be so? The desert makes everyone *odd*. But no need to feel threatened, Ernest.'

'I'm not feeling threatened, not in the least.'

'And he's useful to us at Fennings; I can't say he isn't useful. He picks up some of the funerals you turn down, Ernest, so he's really quite a favourite of ours.' It is a criticism of the vicar, of course it is; but Ephraim feels a few home truths might do the reverend some good. He appears to take funerals at his convenience – when a sense of duty might be the better way. Death requires careful, rather than casual, handling. But Ernest, one has to say, offers only the latter.

'As we all know,' says Strutt, 'good news for one is bad news for the other. Think about it: if you get the job, it means I don't. You celebrate and I weep. But if I win the cup, *I* celebrate and you weep. It is the way of the world and good news for Squires is bad news for Elizabeth. She is indicted for perjury and imprisoned in Newgate – less than salubrious accommodation.'

'Good riddance to her!' declares heart surgeon Fairburn. 'Never liked her, anyway. She whined too much for me! Women are always making up stories.'

'Other opinions are also available!' Strutt finds himself in a mine field.

'Only misguided ones.'

'But she was at least fed and clothed by her supporters – and indeed, while imprisoned, painted by the artist Hogarth.

'Hogarth of *Gin Lane* fame?'

'The very same; he did love a cause, Mr Hogarth – though his greatest cause, I suspect, was Mr Hogarth...always an attention-seeker.' A mischievous smile from Strutt. 'Canning, when her turn came, was found guilty of perjury and sentenced, not to hang – she wasn't a gypsy – but to be transported to America for seven years.

'America?'

'It wasn't just Australia who got our low-life. We also gave generously to the States. But guilty or not, she remained a celebrity in this country with huge support; and before leaving, was given £100 spending money for her American adventure, a vast sum raised by friends and fans.'

'Do we know what happened to her?' asks Peter.

'She found a nice American man and got married.'

'I do hate happy endings,' says Fairburn, who had hoped for a troubled hanging abroad, her legs kicking in slow and painful extinction on the end of a rope. I mean, where was the punishment in going to America? He had hugely enjoyed his weekend in New York recently on a medical conference; and he did like people to get their just deserts. He hoped Cathy would get hers. Oh yes, he hoped that very much indeed, something much worse than America for Cathy; and really, anything he could do to help...

'She reputedly had four children in the States,' adds Strutt, 'but never returned to England, dying at the age of 38.'

'Good,' says Fairburn.

'But hers was a case which divided the nation, as it has divided us. The two opposing factions were known as "Canaanites" – those who supported Canning and "Egyptians" – those who supported the gypsy. And no one was allowed to sit on the fence. As is today's way, it was love or loathe, no in-between.'

'I'm mainly for loathing,' says the reverend under his breath. 'It's more evidence-based.'

'And so we return to where we started, my friends: the fragility of the single human testimony. Can it ever carry weight in a court of law? The single testimony of Elizabeth Canning could have had Mary Squires hanged – indeed *would* have had Mary Squires hanged, if you had been the jury! You believed the young girl's tale – *ahh*, the innocence of youth! Yet her crime was of the most enormous magnitude – that of endeavouring to swear away a life, in order to cover, perhaps, her own disgrace – for yes, some people thought that she had been debauched in her absence, perhaps a brief but unfortunate dalliance; and that the whole story was a concerted attempt to conceal it. So now I ask for another show of hands, please, with the story complete. Are there any here who now believe Mary Canning innocent? Are there any Canaanites in the Undercroft? Or are we all born-again Egyptians?' Strutt peers into the darkness and sees no hands at all.

'My goodness, we are a most certain bunch now, are we not? Our support for young Elizabeth dissolves like water in the desert! But it remains the mystery today that it was in 1754; and perhaps the truth of it, my friends, will never be known – or not until that great and glorious day of judgement, when the mist shall be wiped from our eyes and all things hidden made clear! I'm sure we all look forward to that great reckoning and that great glory!'

But while the speaker craves that day, others are less sure. Few here tonight look for hidden things to be made plain; everyone's life has corners which neither receive nor offer light.

'But, in the meantime,' he adds, 'for we know not the day or the hour – I am most happy to take questions.'

With the talk finished, some shuffle hastily for the exit; those eager for bed, and who wouldn't be tonight? Though not all are ready for the sandman, some stay; and from the dark, John asks a question: 'What have legal systems done with this issue, Professor? I mean, given the deficiencies of the single witness, which have become so apparent tonight in your excellent talk – and thank you again for coming. But what significance does the law give them?'

'None, John, none! That's the short answer.' Strutt looks overly-excited, knowledge ejaculating. 'It is an ancient principle that the single witness is not to be trusted. It's there in the Bible, of course, in early Jewish law – the Book of Numbers 35:30 "If anyone kills a person, the murderer shall be put to death at the evidence of witnesses. But no person shall be put to death on the testimony of *one* witness." So one witness was regarded as insufficient and something open to abuse, long before the story of Elizabeth Cannings... a principle later enshrined in Roman Law as well – *"testis unus, testis nullus"*.

There are more sniggers; they can't help themselves when the naughty appears at their gate. Most would blame their public schools, but it's been a while since they were there. 'Testis *what?*' asks Fairburn, the surgeon, ever keen to surf the comedy wave.

'"*Testis unus, testis nullus!*" One witness is no witness. From which – for those who can do the maths – we also get the word 'testicle'. Like witnesses, there do need to be two of them.'

And afterwards, the Professor seems in no hurry to leave; enjoying the complimentary words which his wife so fails to deliver at home. 'A fascinating talk,' says the abbot.

'Well, I'm glad it tickled your fancy. And er, where are you a monk, by the way?' The abbot's habit leads to this question; it's his own fault. 'A dear friend of mine, a most dear friend, is a member of the community at Worth Abbey.'

'I was a little further afield.'

'Surrey?'

'Middle-Egypt,' says Peter, wondering where Surrey had appeared from, and keen to stop the guessing game at source.

'Middle-Egypt, eh?' Strutt draws his belly in for a moment. 'Where the monastic movement began in the 4th century!'

'A little before my time.'

'You weren't at the wonderful St Catherine's, were you, at the foot of Mt Sinai?'

'I wasn't at St Catherine's, no.'

'It has a library to die for, apparently...absolute dream of a library. Never been there myself, too bloody hot, I'd melt like a wax doll.' Peter looks at Strutt's shirt, the sodden armpits and concurs: he would struggle in the desert. Visitors never brought enough shirts to Egypt...too many bibles, not enough shirts. And then, as an afterthought, Strutt asks: 'So where were you?'

'I was at the other end of the valley.' Peter finds himself feeling defensive. 'The less well-known end; shabbier and less visited than St Catherine's...the monastery of St James-the-Less.'

'Oh.' The disappointment hangs in the air. 'Still...'

'The noblest place on earth,' says Peter.

Strutt is feeling around for conversation. 'And, of course, that's a desert with some history, abbot.'

'It's true. Any cave painting less than 2000 years old is dismissed as modern art.' Strutt's eyes are seeking someone more interesting. 'Though I was just thinking...'

'Always dangerous!'

'Just thinking that the single witness must be as problematic for historians like yourself, as well as for juries.'

'Oh indeed, indeed; this is quite so, quite so.' He puffs his feathers like a seagull in the wind, glad to be the expert again – the sun with its planets circling, dependent and seeking light. 'You know, I always feel historians have much in common with astronomers looking at the Pole Star.'

'The Pole Star?'

'Neither can actually observe the object of their study directly! You see?' Peter nods...yes, he sees, but the professor will still explain. 'Astronomers can only look at light emitted four centuries ago; not at the star itself. And similarly, historians have access only to written sources and archaeological remains. They can never quite get back to the actual moment.'

'So observing historical facts is as impossible as observing the Pole Star?'

'Quite, quite. We can never be there ourselves...only investigate by means of the fall-out, the debris, the light, the consequences they produce...which means that historians can never be scientists, who can check and re-check the facts.'

'Because for historians, there are no facts – just possibilities?'

'Take Caesar. He was murdered just once.'

'People tend to be.'

'But what evidence do we have? No forensics from the Senate House, no CCTV, no Roman phone records. So who or what are we to believe?' The abbot nods. 'History is told by the winners, but when did they ever tell the truth? *Never.* Fortunately we have various written records of the assassination. But imagine if we had but *one* witness to the event, with no ability to check; with no – what we historians would call – *information control.* With only one witness, truly, we know not whether we stand in the presence of light or darkness, deception or truth. And with Elizabeth Canning, I suspect they stood in darkness.'

'They could be utterly reliable, I suppose. Some young people tell the truth.'

'But most lie through their teeth, abbot. "Testis unus, testis nullus,"' he says with a wink.

And Peter feels overwhelmingly sad, almost winded, as if some unknown bereavement passes through him, a young voice crying out to be heard, to be believed, to be honoured in some manner.

2

'**M**urder or suicide, abbot? Which is it?' The question is an attack, a gauntlet thrown down by Tamsin; this is an interview to determine his fitness to serve. 'Or put another way, who are we to believe – young Billy Carter or the vicar? Because that's what it comes down to in the end, a fairly simple choice.'

'If it *is* the vicar,' says Peter. He doesn't see it as simple as that, despite the detective's impatience. She's 'leaping to conclusions' as they say; mad leaps, mad conclusions.

Tamsin fights back, she always does. 'It's a fair inference from Billy's suicide note. He does name the vicar, the clues are there.'

'So you've solved the case, Tamsin!' declares Peter. 'Well done and congratulations. Brilliant police work...so much to admire about the procedures.' Should a monk be sarcastic? Who knows? It's not one of the seven deadly sins; and in the face of stupidity, perhaps even a virtue?

'Sometimes it happens, abbot. The answer is staring you in the face, with no attempt at disguise. "Yes, OK, it's a fair cop. I'll come quietly." It's not always a mystery.'

'Then I'm happy for you, Tamsin.' He isn't happy for her. 'You can drive away from Stormhaven with undisguised relief

– remove the pebbles from your shoes and brush the wind from your hair, with yet another successful investigation to your name. Celebration all round with your police chums. Though you won't, of course – celebrate, I mean – because you don't have any police chums and nothing makes you happy; and if it did, you wouldn't share it with anyone else anyway.'

Harsh. Tamsin manages a 'have you quite finished?' look but Peter continues. 'What *is* clear, amid much that isn't, is that you don't need *me*.' He's decisive. Tamsin stares. She hadn't expected that last bit.

'Perhaps I don't.' She shrugs.

'Quite. So you can now go back to your glass-panelled office, close the door, write up your report – or whatever it is you do – and then ring the CPS tomorrow, who, like a puppy, will jump into your lap and ease the courts into action. Job done! And the vicar goes down like a lead balloon.' He drinks a little more of his coffee, toasting her with his mug, as a retainer might toast their master, in ever-so-humble subservience. 'Which just leaves me wondering why you dropped by. I don't imagine it was for my hospitality.'

'Well that's obviously true.'

'So?'

He holds her gaze and is shocked to witness the stress-strains appear in her confidence, like cracks in a new build – small but everywhere.

She says: 'That's obviously the way it *looks*, I agree; how it appears. I've presented the obvious conclusion, one that anyone can see, even a fool in pyjamas.'

'Sometimes the fool's in uniform.'

'But I'm always interested in other opinions.' Peter starts laughing, can't help himself, for this is too absurd. Tamsin interested in other people's views? Say that and keep a straight face; though she does. Her eyes are lost, though, she needs this conversation. So he helps her. 'You refer to the note found in – where was it, Billy's bedroom?'

The abbot likes to know where things were found.

'Yes,' says Tamsin.

'Read it to me again.' Her look asks him if this is really necessary. 'I mean, I know the case is solved and the Reverend Ernest Hand is facing the thick end of twelve years in gaol – but humour me, Tamsin.'

'OK. But I'm afraid the bad language hasn't disappeared.'

'I can cope.'

Tamsin reads from the small piece of paper in her hand. They sit in silence for a while, before Tamsin speaks. 'And now it has happened. The prophet was right. Billy is dead – and I think we know who did it.'

Peter nods. 'Well, that's possible; it has to be possible. Though I'm not sure I hear it in quite the same way as you.' Tamsin dismisses his observation with a shake of her head; dark hair swinging across her stunning Arabian face. She's too beautiful really, and it's a problem. It's a problem if you're male. Her colleagues just do not know what to do with it. If you don't bow to her, you have to attack her, slag her off, call her a bitch, because you cannot be neutral – even though you'd love to bow, and would do so in a moment, if she asked you over for a glass of wine. But she won't ask you over, she absolutely won't, because she only relates to success and how is a shared glass of wine going to further that ambition? She enjoys the power her looks bestow; but somewhere inside fears the fakery they might hide. What if her looks got her this far? Would a plainer woman have had such impact? Tall men can better command attention – they might be fools but they have the height. And Tamsin? Is she a fool in disguise – a fool saved by her beauty? These are the shapes in the shadows within, determinedly ignored, for she doesn't wish to know and wishes no one else close enough to find out. 'You're presuming some paedophile element?' says Peter.

'The thought may have crossed my mind.' Sarcasm returned, one-all. 'He *is* one of the very few priests in Sussex presently *not* in gaol for offences against children...*and* he's unmarried.'

'The assumptions do pile up, Tamsin.'

'This is an evidence-led investigation.'

'No, it's assumption-led. Your assumptions shape the evidence you choose to use. You're assuming the note accuses a priest.'

Tamsin gives him a look. 'I've only been here five minutes and already you're so irritating I could throw you off the case.'

'A small issue and I don't wish to be a pedant...'

'God forbid.'

'But before you can throw someone off the train, they have to be on the train.' Tamsin's face says *what?* 'If they're not on the train in the first place, however much you dislike them, they cannot be thrown off it. A *non sequitur*, as my old Latin master would call it – a man who was undoubtedly a paedophile.'

'Not *Tom Brown's Schooldays* again.'

'Given your present irritation, you could ask me not to get *on* the train. But until you do, and until I have, you can't throw me off.'

'I want you to get on.' The words take the breath away, like the simple request of a child. 'I want you to get on. So would you like to be on the train?' she asks, feeling suddenly tired.

'Not if it's *Southern Rail*.'

'And a proper answer?'

'Anyone getting on a train has to weigh up the chances of being thrown off. What are the current odds for that happening?' Tamsin pulls a face, as if he's asked a quite impossible maths question. 'At least take your coat off, Tamsin – it'll help me relax.'

'And while you relax, I die of cold. Is the heating on?'

With no greeting, she had been in his face since arriving at his small seafront home. She'd started talking as if they had been sharing the house for days; as if she wasn't a surprising invasion.

'The wood burner needs some logs.'

'So it's *you* who's destroying the planet. No wonder they can't breathe in Beijing.'

'Just take a seat and I'll make some tea.' He wears several layers beneath his habit to save both the world and his bank balance. Laura, his neighbour, is always complaining about the cold. 'It's bloody freezin'!' she says. But she wears nothing, or next to. She'll wear a t-shirt and skimpy jumper, no protection around the neck and say things like "I need a new heatin' system." No, Laura, you just need to wear more clothes; it's what they're for. He hasn't said it yet, but perhaps he will. How long do you collude with a fool for politeness's sake? 'And I mean the *comfy* chair,' he adds. 'You can have the comfy one today, Tamsin.'

There is only one comfy chair in the abbot's small front room. The other seat is a wooden crate, which once held herring. She had once questioned this.

'The seating arrangements are designed to limit visitor footfall,' he said, going on to explain that one human being is manageable, and sometimes a joy. 'But as politics reveals, the larger the group, the more stupid people become and I don't wish for that now, really not.' In the monastery, he'd seen sensible men become idiots in a group, stirring each other up about some particular, theological or otherwise, and becoming absurd in the process. 'I don't wish to encourage such decline in human glory – certainly not in my home.' Hence the one comfy chair.

'Not much cop for family gatherings,' a neighbour had said. But actually, it was fine for family gatherings, quite perfect in fact; because Tamsin was his only family – his niece...though what that label meant, he wasn't sure. Blood line? Intimacy? Respect? Joy? Honesty? He remembered a conversation with his vicar.

'Sometimes "family" is more of a label than a relationship, vicar.'

'I'm not sure I understand.'

'People say, "They're family" but that is not the same as saying "I find life and joy in their presence."'

'Family can be a great support to people, abbot.'

'I'm sure they can – family *might* be life-giving. I'm simply saying it's far from certain, and should never be assumed. Society *does* assume it, of course, and that assumption causes psychological contortions of a most painful nature. Families destroy as many as they save.'

With Mothering Sunday approaching, and a saccharine sermon written, the vicar had not been impressed and removed himself in a sulk. And no matter anyway, because the abbot *does* like Tamsin; though he doesn't know why, as she tends to bring grief to his doorstep. But they laugh together, on occasion, and have shared in some nerve-wrenching investigations. They met only a few years ago, with the crucifixion of the vicar – the previous one. It was a messy business, recorded elsewhere; but that was their meeting and their start. So they had no history together, no childhood memories to share; no fading photos of fish and chips in Whitby or the gorse above Loch Ness. They grew on different continents, in different soil and in deep ignorance of each other, with no cousins or aunts knowingly shared. They really do only have each other, which is maybe the draw; they have little else in common.

Tamsin's visit this morning, however, is entirely professional. Today she is 'Detective Inspector' more than 'niece' – some achievement for an immigrant in her late 30s. And with flame taking hold of the logs, a cup of coffee in her hand and short cake biscuit available, the abbot invites her to explain the case, from the start.

'Billy Carter was found dead at Splash Point this morning.'

Splash Point, half a mile down the road from Peter, is the final bay before the white cliffs rise out of reach of the town; and where, made angry by the sea walls, the tide smashes and crashes ferociously in the wind. Splash Point could be as calm as a Buddhist; or as turbulent as a demented dog.

'OK. Suicide?'

'He was drugged and his foot, in some manner, was held or trapped in a gap in the concrete promenade, where he waited in the cold for the dawn tide to rise and cover him. The pathologist suggests he might have been there for six hours – we'll know more after the reconstruction.'

'A long wait for death.'

'He may have been unconscious.'

'And murder?'

'Some abrasions on his wrist and ankles which could suggest he was carried to Splash Point; but they could be there for any number of reasons; no one willing to be definite. Again, the reconstruction will help. His body was knocked about by the water once it arrived, which makes things a lot more difficult.'

'Water does a great clean-up job for the murderer, supposing there is one. Carried by one person?'

'It's possible, one strong one...though it could be two. Or it could be none.'

'And therefore just another suicide in an area not unfamiliar with them.'

There is a loud knock on the door. Tamsin jumps but the abbot makes no move.

'It'll be Hafiz.' Hafiz is his pet seagull, if one can call a seagull a pet. Certainly Hafiz is unaware of the label, having no regard for the abbot. He shits freely on his windows and washing line. But he will not now be ignored, knocking heavy blows on the glass kitchen door with his beak.

'You don't feed him, do you?'

'Occasionally.' The full extent of the feeding could be withheld for now. Tamsin would not be impressed by the breakfast and supper routine. She was against all forms of compassion.

'You do know they are vermin...I mean, they're hated in Hove.'

'All the more reason to like them. In fact, I may have that written on his tombstone: *Here lies Hafiz – Hated in Hove.*'

'He looks cross.'

'He's always cross, whatever you give him, it's never enough. Life is a constant affront to his dignity, and every encounter with me a disappointment.'

'Well, there's a thing.'

'Though how he survives the cold, I don't know. He sits on the wall, surveying the sea, in a wind that penetrates all five layers of my clothing.'

'It's probably warmer out there than in here.' Peter regrets giving Tamsin quite such an open goal.

'So who was Billy Carter?'

'I don't know why you feed him.'

'And Billy Carter?'

'They're meant to be wild.'

'And Billy Carter?'

'He was eighteen, a local boy – lived with his mum in Chyngton Road.' The same age as Elizabeth Canning, thinks Peter; and it somehow makes the boy more interesting. 'He did casual work for an undertaker in the town, the one opposite the hardware shop.'

'Fennings.'

'Fennings, yes.'

'Run by Ephraim Fenning, Stormhaven's *Man of the Year 2017*.'

'A highly competitive field, no doubt.'

'Well, er...' The Abbot's throat tightens.

'Is something wrong? Is something lodged in your throat?'

'No, I mean... yes, no – and it's of no consequence, none at all – but I was actually shortlisted myself that year.'

'You?' She breaks out into delighted laughter, usually saved for lottery winners. 'You were shortlisted for Stormhaven's *Man of the Year 2017*?'

'I was, yes.'

'An unemployed monk and an undertaker? Who said Stormhaven wasn't a town on the rise?'

'I don't know why you're so surprised.'

'Or why you're so ashamed...you never told me.'

'And what would telling you have achieved – apart from the scorn and derision presently on show?' Tamsin shrugs.

'I could have supported you with a banner and chanted your name in the high street – if Stormhaven has one.'

'Precisely...scorn. And yes, I am aware that it's not exactly the *Oscars*.'

'I can confirm that, abbot.' A sudden gust of wind shudders the windows.

'It was during one of your "desert" times, anyway, when you disappear off the radar...or my radar, at least.'

'I was probably working.'

'And not calling for months, which is fine – absolutely fine. I don't sit by the phone.'

'You don't answer the phone.'

'I do answer the phone.'

'You don't. You never answer the phone.'

'You never ring.'

'I have rung.'

'I answer in my own time.'

'That's the same as not answering. A phone call is not like a holiday you schedule six months in advance. It's a spontaneous thing.'

'The phone is a gate-crashing tyrant.' *That's telling me.* 'It was after the school murder – just supposing you're interested...'

'What was?'

'The shortlisting.'

'I was hoping we'd moved on. So how short was the short list? How much *list* was there?'

'It wasn't long.' Tamsin waits. 'It was just the two of us, I believe.'

'And he beat you?'

'Who?'

'Mr Fenning. Ephraim Fenning was Stormhaven's *Man of the Year* 2017...and you were, well – nothing. Second *is* nothing. I can also confirm that.'

'He hardly beat me...it's not a competition, Tamsin, it's not like that.'

'Of course it's a competition! How can *Man of the Year* not be a competition? Life is a competition – every competitive second of it.'

'It was a sort-of competition, I suppose.'

'And he beat you. So I hope you hate him.'

'I don't hate...'

'And I look forward to our joint interview with him, with no hard feelings on show. You are going to help me on this case, aren't you?'

'I don't know, Tamsin,' says Peter with a sudden sigh. And this is a genuine sentiment rather than some vain bid for praise. 'We might fall out again... your behaviour is often appalling.' Tamsin acknowledges this; to a degree. *Moderately* appalling. 'So, couldn't we just live on our memories, which I am happy to doctor if necessary? And, I mean, we've had some successes, which add a happy glow to everything. I wouldn't want this one to ruin it all. We could just live in the past.'

'"The past is stale bread, the future is no bread, the present is fresh bread." Isn't that one of your lines, abbot?' Sadly, it was – and it did rather spike his attempt at escape. 'You cannot live on stale bread. And just think of the money,' she added.

'It's minimum wage...very minimum.'

'But maximum drama...and so much better than no wage at all. And a generous travel and supplies allowance to consider. You could stock up on stationery, which I know you like... though who you write to, I have no idea. It certainly isn't me. And perhaps another log or two on the fire? I said goodbye to a sense of my feet some time ago, I miss them. And my neck and jaw are sore...'

She looks in genuine discomfort.

'You could go and see a doctor.'

'Or you could simply warm up the room. The human body needs heat.'

He takes two logs from the basket, both from the beach, opens the wood burner door and throws them in.

'You need also to consider your stress levels, Tamsin – before making the decision, I mean. You do always regret working with me. You were regretting working with me just now and we hadn't even started. We're usually fine at the beginning and then you start to feel threatened and sense a loss of control, which doesn't play out well inside you.'

'I know I do, I *know* – but then time passes, and I forget how bad it actually was, how truly awful.'

'And that's why I'm reminding you now...because it is usually *you* who makes it so bad. In the murder at the school, it was me who...'

'...solved it in the end, I know, I made an error of judgement.' A few simple words, but also a shift of tectonic plates; never before had the abbot heard a confession on the lips of Tamsin. Nothing close. 'I "make my own suffering," you don't need to say it...though my police colleagues were imbeciles.' And it was true; they had been, but that really wasn't the point. She brought them in, and they danced to her tune; a queen cannot blame her advisors. 'You know how they struggle with my success.'

'But not as much as you struggle, keeping all the plates spinning. No one does it like you, Tamsin – but it must be an exhausting game; rather stressful, I'd imagine.'

'It has been difficult recently.' Her body slumps as she speaks – uncharacteristic. She ages ten years before him and sips her coffee, almost for comfort. 'Shoreham.'

'Shoreham?'

'I don't wish to speak about it. It wasn't good. And Geoffrey Sitwell is a shit. You're not to say that to anyone. Actually, you can.'

The abbot has never seen her defences so low; though they'll not remain there for long.

'Tamsin allows herself neither weakness nor failure,' he recorded in his journal soon after they met; and since then, they'd worked together on a number of cases, supported by the Sussex police's 'Trusted citizen' scheme. This was a local scheme which permitted civilians to be brought in on police investigations where their experience and knowledge was deemed helpful to the enquiry. The partnership between the abbot and Tamsin had not always been easy, as both knew; and neither had Police HQ at Lewes always looked kindly upon it. They'd no wish to be represented by 'a bloody monk'; it wasn't their idea of modern policing at all. But they couldn't argue with the results, and as Chief Constable Wonder reminded them – and with some regularity – from behind his large desk, 'Policing is like Premier League football – a results-based business.'

'Though the Chief's more Allardyce than Guardiola,' as one sergeant joked.

The fact that on their first investigation, the abbot had discovered Tamsin was his niece – indeed, his only relative in the world – had not changed matters a great deal. Both wished to keep family at a distance; it was the murderers they wished to get close to. And now with the offer of a new case before him, Peter is thinking about money; for while the love of it is the root of all evil, its absence can make survival tricky. The winter gas and electrics bill had been high...very high, and now this late February freeze is making things worse. Who knows what next month's bill will be? *Don't even go there!* as next door would say. And next door on the other side, their pipe's burst yesterday, water everywhere; the carpet in the front room ruined. So are his pipes quietly splitting even now? Have they ever been appropriately lagged? He has no idea. And how could he ever afford a new carpet?

He does his best to earn something; but there's limited demand for a monk.

'I suppose you are a bit niche,' as a car mechanic had told him. He'd taken a few funerals for Fennings, earning £100 for each...£100 for solemnity, kindness and hope, which is cheap at the price, really. He preferred funerals to weddings – but then doesn't everyone?

He'd also managed to get himself on the exam invigilation rota at Stormhaven High; some kind friends had organised it... but while the remuneration is decent for doing nothing beyond staying awake, like fruit picking and fun fairs, it is seasonal work. And with the mock exams now coming to an end, some spring income would definitely be helpful.

'We will need to start with Billy Carter's mother,' says Peter and Tamsin smiles. The abbot is on board, he has got on the train; and she can always throw him off, if necessary.

'Obviously.'

'Did she know about the note that Billy wrote?'

'She says she didn't.'

'And then there's the priest.'

'The priest, yes,' she says, with enthusiasm. 'Looking forward to that. I've developed a good strategy with vicars over the years.' She gets up and reaches for her coat. 'I have a mantra as I sit down with them.'

'And that is?'

'What is this lying bastard lying about today?'

'It may be wise if I talk with the vicars.'

3

They're driving towards grief, Tamsin and the abbot, towards the dead boy's mother.

She gave birth to the boy who either froze to death or drowned or maybe a little of both; the boy who maybe chose to end it all – or endured a decision made by another. Though really, who would want to kill a boy? What harm could he have done? There were no drugs wars here and plenty of teenagers kill themselves in a confusing, difficult and overwhelming world. They don't have the resources, they just have to go. But lying on freezing concrete for six hours before death in icy water? Hardly the suicide of choice; not for anyone – better the noose than that, better the leap from the cliff. This was how men did it, no messing around with an overdose. And it was only half a mile to the top from Splash Point – an easy jump, a brief end. So suicide seemed unlikely. But if murder, then who and why? Murder is the first resort of the visceral and the last resort of the calculating. Which of the two had Billy met?

They're driving towards grief in Tamsin's smart car, charcoal grey, a BMW, with no neon stripes and no blue light. Like the driver, it has only a loose affiliation with the police force. She will bless them with her presence as long as success is assured.

'Cathy Carter lives in a two bedroom flat in the Chyngton area of Seaford,' says Tamsin. 'Chyngton Road, in fact – and according to Rightmove, we're promised fine views across the golf course.'

'Is the estate agent coming along too?'

'Very funny. It's background.'

'And that's all we know of her?'

She has picked him up from home and they've driven in silence, tense at the beginning of an investigation. There is so much unknown; and unknowing puts Tamsin on edge, her body tight with stress. The dark glasses hide her eyes, but not the strain.

'Her son was alive yesterday, for God's sake, looking forward to the weekend – which I'm told some people do. While Cathy was – well, I don't know what she was doing – planning a shopping trip to Brighton or a theatre show in Eastbourne.'

'Nothing going on in Hove? Shame.'

'How *would* we know anything about her, abbot?' This was her point. She had taken his query personally, as some black mark against her, no information on Cathy Carter. 'She's neither a crime lord nor a druggie. We don't know her from Adam.'

'Or Eve.'

'Whatever.'

'Though she may be a crime lord who has simply slipped under your radar. It's what the best crime lords do.'

'We're starting from scratch with Cathy Carter, she's clean – no finger prints, no DNA and no other crimes to be taken into consideration. She could be Mother Theresa – but she isn't Al Capone.'

'And so remember, Tamsin, that while we're starting from scratch, she's starting from shock and pain.'

'And your point is?'

'Think *sympathy*.

'I'm mainly thinking *information*. I don't remember sympathy ever solving a case; though I remember it cocking up a few. Emotional involvement clouds judgement. Not to be encouraged.'

'Is this also your life motto?'

'It's called police work, abbot; at which I've been remarkably successful.'

She feels strong irritation; and she's regretting asking him to join her. They haven't even started work, and she's regretting it. He's trying to take control, when he shouldn't; because she's the professional here and she needs to make this clear from the beginning. She's had enough stress recently, way too much – particularly that last case in Shoreham; she wouldn't be telling Peter about that. But this is straightforward and let's keep it so: a simple suicide, probably a vicar involved, a few loose ends to tie up – that would be good right now.

'Nevertheless, keep it somewhere in your mental notes.' He says it quietly but firmly, almost like a parent. 'Keep it in large letters, across your mental wall, between your aggressive thoughts. You never know, it might even help on the information front.'

Something in Tamsin relaxes.

'I don't mind sympathy; I'm not against it as such...'

'And on that bombshell...'

'But if she starts lying – if she starts playing silly buggers, then the contract is ripped up.'

'Which contract?'

'The sympathy contract.'

'Torn to shreds at the first sign of dissimulation. I understand.'

'I just don't have the energy for that sort of nonsense today.'

'And you usually do, of course.'

'I'm too tired, really I am. The case I've just come from, well – I don't even want to talk about it.'

'Yet you just have, so there's a mixed message.'

They drive in silence for a while.

'All I'm saying is if Cathy Carter starts sodding about – I mean, we're trying to help her, for God's sake.'

'You're getting angry with her before we've arrived. The mind does rush ahead sometimes. Are you OK?'

They pull up outside a large house.

'Big house,' says Peter.

'Theirs is the ground floor flat.'

'Ah.'

'She knows we're coming.'

And Cathy Carter – mother of Billy, recently deceased, drowned at Splash Point – opens the door.

'Hello,' she says. Clear skinned, five foot four, forty-ish with a blond bob, she is neither skinny nor fat, with tight jeans and red shoes. She lets them inside with a silent nod... but no sense of the hostility sometimes found in the bereaved, when officialdom arrives to trample clumsily across their carpet and through their lives. Officialdom is generally the first person they can blame; and everyone likes a target.

'Tea?' she asks.

~

'I know he's a bloody monk. The clues are there!' Chief Inspector Wonder could well do without DI Geoffrey Sitwell this morning – or indeed any other morning; but Geoffrey, it seems, can't do without him.

'I just query DI Shah's approach here.'

'You don't like her, do you?'

'It's a professional observation – nothing personal.'

'She's simply using the *Trusted Citizen* scheme, which we have piloted here in Sussex. Something of a success story, actually.' *Stay calm.*

'Well, you'll have your own view of that – as I'm sure we all do, Patrick.' He hated being called 'Patrick' by anyone at work. It was a liberty; and Sitwell hadn't earned the right; not by a long way. 'I mean, I can't comment, of course, because it was before my time, so my hands are clean. And perhaps the thinking behind it was more obvious then.'

'Geoffrey, not everything was bad before you arrived, though you seem intent on making it so.'

'This is not about me, Patrick.'

'Geoffrey, everything is about you, and one day, someone will notice.' He can't keep it in. 'You and the greasy pole. Loyalty is under-valued.'

'Always loyal; where I can be.'

'But obviously not in the canteen, where I hear you sniggered loudly on hearing me compared to Sam Allardyce. "More Allardyce than Guardiola." Remember? A little bird flew by and told me.'

'Just banter among the boys, Patrick.' Geoffrey is blushing, just a hint; he doesn't like being caught out. But the opportunity had been too good to miss, so yes, he'd discretely surfed the canteen disrespect, a leader able to laugh with his foot soldiers, the common touch, 'a man of the people'. 'Everyone's behind you, Chief Inspector.'

'I'd prefer you in front of me, Geoffrey. This isn't Kent, you know. And the *Trusted Citizen* scheme has got results. Local people know things. These two have worked together before. And he's *cheap!* You wouldn't get out of bed for his wages.'

'But DI Shah is a spent force, Patrick – you know that and I know that. Shoreham was a mess.'

'And made messier by your intervention, I'm told.'

'Shah was all over the place. And now her decision to work with a monk on the suicide gig? I mean, no offence, but what's the opposite of a dream team?'

How Sitwell can smirk, thinks Wonder. *He'll take us all down one day.*

~

They warm to Cathy's offer.

'Tea would be nice, thank you,' says Tamsin and Peter applauds her with encouraging eyes. However hard it might have been, she has managed sympathy – so far.

They are led through into a light front room, wooden floor, red poppy throw over the sofa, homely...and Rightmove wasn't wrong – there's a very fine view of the golf course.

The room feels larger than it is; a sense of space. And Cathy reads their minds.

'Borrowed landscape,' she says. 'The view doesn't belong to the property, but it makes the property a great deal more pleasant. I've always liked light.' She goes into the kitchen to make the tea, while Tamsin and the abbot sit in silence. They note photos of a boy growing up, a serious boy; and a man with big hands and a confident gaze in one of them, taken when Billy was younger. Peter has seen the man somewhere before.

'You will have been looking at the photos,' she says on her return. 'I'd be doing the same. So yes, that's Billy. And the man is his father, James.'

'You're not...'

'No, we're not together, thank God. I don't know if we ever were.'

'I seem to recognise him from somewhere,' says Peter, hopeless at faces.

'He's James Fairburn, the surgeon. You might have come across him. He doesn't mind attention, not averse to it at all, as long as it's *good* attention.' *Nothing too unusual, thinks Peter.* 'He's not a man to hide his light beneath a bushel, James – neither his medical brilliance nor his endless charity marathons. You can get bored of charity marathons, I find. He *is* a good surgeon, though, if you ever need some interior plumbing.'

Peter doesn't know what to make of Cathy. It doesn't feel like he's speaking with grief – no tear-swabbed eyes or the slow body movements of shock and despair. This doesn't look like the emotion of grief. Or has grief just been put away for another time, when the flat-footed investigators have left? Is it too precious for now? Is she in denial or a rare and remarkable glimpse of sanity in crisis?

'I saw him last night at the Stormhaven Historical Society,' says Peter.

'When I'm sure he asked some very intelligent questions.' Peter mainly remembered the one about women's underwear, but he'd leave that for now. 'Do also remember, before you fall in love with him and join his crowd of worshippers, that he once made me eat baked beans for a week as punishment for upsetting him.' Peter has often eaten baked beans for a week; but that was choice rather than punishment, so that was different – and Tamsin is suddenly energised. Blatant and shameless abuse of power and she hopes she'll be able to destroy Fairburn along the way, whatever his involvement in the case. Forcing his wife to eat baked beans? She hopes this is murder and she hopes he's the one.

'It was early in our relationship, when Billy was a few months old and I was young and stupid. I knew nothing. Who does at that age? Though I knew even then that life was unfair, that it wasn't going to be happy-ever-after...that I'd made his bed and I was going to have to lie in it. For now.'

This was marriage talk Tamsin could understand – the hopelessness, the despair, the deep frustration, the sheer impossibility of it all. It was the 'honouring' and the 'working-things-out' and the 'loving-through-thick-and-thin' bits she struggled with.

'I'd always keep a small kitchen knife down the side of the sofa, where you sit now.'

Peter nods thoughtfully as if this was entirely normal, as if everyone had a knife secreted somewhere about their furniture. But he is inwardly surprised, not by the knife but by the delivery. This was some way from the hysteria he had expected and the revelations continued, crisply offered, almost like a confession, as if she had been waiting for this moment.

'I don't know why I kept it there, I never thought of using it, though who knows, perhaps I did? And now I'll never know. It was good to know it was there.'

Both Peter and Tamsin sit a little less comfortably, each wondering who has the "knife side" of the sofa.

'I suppose it's about taking back control,' says Peter. He's trying to normalise the situation; as if Cathy has said nothing surprising and done nothing odd. 'It's about feeling there's something we can do, a door we can leave by. That's important. We all need a door we can leave by.'

'I never would have stabbed him; I couldn't.' Is she trying to convince herself now? Is the peace-loving and reasonable self-image attempting a comeback? 'But I knew I didn't want to be with him – and maybe it was just a physical reminder of that, a symbol of my disillusionment, buried in the sofa where he used to make me have sex.' Again, Peter moves a little uncomfortably. Every sofa has a story and this one, it seems, more than most. 'Don't worry – it's been cleaned.'

'Quite,' says Tamsin, raging inside; she's still with the beans, used as punishment, and now looks at the smiling face in the photo with different eyes. Suddenly a monster has appeared through the smile; she sees it now, though she missed it before.

'And now I'm a stain on his reputation, of course, which is not a comfortable place to be. His reputation is rather precious to James; the perception of others matters a great deal to him. He wishes to be in good standing; perceived well. So if you threaten his reputation, then he will come for you...just a warning, folks.' She smiles.

She's very angry with James, thinks Peter.

'We'll take note,' he says while Tamsin looks forward to the day. 'Though reputations are a house of cards in my experience and tend to collapse quickly when exposed to the nudge of truth.'

'And we're very sorry about Billy,' says Tamsin, aware that she hadn't yet spoken of him. 'It must be...'

'Unbearable,' says the abbot.

'I'll tell you in a few months' time,' says Cathy. 'Or perhaps a few years' time. At the moment, I feel very little...shock is kindly shutting the body down.' Is she always so matter-of-fact? Such calm analysis of her predicament is slightly unnerving. 'Which is why you're getting tea. It isn't a welcome or even an act of kindness; it's just something to do.'

They sit in silence, while the information bug eats away at Tamsin.

'We will find the murderer,' she says when Cathy returns with a small tray of cups; and then regrets it.

'So, it was murder?' She puts her tea down.

'Well, yes, we have reason to believe so. Your son was drugged, Mrs Carter...so he probably knew nothing.'

'It's very likely he knew nothing,' adds Peter. 'Whatever happened.'

'Did your son take drugs, Mrs Carter? Or have access to them?'

'It's not a judgement,' says Peter quickly.

'But it would help us to know.'

'Not to my knowledge.' But she's distracted in her mind. 'It was paralysing last night, the cold, I mean.' They couldn't argue. 'I'm just thinking of him... lying there, the wind biting, the sea rising...' She looks away.

'I'm sure he didn't feel anything,' says Tamsin.

'And I'm grateful you attempt to make it better; but you can't make it better.'

These words are spoken simply and without aggression.

'No.'

'But if I can help in any way in what you must do, in your investigations...he was happy.'

'Quite.' No parent wants the suicide verdict.

'We really just need a sense of his life,' says Peter. 'That would be a great help. It's always the same with a tragedy like this: we don't know what we're looking for; but we do know we'll find it.'

'And forgive me, but you're here because? You're not from the undertakers?'

She looks straight into his eyes.

'Well, I'm...'

'I should have explained, Mrs Carter.' Tamsin steps in quickly. 'He is not from the undertakers; or not on this occasion. The abbot is working on this case with the Sussex police. He has been an associate on a number of cases in the area, and proved...helpful.'

Is that all?

'Well, isn't life endlessly surprising?' says Cathy. 'The Sussex police employing a monk.'

'Ex-monk,' says Peter.

'But still in uniform, I see...interesting.' No judgement; just an observation.

'Old habits die hard,' says Peter, risking a joke and regretting it; regretting it before he'd even said it...anticipatory regret; yet still stumbling on, when it really wasn't the time.

'The past is not easy to let go of,' says Cathy. 'For any of us. We're all clinging to the remnants, like survivors from a shipwreck. I'm certainly clinging today.'

'What was Billy doing yesterday?' asks Tamsin, wishing to ease away from the self-help and focus on the case, though the word had never felt so full of meaning. *Yesterday*...so final and so gone.

'He gets some work with Fennings, the undertakers. You probably know them.' Peter nods.

'I've worked for them myself,' he says. 'The odd funeral... maybe I met Billy.'

'Maybe you did.' She likes this idea. 'Billy is one of the coffin-carriers – he *was* one of the coffin carriers.' She pauses. 'Who will carry him, I wonder?' Another pause...Peter indicates to Tamsin to keep quiet. 'He'd get £70 for a funeral, cash in hand, which was useful. And he was friends with Ralph, their son.'

'Whose son?'

'The Fennings – Ephraim and Sandra, they have a son called Ralph... so Billy would sometimes 'hang out' there, as he'd say.'

'Was he there yesterday?'

'He had a funeral in the afternoon. And he was sexually abused, I think...when young.'

My goodness, she doesn't withhold her punches, thinks Peter. And Tamsin is on high alert.

'OK. And why do you say that?' she asks, in some sort of seventh heaven at the mine of information on offer. This had to be a paedophile case, surely? The vicar's days were numbered.

'It's just a feeling; and he never spoke of it to me. So, it is just a feeling... and not an accusation. I have no evidence, no suspects. Just a feeling.'

'He never spoke of it?'

'I'd always say to him that if he ever wanted to tell me anything, he could...and that I'd never judge him, and that sometimes people did bad things to children. But he never said anything. He'd just nod and suggest scotch eggs for tea or ask for some new trainers.'

'You say it's not an accusation,' says Tamsin, 'but in a manner, it is.' And not just in a manner. 'I mean, is there anyone you suspect?'

'Like I said, I don't know. I have no idea. And that's why I don't accuse. He stayed with his dad quite a lot and sometimes they shared a bed, Billy told me. I wasn't happy about that, privately, it just seemed inappropriate – and with the number of bedrooms he has in Rodmell, it was hardly necessary...but Billy said it was his idea, because he was nervous in a strange house. And it is a strange house. I haven't been inside, but I've seen it from the road and it's not exactly cosy – so that may be so.' She pauses, weighing her own evidence. 'He loved football, of course, and he was good at it. He played his way up through the various youth teams. Nick Hallington's in charge of all that...and yes, there were rumours about him with regard to...well, there *are* rumours about him.'

'What sort of rumours?'

'Sports coaches. Need I say more? The press hasn't been good for them recently, has it?'

'No.'

'Now we've imprisoned all clergy, scout masters and teachers at private schools, it's the turn of charity workers and sports coaches. Abusers pretending virtue; I find it quite repulsive... and talking of priests, Billy became involved with St Botolphs in Lewes, which surprised me.'

'He knew the vicar there?'

'It was a particular circle of school friends, I think. Though he's been less committed of late, maybe growing out of it. I mean, belief in God when you're young is fine, as long as you grow out of it. No offence.' She looks at Peter. 'But who knows? It's a secretive world, child abuse...no one rings up the mother to let them know how it's all going. And as I say, it's only a sense I have; no evidence.'

'You kindly gave PC Lennon permission to look in Billy's room this morning,' says Tamsin.

'Seems a long time ago. Did she find anything apart from dirty boxer shorts? She didn't say she'd found anything. But I don't know what she was expecting to find.' She's talking too much, she's frightened. Perhaps she knows.

'She found this note.'

'A note? She didn't say anything to me.'

'I don't think she wished to upset you.'

Cathy shakes her head. 'Upset me?' Her voice breaks a little. 'I think the bar for upset has been raised a little over the last twenty-four hours. Don't you?'

'She didn't wish to upset you *further,* is perhaps what she meant,' says Tamsin, unusually supportive of the suspect, which is how she regards everyone.

'I don't mind crossing people off my list,' she told Peter when they started to work together. 'But everyone starts there, everyone is *on* the list, whether it's the dustman or the Dalai Lama...particularly the Dalai Lama. I'm sure he has a secret.'

'If he has only one, we should all applaud.'

But she's handling Cathy carefully today; as carefully as she can handle anyone.

'She's young, still learning her trade, if you know what I mean. PC Lennon is more familiar with community policing – school assemblies, that sort of thing.' And Peter knew what Tamsin thought of 'that sort of thing'. 'Would you like me to read the note to you...or perhaps you'd like to read it yourself.'

'No, you read it.' She can't bear to read his writing today; it is a step too far. She notes the strong feelings that arise in her, another wave of sadness, quite unbearable; though she must somehow hold back the flood, gazing down into her lap, holding back the tide that could swell and destroy everything in its path. Tamsin finds the note in her bag.

'We have copied it, this isn't the original, but it says – and she pauses, 'Are you ready?'

'I'll never be ready.'

'"*He's done bad things to me.*" This is what he wrote. "*He's done bad things to me. Speak to the fucking priest at Lewes, speak to him. He's evil. And now he's going to kill me.*"'

Cathy doesn't move but breathes deeply, in and out; in and out. Anxiety has made her breathing shallow. She tries to deepen it, though it's difficult to say what she heard. Peter's guess is *almost nothing.*

'You don't know who he might have written that to...or about?'

'Could you read it again, please?'

'Again? Yes, OK. Here we go: "*He's done bad things to me. Speak to the fucking priest at Lewes, speak to him. He's evil. And now he's going to kill me.*"'

Again, silence.

'It looks like you'll be visiting St Botolphs,' she says. 'I don't think I have anything more to say to you today.'

'No,' says Peter, getting up from the sofa and Tamsin follows. She doesn't wish to follow, but the abbot's probably right. Their welcome is over, and today, that means they leave. Cathy thanks them for their time, she shows them out, she closes the door, she puts the chain across it, returns to her front room, kneels down, looks out on the golf course and cries.

What else can her body do for Billy?

4

〜

'The vicarage is a crime,' as the vicar will say to anyone who visits. 'A murder without the mystery. And a murder with very thin walls.'

And now the police are coming round for some reason or other; and he hopes it's nothing too horrific and nothing too close to home. It's probably some naughty parishioner – that would be good, the police wanting some background. He doesn't know DI Shah and neither is he certain a woman should hold such a post. She is maybe the pastoral choice, for when someone has lost their cat, that sort of thing; a soft presence, a motherly figure, a shoulder to cry on. Well, he'll look after her as well as he can. It's what vicars do. The doorbell goes and he is up from his desk, out of the study, across the hall. He can see silhouettes on his door step. She has brought an odd-shaped companion. What *are* they wearing?

'Greetings!' he declares, as he always does when opening the door – though it's usually a lie; and certainly so today. He plays the beneficent priest in magnificent and warm-hearted welcome and hopes that one day it will be true. Today he feels only the cold air rush in and rush past, as the silhouettes become flesh, with one at least is a surprise. 'You must be DI Shah. And a monk?' he says, clunkily. He's taken aback, pauses for breath. 'Is this a ploy to calm my nerves or something? "Bring along a monk! It's what those reverends like!"' he says, affecting a sort-of cockney accent. 'Does he break out into Gregorian chant if things get a little stressy?'

'DI Tamsin Shah,' says the woman, holding up a card. She's not the caring type he was expecting; but a woman who could frighten a snake. 'And this is Abbot Peter, who is assisting me on the case.'

'It all sounds very ominous!' says Ernest, a large man, with hair thinning a little and slightly camp. 'And which particular case is in need of assistance today?'

'Can we come in?'

'Of course, of course, I'm sorry! I don't want you dying like my daffodils. Oh, the tragedy! They absolutely don't know what's hit them and they lie *très désolée* in the flower bed.' He's ushering them into the hall and closing the door on the world. 'They simply cannot stand in this temperature, poor things. They lie down, they actually lie down – I do believe I can hear them crying.'

The reverend is irritating her; he irritates her intensely but his hall way is warm, which is compensation. *Here's someone who doesn't pay his own heating bill*, thinks the abbot.

'And do remember what a heated house feels like,' says Tamsin by way of instruction, as they are led through into Ernest's study. 'This is the sort of temperature to aspire to, abbot.'

'Was that the old vicarage we saw down the road?' asks Peter. '"The Old Rectory"?'

'The *true* rectory, yes,' says the reverend. 'I live in the diocesan-approved builder's hut.'

'A decent builders' hut – as builders' huts go.'

The builder's hut is a new-build, functional space with pretend Tudor beams...while three doors down is the glory that might have been his, the beautiful old Georgian rectory, with its walled garden. This is where the Reverend Ernest Hand could have lived had he arrived in the parish a hundred years earlier. Sold off by the church to raise funds, it is ever-more beautiful with the passing of time, draped in wisteria and now worth millions – way beyond the sad reach of Ernest. He shouldn't complain; of course, he shouldn't complain, and he tries not to in public. Most think his house more than adequate and wouldn't mind living there themselves.

'Some house you've got there, reverend!'

He has the statutory four bedrooms, one dining room and a study, so hardly a slum...but with the real thing so close, so tantalisingly close, so *painfully* close, there is always a hollowness to the home, a gnawing regret for what might have been had he not arrived so late; two centuries too late, in a way.

'To compare oneself or one's house or one's situation with those around you, is just the best recipe for unhappiness,' he told a parishioner. 'And I'm afraid I do it *all* the time. I never stop!'

'Weren't you at the lecture, abbot? "Testis unus, testis nullus" and all that?'

'I was, yes.'

'I didn't think there could be *two* monks in Stormhaven. One feels enough somehow, no offence! And you being teacher's pet at the front.'

'I have an aversion to the backs of peoples's heads.'

'And both of you there doing your homework, no doubt. Who to believe and all that.'

'Unfortunately the DI here couldn't make it; she was otherwise engaged; so I'm afraid we must endure her ignorance.' He offers Tamsin a sad smile. 'But it was certainly interesting. Just who is telling the truth? The eternal question, I suppose.'

Peter looks straight at the reverend.

'Well, quite, quite. Hypothetical now, of course,' he says uncomfortably. 'But not back in the 18th century, no. So was Elizabeth Canning innocent or guilty, abbot?' He feels safer talking to the abbot. 'I have to say I had her down as a young liar from the off. I find the young to be first-rate liars. I lied all the time as a child!'

'We wanted to ask you about Billy Carter.' Tamsin takes control. 'It's the more recent crime, I believe. Seen much of Billy lately?'

'Sit down, please.' He pulls out two easy chairs, as he might for a couple come for marriage preparation...'though don't be fooled by the name because really nothing prepares you for marriage; least of all me.' He'd usually say this to the couple, just in case they thought he was the answer. He had never been married himself; but had seen the difficulties of those who attempted it. No one could prepare you for that cataclysm.

'And Billy Carter?'

'Billy? Yes, well...' He cannot hide his unease. 'Why do you ask? I mean, he hasn't been around St Botolph's for a while, so I'm a little "out of the loop", as I think they say. He's all right, is he? Hasn't done anything stupid?'

'And Billy?'

'Well, lovely boy, bit of a dreamer, obviously – slightly unattached to the world, makes up his own world, I think – and who can blame him for that? The real one's pretty ghastly! He's growing up, of course.'

'Meaning?'

'Well, you can't be an altar boy forever,' he says. 'The excitement wears off after a while.' Tamsin hides her smile, unsure if he's joking. 'And there's exploring to be done, some freedom required from the shackles of the church. Not that I feel shackled, of course; but the young might feel so, might they not?'

'Which particular shackles did Billy need to be free from?' asks Peter, and the reverend turns towards him in mock surprise.

'"Clowns to the right of me, jokers to the left!" You arrive from all angles!'

'And the shackles?'

He is now wondering why they are here; he realises they haven't exactly stated their business, a little odd. But then he's enjoying the company to be honest. And he has nothing to hide; nothing that these dear folk will ever know about.

'Well, the church can be very prudish with its do's and don'ts, can it not? I'm sure you don't need me to tell you that, abbot. I mean, perhaps you aren't a "do's and don'ts" person, I wouldn't know, but there are plenty who are!'

'Do you feel shackled, reverend?' Now it's Tamsin's turn.

'Ah, well, I say I don't, of course; but what would any of us do if we knew we'd get away with it? That's the question; even for you, Detective Inspector. That would test our virtue, would it not? If we knew we'd never be found out.' There is longing in his words, he is greatly excited at the thought; as if very little of his life would be left as it is, if only he knew he'd never be found out. 'The shackles imposed on us are many and various.'

'We put them there ourselves,' says the abbot.

'I believe the ten commandments play a part,' replies the vicar in jokey retort.

'If the church ties us up with her rules, it's only because we let her. We have to give our permission before anyone can tie us up.' The reverend shrugs.

'What would you do?' asks Tamsin. 'If you knew you'd never be found out?'

'*Moi?*' He blushes and edits in a moment; men *can* do two things at the same time if their survival is threatened. 'Oh, I'd give myself breakfast in bed more often. And not answer any emails, none at all. I'm sorry if that's a rather dull answer.'

And also unbelievable so Tamsin changes tack. 'Billy stopped coming to St Botolphs?'

'He did, yes.'

'And you were OK about that?'

'I always say – and I know it's a cliché – but if you want them to return, you have to let them go.'

'Very fridge-magnet.'

'Not that they do return.' The reverend is suddenly sullen, sinking in self-pity; his lips turn downwards. 'Not in my experience, anyway. Everyone goes – and no one returns!'

'Was Billy happy?'

Something is up; he knows when something is up. 'Why the great interest in Billy? Is he in trouble of some sort?'

'So was he happy – when you knew him?'

'Happy?' The reverend looks suitably bemused. 'Are you happy?'

'Was Billy happy?'

'Is any youngster happy? There's such a lot of pressure on them these days – and with nothing to believe in but a phone.' In Pavlovian response, Tamsin instantly feels for hers. There's something reassuring about its presence. 'Billy was a gifted footballer, I believe. I know nothing about football – lots of people running around in meaningless pursuit of a ball. But I'd go along to watch him on occasion, to show support...shame about his parents, obviously.'

'Why a shame?'

'Well, I mean, we won't gossip and who knows the truth of these things anyway? But they separated when he was five, all rather acrimonious...or so I'm told. Rather a forceful woman his mother.'

'Do you not like forceful women?'

'I have absolutely nothing against them,' he says, 'but Catherine Carter, she may be all calm and lovey-dovey in the therapy room, who knows? But as soon as the session is over, well...not a woman to be crossed, shall we say.'

'So you crossed her?'

He shakes his head. 'Not me, but you hear stories.'

'And I love stories,' lies Tamsin.

'Me and my big mouth.'

'So who tells them? Who tells these stories?' He hesitates. 'You will need to tell us.' The friendly encouragement is over.

'James Fairburn, if you must know, the surgeon – he was very harshly treated by her.'

'There'll be nothing one-sided about his telling, of course.'

'He was a consultant in his thirties, I believe.'

'What's that got to do with veracity?'

'Look, I'm just saying that a top surgeon was clearly not good enough for her – when most people would have been rather pleased at such a catch!' Tamsin's opinion of the reverend spirals further down; and it hadn't started high. *Such a catch?* 'So, the boy shuffled between the two of them.'

'And he had friends at St Botolph's?' asks Peter.

'He did, yes...a number of them, all away at uni now.'

'But not Billy?'

'He always said uni was a waste of time. "Why would I want to go to Nottingham, when I can masturbate at home?" he said, which rather amused me. He wanted to be rich, of course, like the rest of them – but felt you didn't have to work to be rich. He read ridiculous books like 'The Four-Hour-a-Week Millionaire.' It's a new genre...all about you sitting in your room with your computer earning vast sums of money, in property or such like. All very dodgy. When I once talked about people going to work, he called me out, "That's the old order, reverend, it's history! Who needs to go to work to be rich?" There's something un-tethered about Billy, a little grandiose, perhaps...but the young must be allowed their dreams and illusions, I suppose.'

'If only to keep you company.'

Peter steps in. 'So, he left St Botolph's, and his friends left for uni – the end of an era, in a way?'

'It happens in parish life,' he says. He is still smarting. 'People come and people go. It's bane or blessing, depending on who it is. We can all do without some people.'

'And sometimes they leave quite angrily, I suppose.'

'Well, one can't get on with everyone...or please everyone. We all know that. I mean, try and please everyone, and it's an early grave for you – no, really. And some will never be pleased, even if you give them the moon!' He pauses for a moment. 'I'm not to everyone's taste, I know that.'

'You don't seem to have been to Billy's taste,' says Tamsin. The abbot watches Hand.

'Oh? I did everything I could in terms of support...'

'He was murdered last night, did you know that?'

'Murdered?'

'He was murdered, yes.'

'And you're sure it was actually – I mean, he might have... *murdered?*' Hand's face is a haunted pinky-grey, as if energy has left and fear has moved in. 'I mean, you're sure it was murder; sure it wasn't suicide?' He's finding it hard to breathe, but tries to gather himself. He gets up from his seat and looks out the window. 'The poor daffodils,' he says to a silent audience. '*They've* been murdered, you know. Look at them! One hopes they'll recover, rise again and all that; but it's hard to imagine, so sad.' The reverend turns back into the room. 'He always had that look, Billy – sad eyes, slightly hang-dog; angry, of course, I always knew he was angry and suicide is so often angry – the most punishing thing you can do to those left behind...'

'We found this note in his bedroom,' says Tamsin. 'Would you like to hear what the note says?'

'Well...'

'Let me read it to you. It's not without interest or relevance. Are you listening?' The reverend nods. '"*He's done bad things to me. Speak to the fucking priest at Lewes, speak to him. He's evil. And now he's going to kill me.*" She allows the crude words time do their do their work. Hand is speechless. 'So we're now speaking to the fucking priest, which presumably is you. That's why we're here. Unless there's another fucking priest?'

'No, I don't think so.'

'Who is it who is evil, reverend?'

5

Peter is hurting, he has never been so cold, his habit is gusting, it as a life of its own. The wind screams in his ears, numbing thought without immediate chance of relief. There is no chance of thriving, here beneath the white cliffs; he must simply survive – button-up, hunker-down and stay alive... and be polite if possible.

'Sometimes you learn nothing and sometimes you learn everything.' Tamsin is shouting in his ear, her face creased against the gale; it makes her dark skin pale, almost luminous, finding crevices in genetics made for warmth. And while Peter has stood here at Splash Point many times before, he has never stood like this. And he is sad at the loss of innocence; for he stands not at a beauty spot but a murder site where history will always have its claim.

Until today, he has thought of Splash Point as a 'thin place'. Whether 'thin places' exist on earth, Peter isn't sure and he doesn't speak of it. People do speak of them, places of special revelation, generally up mountains, in fields or by the sea. (Never a shopping mall.) TS Eliot spoke of *Little Gidding* as a thin place – a space where the veil between heaven and earth is somehow removed; where the spiritual has easier access to mortal earth. Instinctively, Peter doesn't believe the hype. He finds something pompous in the claims made, something needy; and it is a well-known marketing tool for retreat houses. It does no harm to business to be known as 'a thin place'. People had sometimes spoken of the desert as a thin place; 'you live in a "thin place", abbot!' But Peter had never encouraged the idea, despite the commercial cost. 'If the prison isn't a thin place, if the street isn't a thin place, if the office isn't a thin place, if my bed isn't a thin place, if Golgotha isn't a thin place – then we might as well all pack up and go home.'

But if there *is* a thin place in Stormhaven, if such places exist, then perhaps Splash Point is that place for Peter...the battered rocks, the crashing waves, the stained white cliffs beneath majestic clouds, scudding across the long horizon. It is never the same – serenity and violence, beauty and danger, still one day and loud with terror the next. Here there is no past, no future...only this moment. It had been his first walk on arrival, eating fish and chips; and his place of inner reference ever since.

But now it is changed. Can it ever recover from the death of Billy Carter? Can this rough shoreline ever be a thin place again? He wonders this, as the reconstruction is enacted before his eyes, the coast now a stage; and the play – the saddest and most spiteful of deaths.

The part of Billy is played by a stand-in from a local college, earning beer money; though he may spend it on hot chocolate today. Peter watches as he is laid down on the rocks.

'Who's she?'

He sees a small lady in wellington boots and a stout coat, self-contained but holding sway, like a theatre director, coaxing and ordering around.

'The one to whom all must bow.'

'So, God is a woman. There were rumours.'

'She's the CSR – Crime Scene Reconstructionist. Mary Houseman. She's very good.'

The abbot feels the pain in this admission by Tamsin. The bestowal of a compliment is no easy matter for the DI;

especially on one with some professional overlap. Praising her handyman is easy; he is, in no sense, a rival. But someone else in the crime game?

'What is she good at?'

'The only thing you have to be in her line of business: interpreting the evidence in context. A CSR doesn't have to be a specialist in any *one* area.' She still shouts a little to cut through the wind and the scarf Peter wears around his ears. 'She'll be a forensic scientist of one sort or another, I'm not sure which; but mainly, she has to understand how and where everything fits in.'

'I see.'

'Everything's material for the reconstructionist – the DNA, the state of the stones, recent tyre marks, the nature of the journey from the car to the point of death, the weather and temperature on the night, the weight of Billy, the degree of difficulty in carrying him, the tidal patterns – and if he *was* carried, any physical evidence of carrying or tying. We know from the lab he was drugged – something he drank, probably tea – so it is likely he was carried in some manner. How easy would that have been? Could one person have done it? Or would it take two?'

'It looks like one has done it – with difficulty.'

A young policeman has managed to carry the student Billy by himself. He has staggered from the beach huts, where the car was reckoned to have been parked, to the concrete promenade, which is completely covered when the tide comes in; and in winter, never dry – the seaweed and moss slippery and damp. Mary has a word with the policeman. She hears his story, pats him on the back, a job well done; and he now makes his way back up the raised walkway where Tamsin and Peter stand, surveying the scene.

'That's a bloody difficult walk,' he says. 'If that was a woman doing the hefting, then I'm the Pope.'

'We all look forward to that day, constable,' says Peter. 'A fresh start for Christendom.'

The young man looks blank and Tamsin steps in: 'These reconstructions can't always tell you what happened.'

'I suppose not.'

'But they can often tell you what *didn't* happen...which is almost as good. It's unlikely a woman carried Billy.'

And now Mary Houseman is stepping forward. Her grey hair is flying everywhere; she should really have a hat. She clambers up onto the moss-covered jetty where Billy spent his final hours. The theatre director, previously shouting from the back, is now stepping onto the stage; she becomes an actor, drawn to the space; to the place of revelation. Peter is amazed.

'What's she doing?'

'I don't know. She's not happy with something. She's never happy with anything, which I suppose is a strength.'

Peter wills her not to slip; the sea around the jetty is disturbed, traumatised and devilishly cold. But Mary is on her haunches, looking intently at the rock and concrete, like a rock pool enthusiast, peering down into the gap, it seems, where Billy's foot was fatally stuck, making escape impossible. And now she's leaning forward, and like Doubting Thomas, placing her gloved hand in the stone wound, feeling inside the crevice.

She leans back and says something to her male colleague, who kneels next to her surrounded by crashing sea. The director is now the star, watched by all; and for this moment, even the cold is forgotten. She pauses, holds her hand in the air, perhaps to steady herself on this narrow promenade of safety, and then leans forward. Again her hand enters the hole, until she stops – and then she's working at something with her hand, her colleague holding her for balance, the easterly wind coming down off the cliffs.

'Has she found something?' says Peter, largely to himself. Tamsin is watching, like everyone else is watching, and then something gives, and Mary Houseman, the CSR on the case, withdraws her hand, some object held – and her colleague is taking it, and, wary of his own balance now, placing it in a plastic bag.

And it's then she falls. Mary Houseman slips and falls – the holding hand of her colleague removed, as a strong gust lifts and throws her, her wellies slipping, they can neither grip nor hold on the moss, she's falling westwards, falling to her right, her colleague holding his own position, but Mary Houseman is tumbling head first off the stage, and hitting the dark water, now lost to Peter's view – but he's running to the edge of the walkway and slipping on the wet chalk descent. He's now down onto the shingle, where two policemen, including the student-carrier, are ahead of him as he runs towards the water. He's looking ahead, looking for Mary in the turbulence, he's taking off his habit – Tamsin remembered it as something done with remarkable speed. But he can't see her, he can't see her in the water; he can't see a flailing body fighting the drag, but she must be there – he knows she must, he saw her fall. She dropped eight feet into the sea, it deepens quickly from the shore line here, but in the mad swell around the jetty's edge, she's nowhere.

And while the police stop at the water's edge, as if seeking further instruction, Peter runs past them, beyond health and safety, crashing into the water, taking the hit, enveloped by the freeze, but in some manner beyond it, the passionate mind beyond matter, though his heart stops as he plunges forward towards the place where she must be... and now he's swimming, or trying to swim, and seizing up...his body seizing up as he sees an arm, an arm in the foam and grabbing hold, he pulls hard.

'I've got her!' he's shouting, though he has no breath, and no one hears, the wind too strong; and now there's another figure alongside him, the one who would be Pope – that may have to wait – and he's pulling at Peter, he feels the tug as Peter pulls at Mary, though he has no footing and she has no footing, and whether he'll live, Peter cannot tell, his body closing down and entirely red, he remembered this, the red skin – no, purple – but holding onto Mary...he must hold onto Mary...

He also remembered Tamsin calling him a show-off.

6

'Let me make you some tea, Cath. Sometimes you just need a cup of tea.'

'It's no consolation for me, Sandra. But if it helps you to be doing something...'

Sandra Fenning has dropped round to see Cathy, because it must be terrible to lose your son like that and if she can help in any way, she'd like to help, because it's not like they don't know each other – and she must need help at this time.

'I mean, Ephraim is absolutely distraught, Cath. He has never – like, *never* – closed the business for the day. But he can do no other, that's what he said. "I can do no other, Sandra, on a day such as this." He said that.' Cathy acknowledges the news with the half-smile of indifference.

'I don't care whether he opens or closes, to be honest.' What the world does or doesn't do right now means little. And she has no desire to see Sandra, who has turned up unannounced and certainly uninvited. Cathy's long-standing assessment, noted somewhere private, describes 'an anxious woman who'd put a sloth on edge, who feeds on drama like a parasite in a wound.'

'Billy was with us yesterday, you know.' Sandra has made the tea. 'You do know that? He was with us yesterday for the 2.00pm cremation in Eastbourne, carrying the coffin, there in Eastbourne, he was – Mrs Dowd, God bless her, not a heavy woman, surprisingly long but not heavy; well, not a lot of her at the end, quite wasted away...and his last day on earth, who'd believe it? You can't believe it, can you? Very cold, of course, and a bitter wind... well, you know that crem...not the warmest, at the best of times. He wore gloves obviously, we insisted he wear gloves...and faultless, he was, *faultless*...he never missed a step on the entry, holding the coffin high, Billy, you could always rely on him – never missed a step.' She slows for a moment. 'It doesn't seem real; really, it doesn't... does. not. seem. real.' And after a pause. 'He was, of course, like a second son to us – to Ephraim and myself.'

Sandra and Cathy have known each other a long time, though this is not be mistaken for friendship. Sandra had child-minded for Cathy in those early days of the business, when she was getting underway with the psychotherapy. She had tried to keep office hours, but had had to see clients some evenings and Saturday mornings. You do need help sometimes and you go where you can find it; and Cathy found it in Sandra, wife of Ephraim Fenning, the local undertaker.

'I know,' says Cathy. She's aware he was around there a lot. 'And it's kind of you to come round, Sandra, you mean well, I'm sure, but...'

'I couldn't *not* come round, Cath.' She *hated* being called Cath. It's what her mother called her. 'How could I not come round? I had to come round, Cath. And I mean, if there's anything, like anything, we can do, you only need to ...'

'I'm sure there will be, Sandra. But I don't expect the body to be released for a while. It's evidence.'

'Oh don't, Cath, *don't* – don't even...*evidence*?'

'How did he seem?' She suddenly wants to know.

'Sorry?'

'How did Billy seem yesterday? You were with him. How did he seem? Was he laughing? I liked him laughing.'

'Oh well, he was laughing, all right, oh yes! I mean, not when carrying the coffin, obviously – height of decorum when carrying the coffin, always. You can't be laughing when you're carrying a coffin, a time and a place. But Ralph was helping yesterday, so they were, well, you know boys... "joshing", I think they call it.'

'Yes...well, I'm glad they were together. Is Ralph OK?'

'Well, you know Ralph.' *Not really*, thinks Cath. *And nor do you*. 'He takes himself away, he does. Don't see him for days sometimes, with those games he plays. I mean, how long can you sit in front of a screen?'

'Quite a long time, if it's oblivion you need.'

'Not that he's playing games today, I'm sure. Out of respect and that. He's a good boy, Ralph...if a little strange.' She wants Sandra to go now. She has wanted her to go ever since she arrived. In fact, she has always wanted her to go, ever since she's known her.

'You must have a lot to do,' says Cathy, getting up from the sofa.

'Well, we're all here for you, Cath. You'll be all right alone, will you? You don't want me to stay over, I could do that.' Cathy contemplates the horror of the idea and allows Sandra to gather her things. 'Don't want you doing anything...'

'I'll be all right alone. Better alone, I think.'

'Used to be such a nice town, Stormhaven – never, you know, swanky. You couldn't call Stormhaven swanky. But nice, you know, the people were *nice*. Oh well...'

With Sandra gone, Cathy picks up her phone and rings James Fairburn. It's just possible he hasn't got his hands in someone's intestines. And they do need to talk.

7

~

'Fortunately, you have a strong heart,' says Tamsin. 'A small brain but a strong heart.' She had watched the unfolding scene at Splash Point amazed – Mary's slippery slow-motion fall into the water and Peter's insane response; appalling decision making. 'You could have died.'

She is glad to be away from the nick, where the incident de-brief had become soiled, everyone covering their backs and easing themselves from the looming shadow of blame. You could never legislate for Mary, said one, and some nodded – you never knew what she'd do next! And another asked who was holding her, a more pointed question, while another said it was clear no proper risk assessment had been made prior to the reconstruction, and another said that was completely unacceptable, though *what* was unacceptable – the lack of risk assessment or the comment itself – no one was sure or stayed to find out, because everyone saw the storm clouds, everyone knew this was a massive cock-up and what was essential now, as an accountable public body, was that no one was to blame, that angles were covered, false trails laid and safe escape routes planned. *Deny and distract* was the best way.

So Tamsin leaves with relief, driving to Stormhaven, to make sure 'Small Brain' Peter isn't being stupid. He'd refused hospital, where P.C.Banville had been taken. Instead, he insisted on going home, where he now sits in the comfy chair, a bloodless pale after the bright red of the beach. He is well-wrapped in blankets; and hot lemon with honey steams by his side.

'I'd prefer coffee.'

'Drink it.' She has organised the fire – building, lighting and maintenance; and found herself enjoying it. Perhaps she will buy a wood burner herself. Real fire might be good for her, she thinks this. Though her cleaner will need to agree; there will be ash, after all, which no one wants in their home. 'Where's your wood pile?' she asks.

'It's out the back. Mind the hedgehog. There may be a hedgehog in there somewhere; I saw one a couple of years ago. They've probably moved to Hove though. I think they had money.'

She had emptied the paper bin in his study to provide kindling, struck a match and with the ducts open, everything is aglow, the fire hungry to consume and spilling marvellous heat. Perhaps it's simply a matter of paying her cleaner extra for the ash. That's probably the answer.

'You never put enough wood in it, abbot. That's why it's always cold in here. You skimp on the wood.'

'There's none so dull as a convert.'

'But *that's* what the fire should look like. Do you see the difference? And *feel* the difference. I'm modelling good practice.'

Though Peter remembers only the face. They'd managed to pull the body to the shore, pull Mary Houseman onto the shingle; and Peter had straightway rushed for his habit, knowing he needed the warmth, with Banville attempting to blow warm life into the water-smashed face, a small group forming around them, telling him to keep trying, until he couldn't any more, his wet body shivering uncontrollably in the glacial wind; and someone was running down with a blanket from the car.

He was blowing for life but there was no life to find; life had left the body, a parting of ways, the head taking the blow on sharp rocks below the wash; caved in, bloodied and blue from impact. Saved by the cold, Mary Houseman had died quickly but not kindly in the chill turbulence of Splash Point.

And Peter's rage, pressing hard beneath his skin, had warmed him. How anger heats!

8

~

'**A**nd you think *I'm* the one who did bad things – is that why you're back here?' The reverend is hysterical, the man is rattled, his words a strained falsetto. 'You think it's me?' He now points to himself, aghast, like some hammy actor in local theatre, playing the part of a desperate reverend. And he does it well because he is one. 'Is that what you think – seriously?'

They have returned to speak with the priest in his new build. They had left the rectory with unfinished business, to attend the reconstruction at Splash Point. They are still in recovery from events there, they carry the shock and the fury inside, out of view but ready when needed. They had not spoken in the car journey to Lewes until they turned off the A27.

'One of our fucking own.' Peter is shocked, Tamsin never swears; but she repeats it a number of times in unusual camaraderie with her police colleagues. He has never seen a death so unsettle her, so obviously affect her – and they'd attended a few. Some inner sanctum had been invaded by the death of Mary Houseman, a line crossed, a fear exposed. She was disorientated, talking more to herself than to Peter. 'She was just doing her job, just doing her job, for God's sake! And retiring next year...next year she was retiring. Worked all her life, about to retire – and *this*. So what's that all about?'

It had felt like a challenge because it was a challenge; but Peter had said nothing and watched the fields pass by. When people demand meaning it is best not to respond. There is the temptation to rush into words, to rush to their help, to justify yourself with some scrubbed-up reply; but words struggle in such places. They sound tinny, like space-fillers, with no authority to explain 'what that's all about'. It's not about anything but itself; and silence is the better way.

And now they've returned to the rectory to maximise the vicar's discomfort. He must know something; and his whining 'You think it's me?' performance has altered little. He doesn't know what they have experienced today; he wasn't there at Splash Point. He didn't see her fall or witness the drowned body on the beach. So he is also unaware of the steely intent sat before him.

'You can see why we might.' Tamsin stares at him. 'And just so you know, the killer – or killers, who can say? – they lost a few more friends this morning, particularly police friends.' Ernest Hand looks bemused. 'The CSR, Crime Scene Reconstructionist, Mary Houseman, she was about to retire – but she died while on the case, she was killed by it...drowned. Drowned at Splash Point. So we're all looking forward to finding the killer of Billy Carter. And hoping no one lies to us along the way. Will you be lying?'

The reverend's face is like melting wax, shape-shifting. Something dies in his eyes; they hollow out, his skin colour drains to grey. 'Well, I'm very sorry.'

'Someone will be.'

'But I mean, even so...' *Gather yourself, man.*

'Mary Housman, remember the name – as I say, due to retire next year.'

'And I am truly sorry, most regrettable, a tragedy – what can I say? But even so, this is ridiculous.'

'Not from where I'm sitting. We have this note which...'

'No, no, you misunder*stand* the note, you misunderstand it, that isn't what its saying, I've thought about that – the note, I mean.'

'I'm sure you have.'

'*I'm* the one he told them to...I'm the one he told the bad things to, he spoke to *me*. He wanted me to report them to the police, to you lot, but I told him he must report it himself.'

He has their attention.

'Why wouldn't you help him?'

'Well, he was old enough to do it himself, wasn't he? He needed to take responsibility; it would do him good, I thought. And then he got angry with me. "I want *you* to report it, reverend – they'll believe you." That's what he said.'

'And who did Billy want you to report, Ernest?'

Tamsin tries to sound casual.

'He never said.' He blushes as he speaks, but shakes his head to confirm his words. 'He never said who it was. And I didn't ask, may be I should have.'

'Strange,' says Peter.

'I thought so.'

'He's demanding you report it, getting angry that you won't report it – yet he didn't tell you who it was. So what exactly are you meant to report?'

'Well, I did tell him that, I was quite plain with him; no really, I was.....very plain. But maybe it was too difficult for him? It was as if – and this has only just occurred to me – as if he wanted it reported, yet didn't.' Dramatic pause, like he'd sometimes use in a sermon.

'Didn't what?'

'That could be it, you know. Maybe it was someone, shall we say, too close to home. Do you appreciate how difficult that is – to set that particular ball rolling, to take on one's parent in public?'

'His *parent?*'

'Well, that's the last battle, isn't it?' He is rolling again, back on the horse. He can do this, and what a recovery! 'That's what they say. Not my territory, all that psychological stuff, I'd be the most terrible shrink – but don't most kill themselves as a preferable alternative to taking on a parent? There's probably some Greek play about it; it's definitely their stamping ground. You are sure it wasn't suicide?'

'Would that suit you better?'

The reverend is mortified. 'Nothing suits me about this situation! Nothing at all! And I resent the implication!' He's almost out of his chair. 'Are you completely stupid?'

The abbot watches the indignation let out to play. But whether it's the real thing?

'Just so we're clear, Reverend Hand: you're suggesting that Billy Carter was abused by his father, James Fairburn – the surgeon?'

'I don't know what his job has to do with it! As if the medical profession care more than the rest of us! Now *there's* an all-pervasive myth! And quite why Fairburn is paid so much and I am paid so little – I mean, where is the justice in it? Is a surgeon so much more valuable than a priest?'

'Some might say so,' says Tamsin.

'And you do get a house,' adds Peter.

'Not the *proper* house,' says Ernest, with a hint of self-mockery. Even he can see his "Woe is me!" story lacks legs.

'But that's who you think Billy was talking about in the note. You think he was talking about Fairburn?'

Ernest shakes his head, in frustrated mirth.

'Well, I don't wish to do your job for you, lady and gentleman – God, I struggle enough with my own! But, I mean, it's hard to look beyond him, isn't it? I mean really! – the clues are there, with bright neon lights attached, one might say.' He is pleased with his speech thus far. 'Yet who am I but an ever-so-humble parson?' He has somehow gained the upper hand and gives them both an amused smile. 'And if that is all, I now hope you will allow me, like Simeon, to depart in peace.'

He moves to get up and Tamsin, with a wave of her hand, bids him stay exactly where he is.

'Do you know Mr Fairburn?' She doesn't know who Simeon is or why he departed...and neither does she care.

'Do I know him? Well, what is it to know someone?'

'I left my patience at the police station, Mr Hand – where you will soon join it, answering questions in less grand circumstances.'

'I mean, our paths might have crossed; paths do this.' She is still waiting. 'He may have sneaked into a service with a bag over his head occasionally, too embarrassed to be seen.'

'He came to St Botolph's?'

'Or bumped into me at the football. We both took an interest in Billy's football – and, of course, he lives in Rodmell, in a very large house next door to Virginia Woolf – so not a million miles away, just up the Lewes Road.'

'You know where he lives.'

'I know where the queen lives, Detective Inspector, but we're not close. And more's the shame. I mean, James and I, we haven't sat in a pub together, just the two of us, and enjoyed a drink – which, I believe, is friendship's most basic test.'

This feels a contrived explanation to Peter, manufactured – a small truth offered to avoid a greater lie?

'I wasn't asking if you are friends,' says Tamsin, 'and clearly you aren't. Because the other basic test of a friendship, apart from a drink in the pub, is that you don't sell them down the river, as you've just sold Dr Fairburn...'

~

'He's lying,' says Tamsin as they drive away. 'I don't know what he is lying about, but he is lying. Do you think he's lying?'

'Increasingly unsettled...in control this morning, but losing it this evening. Genuinely shocked at Billy's murder, and also, I thought, a little frightened by Mary Houseman's death. But what in particular is frightening him? "Desperate" is my word for the reverend today.'

'One of our fucking own,' says Tamsin as they reach the sea. And really, she never uses language like this...

9

He does have very large hands, Tamsin's first thought as James Fairburn greets them in the generous hall way of his Rodmell home; generous in size, but dark, as if a welcome was not in the architect's mind, or indeed, a home; though the garden does its best. The large patio window in the front room reveals an acre of manicured land, crisp and even – frosted grass neatly mown, flower beds clear, all waiting for spring... *and good luck with that.* It's one of those villages where only perfect gardens need apply, and where comment is made if failure is apparent. '"The Corner Cottage" is disappointing this year.'

Though there's no way Fairburn did all of this; if any of it. He'd have a contract with some company in Lewes called 'Green Fingers' or 'Love Lawn' or 'Garden Glory' and they'd come in their van twice a month to cut, prune, plant and clear. Fairburn's only job was to look at it.

'Lovely garden, Mr Fairburn,' she says, unusually charitable. Success is attractive; and James is successful.

'Bit of a beast to maintain, of course – and not all my own work, I must admit. But I don't mind looking at it occasionally.'

Rodmell. Forever associated with one person and it wasn't the surgeon. Peter had talked about it in the car, drawn to its past in some unexamined way. 'Most come here to see *Monk's House*, this is the fame of the place – the weather-boarded cottage where Virginia and Leonard Woolf found some sort of solace in the 1920's and 30's.' Tamsin is checking her phone. 'I've visited it myself, and while not a great fan of her writing, I found it haunting.' She's not listening, thinking instead about the surgeon they're about to meet. But the abbot stays with Virginia. 'And yes, I have done the walk.'

'What walk?'

Why did he expect Tamsin to know? Not her territory at all. 'Virginia Woolf often made it – the six-mile trek through the valley, across the river Ouse and then along the South Downs to see her sister at Charleston Farmhouse.'

'Happy families.'

'Colluding families, possibly. But once you climb out of the valley up Itford hill, which is a bit of a beast and does hurt the legs – I've run it – it becomes a rather merry journey, good for the mental cobwebs, full of big skies and huge views. You somehow expect to meet Ravilious behind his easel, painting it all.'

'Who?'

'A local painter; it doesn't matter. But it's like you're on top of the world up there, the English Channel and Newhaven harbour to the right, the field-quilt of The Weald to the left and ahead, just this chalk-and-green escarpment stretching before you, sweet curves of open land, full of sheep, wheat fields – and hang gliders. Without the hang gliders, you really could be in the 18th century.'

'What a terrible thought.' Pause. 'And what has this all got to do with anything?'

'Well, there was one day in 1941 when Virginia didn't complete the walk; she never reached her family at Charleston.'

'She got lost?'

'In a manner. She was in a deep depression at the time and never got beyond the low ground of the valley. Instead of crossing the footbridge near Southease station, she filled her pockets with stones and walked into the river. Like Mary Houseman, she was overwhelmed by water, never breathed again.' Tamsin doesn't wish to be reminded of Mary. Nor does she wish her compared to some depressed and flaky writer.

'The difference being, she chose it, abbot. Mary didn't.'

'Does anyone *choose* suicide? I'm not sure. It's almost done to them.'

'Nonsense.'

'But I've made that walk from Rodmell. I followed in Virginia's footsteps, with the stark silhouette of Lewes Castle to my left...it was the novelist's last view. And somehow we were *both* there, time melting, myself and her. Quite unnerving...I remember feeling a shiver through my shoulders and spine. Do you believe time can melt?'

'Not in this weather. And shall we focus on Fairburn now? I believe Virginia's case files are closed.'

But not the story, thinks the abbot who feels heavy with death this morning, as if water-logged himself; soaked in mortality, where all seems surreal and nothing much matters. *And this too shall pass,* he says to himself as he ponders their new surroundings, a few doors down from *Monk's House,* the posh home of Fairburn, and it's a clean house, though not cosy. There are wooden floors, expensive rugs, abstract art, various sporting photos from years gone by, tennis rackets and golf clubs in a stand; it is a man's house. And Fairburn does have large hands, what Tamsin would call 'proper hands' – men should have large hands and a firm grip, though not one which crushes. There's no need to take manhood too far. A firm grip is attractive; but no one likes a hand-crusher, way too desperate.

'And thank you for seeing us at such short notice, Dr Fairburn,' she says. Again, Peter notices the unusual subservience.

'Not at all,' he replies easily. 'Let's go through. There's a time for a cold plunge in the winter sea; and a time for a well-heated lounge!'

'You're a cold-weather swimmer, Mr Fairburn?'

'James, please. And yes, I am one of the insane buggers on Stormhaven beach on New Year's Day – if you avoid a heart attack, it's cardiac heaven.'

'And if you don't?'

'If you don't, you probably wouldn't have survived the year anyway. So why not get it over with?'

If you didn't know, you might not guess he had just lost his son to the wild and freezing sea; and the abbot watches Tamsin being beguiled. She can actually be very decent to people if she puts her mind to it. Has she forgotten about the beans?

'And you must be the monk who solved the murder at Stormhaven Towers?' he says, turning to Peter. 'I read about that.'

'Well, the Detective Inspector and I, we worked on the case *together...*'

'A friend of mine is a teacher there, poor sod. Wouldn't wish that job on anyone. But she told me all about it, especially the bit in the forest. You're quite the hero there apparently.'

'Oh, well...'

'"The monk was brilliant," she said.'

'Well, I'm sure you're a hero on a very regular basis, Mr Fairburn!'

One compliment deserves another, feels Peter but Tamsin feels something else. She feels diminished by this exchange, for Stormhaven Towers was not her finest hour. And somehow she is lessened by praise for another.

'She struggles when others are praised,' as Peter once told a friend. 'So if we're together, and you wish for a relaxed time of it, never say a good word about me. She really won't be able to cope.'

But James Fairburn doesn't know the rules; he wasn't there when the guide lines were laid down. So he praises Peter without praising his colleague and Tamsin's tone towards him hardens. Peter watches the freeze in her face. Professional respect and a certain amount of fawning give way to professional competition. It looks like she's remembered the beans.

'We are very sorry for your loss, James,' says Peter, before the attack can commence. 'An appalling tragedy. We've heard such good things of Billy. And we certainly do not wish to keep you any longer than is necessary today.'

'It's only a short walk to the Ouse,' says James.

'I'm sorry?'

'It was Virginia Woolf's last walk, wasn't it? I mean, I'm still a bit new to these parts, but...'

'Oh, I see...well, yes it was.'

'From Rodmell to the River Ouse where the old bat drowned herself.'

'Not that old. I have done the walk.'

'Bit morbid!'

'It is good sometimes to speak with death.'

'Yet you stopped short, and that's the difference. You spoke with death but it couldn't persuade you to join her. Unlike Virginia, you said "No" to the cold uncaring flow.'

'That's one way of putting it.'

'But perhaps there will come a day when you don't, abbot.' The surgeon's eyes fix on Peter. 'Perhaps one day you'll join with her intentions and submit to the water as well. Destroyed by life – if only for a moment, for that's all it takes, one mad moment – you will wade in and let yourself go under. And perhaps one day I will? Who knows?' Tamsin curdles at this self-indulgent exchange. 'I live very close to death in my work, of course; every operation, a few seconds from a fatality. And a surgeon *is* just a plumber...'

'A well-paid plumber.'

'And every plumber makes a mistake sometimes. Entropy – it's the law of the universe, a tendency to disorder. We may get things right for a while; but we don't get them right forever. Though I've never cared, not for a moment.' *He cares a lot*, she thinks. 'You can only do your best, after all. So, it's only the occasional death that affects me. Like the death of my son.'

There is silence in the room at this sudden seriousness, this jerking halt, like the jamming on of the brakes; and something unreal in the words, adrift from authenticity, as if delivered for effect. They are the right words to say, but lack the ring of truth; though the two visitors nod with respect while through the patio window, a frozen lawn stretches away towards fields. A robin hops past the expensive triple-glazing, unaware of the cost.

'Billy didn't live with me, obviously. And that isn't his name, by the way. His name was William.'

'You called him William?'

'*Of course* I called him William.'

'But he preferred Billy?'

'Who knows whether he preferred it? It could have been the concoction of his appalling mother, in order to slight me.'

'You know that?'

'I don't *know* that, no. But why wouldn't it be true? There is some bitterness between us, with her 1950s' morals.'

'"Fifties morals?"'

'I may have slept with a nurse. I mean, who hasn't, frankly?'

'Male or female?' asks Tamsin, pursuing the cold war.

'And I think monogamy may pre-date the 50s', adds Peter.

'When men are different,' continues Fairburn. 'Quite different, it's a fact. Different bodies, different needs. Would you like to sit down?'

They take their place on the leather sofa, which slides too much for the abbot. He doesn't like to slide about on a chair, like some drunk bobsleigh enthusiast; he prefers to be held by it.

'You had an affair?' says Tamsin, crossing her legs and sitting upright, with her notebook in hand, like a P.A.

'I wandered a little.' As do his eyes now. 'Is that the end of the world?'

'That's not our business. But it was for your wife, apparently. And so you parted company?'

'Only after two years of pained distrust – *Oh my God!* Two years of having my phone checked when I wasn't looking...two years of the "text police" at work, the whole excruciating "Who's sending you texts at this hour?" business. I really couldn't be doing with it.'

'William did leave a note.'

'How do you mean, he left a note?' Genuine shock. 'A suicide note?' Rising energy in his body. 'I said all along it was bloody suicide – and I blame his mother.'

'There was no suicide note...just this.' She holds up a piece of paper, photocopied. 'It was in his room at home. Would you like me to read it to you?'

'Doctors can't write but they can usually read.' He reads it aloud as proof. '"*He's done bad things to me. Speak to the fucking priest at Lewes, speak to him. He's evil. And now he's going to kill me.*" I don't know what this is about...but it doesn't sound too good for that tart of a vicar of St Botolph's, does it? As if our prisons need any more clergymen from Sussex.' His large hands shake a little. 'And I did withdraw him from the Under 16's – withdrew him immediately when I heard what other people were saying. But you can only protect them so much.'

'What *were* other people saying?'

'The sports coach there, old "Teflon" Hallington.'

'As in "nothing sticks"?' James nods. 'What was meant to stick? Have people come forward to complain about him?'

'As I say, there are rumours. But I haven't offered you tea.' The note is affecting him, as if slowly dissolving the veneer. 'Would you like some tea? Can't get the bloody staff these days.'

'Do you believe your son was ever sexually abused?' asks Tamsin.

'William?'

'You seem hyper-vigilant on the matter. The vicar's a tart and the youth worker, "Teflon".'

'Any parent is.'

'But with regard to Mr Hallington, Billy – or William – was seventeen; he could probably look after himself, without your histrionics.'

'My *histrionics?*' James is amazed. 'Do you want to get out right now, while I ring my lawyer?'

But Tamsin doesn't want to get out right now. Indeed, she edges back slightly, as if settling in.

'I'm just saying he would have been much more vulnerable when younger, that's all. And I just wondered if you knew anything about possible sexual abuse when he was younger. Or whether you ever suspected it?'

Fairburn calms himself. 'You mean by Hallington?'

'Hallington – or anyone else. Perhaps someone closer...'

James looks hard at Tamsin; and then sneers.

'Is this some line of inquiry being peddled here? Some sort of fishing expedition? I'd be very careful.'

'I'm not aware of any fishing, Mr Fairburn...just the spectre of child abuse, so we need some light, if only to dispel the spectre. And clearly it's been on your mind as well, withdrawing Billy from Mr Hallington's team.'

The robin returns outside the patio window. And James Fairburn sighs.

'Cathy did mention something.'

'When?'

'A few years ago, I didn't take much notice. Therapists see sexual abuse everywhere. If in doubt, its sexual abuse! Bloody hell! There is such a thing as a normal childhood!'

'Is there?'

'There's a lot of it about,' says Peter. 'Abuse – and mostly unreported at the time by the victims. It's unreported because it's too difficult to face, let alone speak of – particularly if the abuser is close to you and they call it "love". It's so hard when the abuser calls it "love", isn't it? Sometimes years must pass before the victim can open that particular can of worms...when the abuse is called "love" and "our little secret".'

The surgeon leans forward in frustration.

'He was just a boy growing up, for God's sake! And there are many explanations for why William might have become sullen...living with *her* for a start. It made me sullen!'

'Did he want to live with you?'

'Who knows what he wanted? I know my way around a body – but not the mind of a child.'

10

~

Sandra Fenning takes the call; like a seagull to food, she is first to the phone, moving with speed, nose-diving anxiety. She likes it to be so, to be first to the phone, first to information, to know what's going on; otherwise Ephraim can be a little secretive, he withhholds things, keeps them to himself and for no other reason, it seems to her, than that he *likes* to – 'which is men for you!' as Sandra tells her friends. 'It seems they need the power.'

'It's Theresa Sykes speaking,' says the voice.

'And how can we help you, Mrs Sykes?' She thinks she knows Mrs Sykes, she recognises the aimless tone. They've probably buried a relation of hers; there's a fair chance. People don't change banks and neither do they change undertakers. She will pretend to remember, if necessary... but she wants Mrs Sykes to hurry up, because she doesn't want Ephraim interfering. He'll ask her to pass him the phone but she can handle Mrs Sykes, whatever it is she has to say. Sometimes he actually takes the phone out of her hand, and she can't very well hold on to it, because what will the bereaved think of a physical tussle at the undertakers?

'I just thought I should ring you, in case *she* doesn't. And you did bury my mother last year.'

'Of course we did, Theresa, I remember you very well,' says Sandra, 'and indeed, your mother.'

'You never met my mother, dearie.'

'No, but you spoke so movingly about her.'

'That sounds unlikely – and I spoke with your husband.'

'Of course, of course,' – *Why did I say that!?* –'but he does sometimes mention the deceased to me, the special ones. I hope you don't mind.' This is becoming a nightmare. Why didn't she keep her mouth shut? And is this woman drunk? It's only 11.00am, so surely not? No one can be drunk at 11.00am. But she does sound a little, well, wayward in her speech – almost as if she's dancing while talking. Is she dancing round the room while talking? But this won't be mentioned, of course; for *relationship* is everything in the funeral business – relationship nurtured carefully down the years. Repeat trade is their life-blood. If you buried their dad, they'll probably want you to bury their mum as well; and why wouldn't they? They want that connection, the hidden trail back to their past.

'I'm not asking you to remember her,' says Theresa. And how could she remember her, anyway? The bereaved remember their funeral arranger, but how can funeral arrangers possibly remember the bereaved? There are simply too many of them; their faces fade. Fennings conducted one hundred and eighty funerals last year. A good year, all targets hit, greatly helped by the flu epidemic which was something of a life-saver for the company; the elderly dropping like flies – though, as a memo advised, while celebrating the company's success, these were not phrases for public consumption or to be spoken beyond the office setting – neither the 'life-saver for the company' part nor the 'dropping like flies'. No one wishes their dead grandma to be remembered as a financial life-saver; or compared to a fly. And now, from what the doctor says, another one's breaking out, 'the flu season', as he calls it. It starts in schools, spreads via the school gate and ends with the panic buying of long life milk and pasta...and coffins, of course. It ends with them as well. They presently have seventeen funerals on the go, which is a great deal of paperwork; another reason why Mrs Sykes needs closing down.

'I just wanted to help,' says Mrs Sykes and there's definitely music in the background; possibly Frank Sinatra. And she does sound like she's dancing.

'That's very kind.' Sandra is barely holding the impatience in; but hold it in she must. 'Calm at all times' is Ephraim's business motto – but it isn't always easy. 'The grieving think they're so bloody entitled!' as she once said to him. 'All the "Poor me! Poor me! I just don't understand why he died!" stuff. Well, one reason, madam, might be that he was eighty-seven and had lungs like tar buckets. He smoked eighty-a-day, – prolonged self-abuse! The only surprise is he lived so long!'

'You didn't say that, dear?'

'Of course I didn't say that. But one day I will, one day!'

'Best to let me deal with the customers, my dear.'

Ephraim would just 'tut-tut' at her complaints, seeming to float some way above normal human emotion. In the meantime, she'd hear Mrs Sykes out, and then get back to the service sheet which needed attention, and had to be signed off by 4.00pm.

'I was just a little concerned about something my neighbour saw last night.'

'Oh really, Mrs Sykes?'

'And it's probably nothing, as I said – I mean, it's a bit comical in a way, but my neighbour couldn't believe her eyes, and I'm not sure I can believe her eyes either, because you just don't expect to see it. Not at midnight. And she did say she'd ring, but just in case she doesn't...I mean, it could be one of yours.'

And when she had told Sandra what she had seen last night, Sandra agreed that it did seem odd.

'There's probably a very reasonable explanation,' she says calmly. 'There usually is. And I can't imagine it has anything to do with us, but I'll definitely pass the information onto Mr Fenning. Are you well otherwise, Mrs Sykes?'

'Mustn't complain, because complaining really is for losers; but perhaps I am a loser! And the ashes, I've still got them, and

I know, I know I should have done something, it's certainly time, and I really don't want them in the bathroom cupboard. But they're safe there, next to her dentures, I wanted to keep those; and I don't, for the life of me, know where she'd want them thrown – the ashes, I mean. She didn't like anywhere really, miserable bitch; so we didn't talk about it. I thought of going to Stormhaven Head, because I do like the cliffs, but it's very windy up there and I didn't want her blowing in my face.'

'No, you don't want that.'

'She was in my face all her life. I don't want her there again.'

And Sandra knows how that feels; her mother was a bloody nightmare – no offence, and a very sweet woman, obviously, God bless her. But now she's irritated again. Why do people call them 'ashes'? They keep calling them 'ashes' when Ephraim and Sandra never call them ashes. At Fennings, they call them 'cremated remains' which has more class; it's more respectful, less tawdry.

They say to the bereaved, 'When would you like to come and collect the cremated remains?' They never say 'When would you like to collect the ashes?' Yet no one hears them and Sandra sometimes feels like giving up, though Ephraim gets angrier than her. He doesn't stay calm about *that* issue!

'They're cremated remains, for God's sake!' he once screamed in the kitchen. 'Cremated remains!' And she'd never heard him scream before.

So, after reminding Mrs Sykes of a forthcoming bereavement service at the church, she says goodbye and makes a note of the strange apparition last night. She will need to speak to Ephraim about it because it was odd that a hearse should be out and about at that time – especially on the night of the murder.

11

~

'**W**as he a troubled boy?' asks Peter, aware Tamsin feels sick. On the way here, he'd asked her if she was pregnant and her look withered all it touched. And Hallington's office isn't helping. She has opened the door, but nothing can free the room of sweat, layer upon layer, dried into the fabric, soaked into the walls, it permeates the room – a pile of football shirts, random socks, a collection of boots and trainers.

'It's amazing what people can forget,' said Nick as they had walked past the shoe pile. 'You'd think if you arrived with two shoes, you'd notice leaving with only one. But it doesn't seem to work that way.'

The small office window, protected by a metal security panel, is closed. And their host, Stormhaven's youth worker, is a small man but solid – both his body and his hair, which is straight and thick, almost like a mouse-coloured helmet. He's well-bristled and all man; but with a slightly higher-pitched voice than you might expect.

'It's like sitting inside a jockstrap,' he says, sensing Tamsin's discomfort. 'You get used to it.'

Tamsin smiles weakly; but knows there is no level of enlightenment available that will help her to get used to it.

And if she ever does get used to it, should that day arise, she would like to be shot. Then Peter asks the question about Billy.

'All boys are troubled,' says Nick. 'Like all adults. Life is troubling, is it not? And when it stops troubling you, you know you're dead – which might actually be a relief. Perhaps it's a relief for Billy.' He offers a sad smile. 'Especially at that age.'

'You recommend suicide.'

'I recommend football. Gets them into their bodies, helps them forget their troubles for a while, gives them access to all that youthful power and energy...they'll lose it soon enough.'

Nick touches his girth, those extra inches that creep silently through the undergrowth of the years, making sudden show in shocking photos.

'Did you like Billy?'

'I don't think I have accepted his death yet.' He sits up on his chair behind the desk, as if in respect. 'You know, there's this feeling of unreality about it all. It's just not real.'

'Indeed. But obviously you'd heard about his death.'

'I had heard, yes.'

'How?'

'Oh, I was rung up by one of the parents, I think.' He stares back at Tamsin. He's lying; he must be lying. You'd remember that.

'Which one?'

'I really don't remember.'

'Shame.'

'I just hoped I wasn't to blame, of course.'

He sags as one battered by life. Is he referring to the rumours?

'Why would anyone blame you, Mr Hallington?' asks Tamsin innocently. But she's not a good actor, she cannot do the poker face; or maybe she can do the face, but not the tone in her voice. The tone betrays her intention.

'Because, as you are probably aware, Detective Inspector, there have been rumours about me.' Suddenly his eyes look tired. The cost of the rumours is apparent. 'And I know who started them obviously.'

'You do?'

'I do, yes.' His throat has tightened. 'But that doesn't make them less hurtful...or damaging. I go to bed with the lies. I wake up with the lies. They're there in the supermarket; they're there in the bath. There's no escape. They're in your head, that's the thing, which is the worst place for them to be. The council is considering my suspension, pending further enquiries. No one in my line of work can survive rumours. I know what Mary Squires must have felt.'

'Mary Squires?' asks Tamsin.

'The abbot will know. He was at the lecture in the Crypt.' He nods towards Peter.

'Yes, I'm afraid the DI couldn't make it. She was unavoidably detained that night; which I know she regrets.'

'Mary Squires was falsely accused of theft and imprisonment,' says Nick, 'and sentenced to hang – until, at the last minute, the king intervened. I don't see it happening for me.'

'She had a rock-solid alibi which put her many miles from the crime scene,' adds Peter.

'But ye gods – what she endured *before* the king stepped in, eh? The crowds and the fliers all baying for her blood because she was a gypsy; and all of them sure that their darling Elizabeth Canning was telling the truth. When, in fact, as the abbot says, Mary was two hundred miles away in Dorset! What was it again, abbot? "Testis" something.'

'"Testis unus, testis nullus – One witness is no witness."'

'All I know is, you don't want to be on the wrong side of a rumour.'

'So who started them? The rumours, I mean. You mentioned one person being the source.'

'Oh, I know who started them.' A smug smile.

'Are you going to tell us?'

Is he going to tell them?

'James Fairburn – he's a surgeon...Billy's father. Or "William" as he pompously calls him.'

'We know Mr Fairburn.'

'He was at the lecture as well, probably rooting for Elizabeth Canning, because she's his sort of girl. A big fat liar!'

'You know that, do you? You know he's the one?' asks Tamsin and Hallington nods. 'But then what are his reasons? How would that lie help anyone?'

'Oh, it's not rocket science. He isn't trying to help...he's trying to hurt. I dropped Billy for the final, so I need punishing.'

Tamsin is lost. 'You dropped Billy for the final?'

'Yes.'

'But what's that got to do with anything?'

'You're clearly not a football parent, Detective Inspector. They're maniacs, half of them. When the child is an extension of the parent's ego, you're sitting on a very unstable volcano. I never have trouble with the boys, but the *parents...*'

'So what happened?' asks Peter.

'It's the *Waitrose Cup*, which a lot of local teams take part in.'

'Does it have a sponsor?' He can't help himself.

'Stormhaven got to the final this year, which was a miracle, given we're about the tenth best team in a league of nine. And it should have been a happy day...we've never got to the final before. And while Billy had done well in the league, I stayed with the group of players who'd got us to the final. And he couldn't cope with that.'

'Who – Billy?'

'No, Mr Fairburn. The hatred in his eyes when he found out! They were pus.'

'And so he started the rumours about you – and people believed them?'

'He is very persuasive – and well-thought of, of course. He's a surgeon, and everyone loves a surgeon. So not a good enemy.'

His ex-wife had said something similar.

'Perhaps Fairburn was pushing at an already open door?'

Hallington takes the hit. 'Sports coaches are the new pariahs, I know that. We're all Barry Bennell, every coach a pervert, we've joined the *"Scout Masters and Vicars"* club...though he did apologise to me.'

'Fairburn?'

'No, Billy. He apologised for his dad, for his behaviour – and said he was going to end it all.'

'End what?'

'I don't know. I thought he meant suicide at first, but it didn't sound like that – I mean, why would the boy want to kill himself? And then I remembered an odd conversation with him. He once asked me if I believed in God. It was quite out of the blue, for no reason and – well, I'd never really thought about it, to be honest. So I said I wasn't sure and he said, 'I don't believe anything now – not after what he's done.'

'Who?'

'He didn't say, he went quiet after that. It was as if he thought I knew, but I didn't know. He often spoke of a priest in Lewes, so I suppose I always presumed...'

'There's a lot of presuming going on,' says Peter.

'Leaving Billy out of the cup final team was not easy; one of the hardest decisions of my life.' Tears appear in his eyes. 'I was very fond of him. And he didn't need to apologise to me, not at all; I knew it wasn't anything to do with him...big-hearted boy.'

'And someone killed him, Nick.'

'We seem to have brought the socks with us,' says Peter in the car. The cold prohibits opening the window to freshen the jaded air.

'And what's a jock strap?'

'A form of support, not case-relevant.'

'And quite a performance back there.'

'You don't think he's genuine?'

She laughs and there's silence again. She regards lack of trust as a virtue. It is the desire not to be taken in; to see through the other, to come out on top. 'There's something about that trio.'

'Which trio?'

'The reverend, the surgeon and the sports coach.'

'Is this the start of a joke?'

'Each of them points to the other, in a triangle of accusation. Did you notice? The reverend points us to the surgeon, the surgeon points to the sports coach and the sports coach takes us back to the reverend. Round and round the mulberry bush, we'll be getting dizzy soon... and perhaps that's what they want. Sow confusion, distraction, fake news. And they all push the suicide story, as though it's likeliest of tales. You sense they'd all love it to be suicide.'

But Mary Houseman's last work on earth had been to suggest otherwise. Her final discovery on that freezing jetty had been to find in the crevice a piece of rubber, used to wedge the foot there. They had then gone back to the body and found sticky traces of tape on the left ankle. Billy had been tethered to the jetty, like a sacrifice.

'We need to visit Mr Fenning,' says Peter. 'Ephraim Fenning.'

'Yes. I can't do it now; the stink in that office has made me feel ill.'

'Do they not sweat in Hove?'

'I'm not right.'

Unusual for Tamsin, thinks the abbot. She's normally feisty in investigations, up and at 'em; not a quivering and sickening soul at all. But if you aren't a fan of stale sweat – and really, who is? – then Hallington's office will have been challenging.

'That's OK, I know him, I can drop in and at least make contact. I'm not sure you'd warm to him anyway; he is a little spooky.'

'That rather goes with the territory, doesn't it? It must take a particular sort to go into the undertaking trade. I mean, who does that? Most of us avoid death as much as possible.'

'Says a DI in the murder squad.'

'We solve it; we don't wash it, dress it, remove its dentures and comb its hair.'

'Ephraim is like a piece of Victorian furniture...reassuring in a way.' Terrible visions of tat pass through Tamsin's mind; furniture ingrained with the stains of other people's bodies, other people's lives, generations of spillage and hidrosis. This was not furniture that would gain entry into her flat; but find itself fiercely turned away at the door by both the style and hygiene police. 'A link to the past, I suppose.'

'I don't want a link to the past.'

'Though what he really thinks, who knows? And it's probably best we don't. The undertaker is one of those roles, like the royal family, where you are not allowed an opinion. You simply offer timeless solemnity and care.'

They are approaching Tesco's, just up from Fennings. 'I have no place for the past,' says Tamsin, baldly. 'I have no place for it on my mantelpiece and no place for it in my front room.'

'So much work for the therapist, Tamsin.'

'The one I won't be employing. I'll drop you off by Tesco's... and tomorrow morning, having sat with the spook and his coffins, I want you to tell me who killed young Billy Carter – the kind boy with grandiose illusions. Do you think you could do that for me?'

She does look ill, thinks Peter. *She's got this wretched flu. And it takes some people very badly indeed.*

'Rest,' he says. 'I don't want to hear from you.'

12

'**A** most tragic day, abbot,' says Ephraim. They sit in the back office of Fennings Funeral Services, an unfortunate acronym, though rarely noticed. There's a door to the reception area, through which their grieving business arrives; and then another door to the side, which leads into the Fennings' own living quarters.

'I was told it was like the Tardis,' Peter says and Ephraim smiles.

'Making me, I suppose, Doctor Who.' He likes the idea of being a time lord.

Their three-storey accommodation, tall and narrow, gives way out the back to a large garage, where the three limousines are housed, as well as the showroom, where coffins are viewed, if customers wish for more than just a brochure-image.

'You must live and breathe the business, Ephraim. There's death wherever you turn; presumably you don't mind that?'

'It has to be a vocation, abbot. One could not survive otherwise. Sandra has come to see that, I believe. She has grown into the calling – slowly, and with a no little help from my good self. But I don't hold that against her.'

He holds it against her. Sandra is younger than Ephraim, and regarded as something of a trainee in the undertaking trade...though married twenty years. Some lessons take a while.

'She's a very good front-of-house,' says Peter. 'I've heard her with the customers.'

'I'm glad you think so. It wasn't always that way, as I say. But she's learning.' He trusts he has been a father-figure to her, guiding her firmly but gently.

'She has an attentive manner about her.' Ephraim nods knowingly. 'And popular, I'd imagine.'

'Oh yes, everyone in Stormhaven knows Sandra! Wherever we go, someone will come up to her and say, "I know you!" She's particularly good at selling headstones and keepsakes,' he says, smiling naughtily.

'Keepsakes?'

'A growing business, abbot; and growing very nicely. I used to laugh at them but I don't laugh now. We even have a keepsakes brochure – always a sign that the company smell money.'

'It *is* a business, I suppose.'

'We are here to serve, of course; we are servants of Stormhaven, I have always said this to Sandra. We are servants above all else. Not Fennings *of* Stormhaven but Fennings *for* Stormhaven. You see the difference?'

'Neat linguistic footwork.'

'But the servant must *eat*, I say that to Sandra as well; so, grief must pay, of course it must. And the cremated remains in a heart locket are popular, very popular. The remains of your loved one nestling at your breast, knocking at your heart all day long! That's how I sell them and it is rather beautiful in its way. Do you not think so?' The abbot isn't sure. 'Or perhaps the deceased's fingerprint on a small and tasteful metal plate... that's another popular one.'

'Their fingerprint?'

'It can be taken post-mortem. Life has left but the print remains, after all. We take the hand and press it onto a plate, which it can be worn easily around the neck thereafter. *The Happy Prints*, we call it. £24.99.'

Peter has no desire for the ashes of a loved one knocking against his heart; nor does their dead finger appeal. But what does he know? And more pressing still, does he even have a loved one?

'Probably not my cup of tea,' he says.

'I always say to Sandra that people must be allowed to grieve in their own way. Their way is not your way perhaps, abbot. But if a keepsake is an aid to those who mourn, who are we to hold it back and say, "This you are not allowed!"'

Peter is familiar with the line: 'People must be allowed to grieve in their own way.' It is delivered by the caring professions, as if some piece of holy writ, a pious mantra, in the noble cause of leaving people to work out their grief alone. Only, it assumes people know *how* to grieve, when most don't, they haven't a clue and how can they? No one shows us how, until it hits us like a brick in the face. We get on with it, in shock, in pain, in ignorance and in rage. Whether we get on with it well, whether our choices are wise, or indeed healing, is quite another matter. He doesn't mention this.

'Are you involved in the funeral arrangements for Billy?' Ephraim assumes this is the abbot's business this morning. 'I didn't know you knew the family, but we will, of course, be pleased to...'

'I do not come about the funeral, Ephraim.'

'Oh?'

'I have another life, you may be unaware. But I am part of the team that is investigating the murder of Billy Carter.'

'Oh?' He says it again. 'Well, most intriguing, I'm sure. But I am not entirely without knowledge of your investigative exploits, abbot.'

'Well...'

'No, I was a great lover of the Bell Theatre where such dark things occurred recently.'

Peter remembered the case, which involved significant trauma. And he still wakes with the nightmares.

'It was all quite difficult.' *An understatement.*

'I mean, what must it have been like to be buried underground? Most of us do not get there until we no longer care!'

Peter has no wish to remember those events; though he remembers them all. They linger in his psyche like untethered ghosts, particularly at night, when they walk through walls. And sometimes they grow, expanding, not diminishing, with time; and rather than moving on, he finds himself more cloyingly entangled.

'But suicide is such a tragedy.'

'Indeed. Though in this case, Mr Fenning, as I say, we don't believe it was suicide.'

'I rather suspected suicide myself, when I heard of it, knowing Billy as I do – as I *did*...I quite imagined suicide. He always struck me as a rather lost soul. Lovely but lost.' He smiles and pauses to allow time for Peter to agree. 'Suicide would not have surprised me, not in the least. But then who am I to know more than the police?' he asks. 'If you speak of it as murder, then murder it must be, abbot. Though we must hope the fool in all this does not turn out to be you.'

'We cannot be sure.'

'A great tragedy, and – if evidence of murder *is* confirmed, which may be a struggle – an unforgiveable crime against a boy who I regarded as a son.' He nods his head to confirm the truth of this utterance.

'And who was with you on the day of his death?'

'Quite so, quite so – and this is the pain of the matter. He was a carrier at the cremation of Mrs Dowd...effortlessly in step, as always.' He is picturing the smooth journey of the coffin into the crematorium – eased from the hearse, then up onto the shoulders, the pause to steady and then the ascent of the steps and measured procession down the aisle. 'He replaced young Jonathan, a sorry tale. His left leg was longer than his right – something he failed to mention at the interview. We should have asked, I suppose; we carelessly assumed equal length. But it became apparent soon enough, at the cremation of Mr Braithwaite, a large man – we almost had a terrible accident.

And that was a shame, quite apart from the complaints of
the family, because Jonathan was a very decent young fellow.
But with leg issues, so perhaps more suited to another career,
maybe behind a desk.'

'And afterwards?'

'Afterwards? Well, as I say, we apologised for the incident
and had to let him go...'

'No, Billy – after the funeral yesterday?'

'Oh, well, he came back here; he usually did after a cremation,
in one of the limousines. He could look very solemn when he
needed to... and we were a second home in a way.'

'So you spoke with him?'

'Cathy made some tea and biscuits then disappeared rather
quickly. We sat here, right where we now sit, abbot – the dead-
in-waiting, you might say.' The abbot's eyebrows rise. 'And then
he moved on, I imagine, as young people do – though how he
got to Splash Point?...'

'You say this was his second home?'

'You may not be aware, abbot,' he leans forward, confidentially,
'but Sandra was his child-minder, as I believe they are called.
When Cathy was trying to get that therapy business of hers
going, she rather "left him here", one might say – when who
knows, the best therapy might have been to be with her boy?'
Again, he seeks agreement. 'But no matter, one does not judge.'
He brushes some dust from his trousers. 'But yes, we did see a
lot of young Billy; and all the more because of his absent father,
perhaps the greatest crime of all. "Lads without dads" as they
say; so very vulnerable.'

'A telling phrase.'

'Billy needed a father, as any boy does; and with Mr Fairburn's
desertion – well, I do believe the young lad was murdered
twice.' Ephraim is aware of the drama in his declaration. He
drops his head, as might the prosecution counsel with their
summing up complete.

'And perhaps you were that man?'

'Who?' He is worried.

'The father Billy never had.'

'Oh, one must not presume, of course! But, well, one does one's best.'

'Care amongst the coffins,' says Peter, warmly.

'I believe Mrs Fenning would be glad of such a thought. Though maybe order is more important for a young lad.'

'Order?'

'I do believe in order, Abbot. When people come to me, when they walk through our door, what they most need is order. Their world has fallen apart, they can't think straight; they don't need my compassion, rest assured, they have others for that; but they do need my *order*. So everything here at *Fennings* is orderly.'

'Though not the death of Billy.'

'Well, that was not here, of course. That was down at Splash Point...some way away.'

'Quite.'

'We control what we can control, abbot.'

'And what you can't control?'

'I find I can control most eventualities,' he says with a smile. 'Dear Billy will receive our order in death, just as the poor boy did in life.'

13

~

'I am aware this is early, gentlemen, but *early* seems best in the circumstances. Shall we sit down?'

Fenning plays the Master of Ceremonies; and after ordering three coffees, an undertaker, a youth worker and a reverend find a corner table in *The Plough*. It is a popular pub in Church Street, offering Sussex beers and a menu of fish and chips, burger and chips, steak pie and mash, 'solid fare' as Ephraim calls it – as well as private space for mid-morning coffee, which suits the guests this morning. The coffee doesn't suit them; you wouldn't come here for the coffee – not a barista in sight. But the privacy does, for apart from the sad or the desperate, no one's in a pub at 11.00am.

Fenning had said, 'It's not that we have anything to hide, gentlemen. But the watching world does not have to watch everything. God gave us eyelids because sometimes we do not have to see.' So they arrived separately.

'I just felt it might be helpful to talk,' says Fenning.

'About what?' It's Hallington. He is unsettled by the sight of Ephraim in a pub; his unease clear. He is a one-trick pony and his trick is death – so what's he doing here? Ephraim responds by trying to make a funeral parlour of the pub; a parlour where he is king.

'I merely say that when the police are busy-busy, the innocent must look after themselves. And I believe we are all receiving rather unwarranted police attention. I sense the direction of the wind.'

'Only doing their job,' says Nick, looking at him pointedly. 'The innocent have nothing to worry about. Do they? *Well, do they?*'

'I sent them straight to Rodmell,' says the Reverend, carelessly. 'I sent them to James Fairburn...seemed the likeliest one to me.'

Ephraim nods. 'And I don't imagine that troubles *you* very much, Nick? I mean, a good stint behind bars for Dr Fairburn wouldn't do your cause any harm. After all, he does rather bully you, I'm told, down on the football pitch. Maybe the reverend has done you a favour.'

Fairburn was on Nick's mind; this was true. Somewhere along the way, the man had learned to push and intimidate; and yes, recently, Hallington had been under his nasty cosh and could see his own ruin down the line. He liked his football coaching. He'd qualified after selling the cafe he used to run in the high street. But in his line of work, it only takes one bad rumour, one sour relationship with the wrong person, and suddenly the scenery is changed. Fairburn, by not doing a great deal, could destroy him.

'I'm saying nothing,' says Hallington, thereby saying it all. And then their coffee arrives, and Ephraim tastes it, declares it lukewarm and sends it straight back.

'This won't do,' he says fussily. 'It really won't do. It seems to have arrived via the fridge!'

'It's just coffee,' says Hallington, who can't see the point of making a fuss. Some things in life matter – and he can think of a few of them right now. The recent death of his father, for instance – dogged by inadequate care for the last few months of his life. Now *that* mattered, that's what had killed him – and Nick had dealt with it. But lukewarm coffee?

'Call me old fashioned, Hallington, but if I pay for something, I do look for some return.' A humble smile accompanies

Ephraim's words; while the reverend is sitting there wondering what's going on; wondering if he's being accused of something or whether they are there to accuse someone else. He leaves half an hour later, none the wiser. He walks to his car which he parked on the seafront, where there's no charge – free parking by the sea, possibly Stormhaven's finest feature. But really, what a strange affair in *The Plough*! He'd attended some odd ones in his time; it was a long list. But this had surely been the strangest coffee morning of them all?

No one had quite said anything, as if skirting round, but never touching, the most awful of secrets.

14

'She was strangled in her flat – in Hardwicke House.' Tamsin gives the information over the phone, and in haste.

'Hardwicke House?' says Peter. 'That's just along from me.'

'So we need to be there.' The local geography is not her concern. 'When can you make it?'

'Strangled?'

'You seem to be one question behind, abbot.'

'I've just woken up.'

It is 5.30am and he has over-slept. He rarely misses the 5.00am news on the World Service. Did his alarm not go off? There's none more lost than an early bird who is late; caught out by the phone, confused and unclear, his mind still drenched in disturbing dreams. His dreams are always disturbing, this is not new. He doesn't wake up screaming – drowning or falling from a cliff. But he does wake unsettled. He has only twice in his life woken up happy, and – because of the rarity of the event – he can remember the exact when and where of both occasions. He's unclear as to the *why* of this disturbance...why all mornings, except two, should offer such traumatised dawns. But for every trouble he has, someone else has two; and for one old lady today, there is no dawn at all.

'Take a deep breath, abbot and forget any coffee, there isn't time.' This is a blow; but Tamsin is enjoying this. She's enjoying getting him up; enjoying being up and about earlier than the early bird. 'And yes, she was strangled...though not the most difficult of tasks. She's as frail as a stick apparently.'

'The victim?'

'We need to be there.'

Oh, the impatience at the other end.

'And you think there's a link?' asks the abbot, beginning to engage. 'I presume you believe there's a link to Billy.'

There's another sigh down the phone. It is fortunate he is not charged extra for sighs. 'When a one-horse town has two deaths in forty-eight hours, a link is the presumption, yes. When can you be there?' He'd been hoping for a run up the cliffs before breakfast; but that wasn't going to happen. 'Ten minutes? I'll pick you up in ten minutes. No coffee.'

'I'll walk, Tamsin. The walk will do me good.' And he'd have a quick cup of coffee.

'It's No.4,' she says, though as things transpire, the flat number is not important. Peter follows the protective gear on arrival, the bustle of high-viz jackets and a chaotic police presence he must assume is organised. Tamsin sees him and calls out to a colleague, 'Are you done?'

'We're done.'

'SOCO are done, abbot, you can come in.' She indicates to a constable to lift the cordon at the end of the covered corridor, which leads residents of Hardwicke House to their sea-view flats. He is handed protective gear. 'We can't have a habit on the crime scene.'

'I'll take it off.'

'Can you do that? I thought you slept in it.'

'I've never slept in it.'

'Come through when you're changed and tell me what you see.'

'Why would I sleep in it?' says Peter, dodging behind a pillar.

'In case you wake up and forget who you are. Isn't that the point of uniforms – reassurance for the insecure? Ready?'

'Or maybe it's the nullification of self.'

Tamsin looks tired; more drained than he has ever seen her. He makes no mention, because no mention will end well. She doesn't like being told she looks tired; it is heard as an insult rather than empathy. They enter the blessed warmth of the hallway of this two bedroom accommodation – a china fruit bowl on the side with shiny china fruit. 'Almost took one before I realised,' jokes a PC, and Tamsin tells him he can get out now.

'The boy's an idiot.'

There's a cuckoo clock on the wall and lace on the display cabinet containing figurines from another time; though the life-size figure in the front room is fresh, sitting back in her arm chair, shocked at the rough hands placed round her neck, gazing at the telly, still playing, breakfast TV, chuckles on the studio sofa, an amusing guest – though no one's amused in No 4, Hardwicke House, her eyes wide open in blue-skinned terror...an elderly lady, strangled while watching TV.

'Last night some time,' says Tamsin, 'between 6.00pm – 10.00pm? I think we can turn the TV off now. At least she never lived to watch this drivel.'

'Every cloud.'

'She's Mrs Truelove. Roberta Truelove – they must have wanted a son, poor girl. Why couldn't dad just let her be a girl and be herself?'

'There speaks little Tamsin.'

'And the attacker wore gloves and took nothing as far as we can see. She has a tin of money and some jewellery which all remain present and correct. We don't believe her drawers have been searched. This isn't burglary. So she let them in, and then sat down with them – that's how it looks.'

'She knew them.'

'You'd imagine...or just very trusting, which may have been her last mistake. There are no traces of a scuffle in the hall or in here. She died in her chair.'

'So we want her address book and her phone records,' says Peter. 'She'll have an address book for Christmas cards.'

'Christmas cards?'

'They used to be traditional at Christmas.'

'Only for the Incontinence Club.'

'Both harsh and inaccurate, Tamsin. And the "Killing of Truelove". No one wants that on their CV.'

'I'm sorry?' Tamsin is checking the windows, already feeling trapped in a flat she could never live in. But no one could have arrived through the window in this second floor home, unless they'd abseiled from the roof, which no one did in Stormhaven. The killer had arrived through the front door and Mrs Truelove had sensed no danger.

'It just somehow seems worse,' says Peter, and he hears his own vague melancholy. 'To murder someone called Truelove.'

'We must hope the judge remembers that when sentencing.'

'I see no immediate link with Billy.'

'There will be.'

'Ephraim Fenning thought he'd committed suicide, by the way.'

'Well, there's a thing. They're all keen on the suicide story, we've been over this.'

'And perhaps they are right.' It is a sudden thought, a hand on his shoulder, before everything gets too messy, before they plunge further in the mire. 'Perhaps he did...people do. Perhaps Mary just found a piece of rubber, unrelated to Billy? Which just leaves one murder – the killing of Mrs Truelove, which has nothing to do with Billy. After all, twelve men commit suicide every day; twelve men a-day leave family and friends shattered. And eight of those have never had any contact with a health professional. Men just do it, out of the blue. Are there bleaker statistics than those?'

'Billy wasn't one of them.'

~

Though they continue the discussion back at the abbot's house, where he has finally laid his hat, after twenty-five years in the desert. Never mind the sea view and two reasonably sized bedrooms, one of them almost a double. It was excitement enough that for the first time in his life, the abbot had his own kettle.

'I have my own kettle,' he'd told a neighbour, soon after arrival and she had wondered if he was special needs. She took to speaking to him more slowly – and louder. But in those early days, after years of community living, the kettle had seemed almost indecent, hedonism gone mad. And he still enjoyed the privilege of going to the kitchen, filling it up, clicking the switch and listening as it boiled the water for the tea. He was even happy to boil it for others occasionally.

'Let's start with the killing of Billy. Who do we believe?' asks Tamsin. 'The Reverend Hand who says it was the surgeon Fairburn? Fairburn who says it was football coach Hallington? Or Hallington who says it was the Reverend Hand?' Or none of the above?'

'Billy spent his last day on earth with the Fennings, helping at a funeral,' the abbot adds.

'So, what did you learn from him?' She is irritated that she hadn't felt well enough to be there; and hopes that not too much occurred. With the best will in the world, she doesn't wish for another Abbot Peter success story – though she's happy for him to contribute to hers.

'I learned that he likes to be in control.'

'Which I regard as a virtue.'

'And which everyone else on the planet understands to be a compulsion, born of an insecure relationship with uncertainty. But that apart, he confirmed that Billy did spend a lot of time there when young. His wife, Sandra, was Billy's childminder; though he clearly didn't approve of Cathy Carter leaving him to start her therapy business. Let me take your phone – you're not listening. It would help us if you let go of it for ten minutes. Just ten.' Peter holds out his hand

'Let go of my phone?' The incredulity is twenty-four carat. 'I wouldn't let go of my phone for *anyone* or *anything*. Why would I do that?'

'Life?'

'And it's still cold in here.'

'That's why I made you piping hot coffee, which you haven't touched. A hot drink helps.'

'As does heating; it's why fire was invented. The walls themselves are cold; they're on my side in this discussion. They're begging for warmth.'

'Not as persistently as you.'

'Was Scott of the Antarctic your uncle?'

He submits. 'I'll light the fire.'

He is cold himself, to be honest, and he is just being mean; so he sets about scrumpling up old newspapers into paper balls, packing them in, kindling wood on top.

'Remember what I showed you,' she says. 'And you'll need some larger logs ready.' With a strike of a match the fire is lit, flame leaping into life and a couple of larger logs quickly added. 'You're learning.'

The difference is immediate, more the mood than the heat. He should have done this straight away when they'd arrived. He is still learning the art of hospitality. Tamsin is visibly happier and even unbuttons her coat.

'And so to return to your question, abbot: do we believe Billy Carter and his schoolboy note about people wanting to kill him?'

'Well...'

'I mean, what if, as you were sort-of suggesting just now, young Billy *was* just another paranoid attention-seeker from a broken home? What if, as you suggest, it was suicide?'

Peter is surprised at this about-turn.

'It's unlike you to change your mind.'

'We only have his word for it, and how reliable a word is that? Just because a number of inadequate men are saying it was suicide, doesn't mean it wasn't. "Slightly grandiose" was the reverend's assessment. "Un-tethered to reality."' She sighs. 'I've met a few of those.'

Her phone goes.

'Yes?' she says briskly. 'Oh they have?...that was quick...*what?*...
really?!...they're sure?...good work...now trawl the neighbours.'
She holds the phone on her lap, pondering. 'We have Mrs
Truelove's phone records, her landline. You'll never guess who
she spoke to last, yesterday afternoon.'

'Enlighten me.'

'Ephraim Fenning. Hold the suicide theory.'

15

'A wasted journey, Detective Inspector – though a commendable one,' says Ephraim Fenning with a smile. He holds a small urn in the front office. 'Cremated remains,' he says, looking at the line of Tamsin's gaze.

'Didn't they used to be called ashes?'

'Not at Fennings, no,' he says, firmly.

'It's considered common,' adds Peter and only Tamsin sees the laughter in his eyes.

'Now excuse me a moment,' says Ephraim. 'There is a cupboard for these. We like to house them together while awaiting collection. We half-imagine the remains talk among themselves; so we're careful as to who is sat next to who! One thinks of those awful wedding reception meals. Ralph?' A boy's head appears at the door, almost too quickly, as if he has been waiting. He is spotty and a little dead in the eyes; but with more of a physical presence than his father, squarer and less neck. There must have been a boxer in the Fenning blood line. 'Ralph, take these to the remains cupboard, could you?'

'You must have known Billy well, Ralph,' says the abbot seizing the moment and Ralph is pleased to be spoken to.

'I did know him well, yeh.'

There isn't a lot of energy to Ralph. The abbot notes that he repeats lines, saving himself the exhausting business of invention.

'All very upsetting.' Ralph nods.

'Perhaps you could take these remains to the cupboard, Ralph?' Ephraim presses them into his hands, but the abbot persists.

'And you were with him the afternoon before he died, I hear.'

Ephraim intervenes with a smile. 'My son is a fount of wisdom, truly he is, but a little busy at the moment, abbot; so perhaps the questions can wait?'

'We will need to speak with him.'

'Of course – I mean, we just have no desire to upset him any further, he is quite devastated, as you can see...'

'And *today*,' adds Tamsin. 'We'll need to speak with him today. So no flannel.'

'Quite.' It is as if he has been slapped; he smarts visibly. 'Time is of the essence, as they say, and the first twenty-four hours of the investigation the most important, I am not unaware of these things, Detective Inspector...though perhaps I bridle a little at concern for a child being compared to "flannel".'

'He's not a child, Mr Fenning. He's a young man, with a very important story to tell.' Ralph is gazing at Tamsin and nodding. He *is* a young man and he *does* have an important story to tell; and he'd mainly like to tell it to Tamsin. 'And we do need to know about the phone call, Mr Fenning.'

'The phone call, yes.' Ephraim waves Ralph away. The boy reluctantly peels himself from the wall and leaves. Ephraim closes the door behind him as if they have just evicted a very dangerous rat. 'Which particular phone call? I make so many.'

'We're most interested in one you received, a couple of days ago. According to our phone records, you were the last person Mrs Truelove spoke with.' She leaves a pause which Ephraim doesn't fill. 'That's quite a thing, isn't it? Shall we sit down?'

And then anxiety enters. 'Oh my God!' says Sandra as she takes in the scene round the table. 'What's this?'

'It's the police, dear. They're just checking one or two things. Nothing to concern yourself with.'

'Had the Fosdykes in today. Remember them, abbot? Nice family. You buried the mother. They've asked for you again.'

'Well, I'm sure something will be possible. But maybe we can have that discussion later...'

'They were very appreciative, couldn't say "Thank you" enough. So whatever you did – '

'I just took the funeral.'

'Well, they liked it very much. So what are you doing here now?'

'He also helps the police sometimes,' says Ephraim. 'So we have to remember that.'

'Helps the police sometimes?'

No, he saves the police sometimes.

'He helps the police, yes. So if that's all, dear?'

'And, of course, you knew Billy better than any of us, Sandra. You looked after him when he was young?'

'Oh, I did, yes, sweet boy – wasn't he, dear?'

'Indeed, Sandra. It's all very tragic.'

'It's all very tragic, yes,' says Sandra, nodding her head – her body, a constant movement, as if wound up and set in motion.

'So we'll need to talk with you as well, Sandra,' says Tamsin.

'Oh, you don't want to talk with me, I don't know anything!' she says, her voice going too high, 'I've always done my best – but not this, not this.'

'Are you OK, Sandra?' asks the abbot.

'I'm having one of my wobbles,' she says, with a grimace.

'It's what the doctor calls it,' adds Ephraim with a smile. "Wobbles are fine," he said to her, "It's how God made you, dear," which has always seemed rather a good answer to me. Maybe it *is* just how God made us sometimes and there's nothing the NHS can do. We can't always be running to someone else to save us, though it seems to be the way these days. Perhaps some rest, dear – God's best cure?'

The doorbell goes in Reception, a customer has arrived; though Ephraim prefers them called 'clients'. Sandra brushes down her black dress, two inches below the knee and moves towards the door. She takes a deep breath, smiles at the assembled cast and disappears to work. She seems almost relieved, like a beetroot leaving the oven.

'There is no story here,' says Ephraim with a firm smile. 'Mrs Truelove simply rang me about a relation who'd died up north. It was a very simple enquiry. Does that answer your question?'

'She rang about a relation in the north because?'

'She wanted to know about costs.'

'You were handling the funeral.'

'No, she was going with the Co-op.' It is clear he doesn't like using the word, as if he blasphemes in some manner. 'They undercut everyone these days, but you can't buy people's souls. They'll get their comeuppance.'

'So where in the north did Mrs Truelove's relation live?'

'My geography is not good beyond St Albans, I'm afraid.'

'And she didn't want *you* to handle it?'

'Too far away, undertakers do not travel well. We know our patch, beyond which we get very lost! So, if that is all...'

'Then why was she ringing?'

'To find out about costs, as I say.' He is slightly irritated at all these questions, when the answer is quite simple. 'She was using me, I suppose, as others might use a website. For information – it's not unusual.'

'And did you help her?'

'Of course I helped her...one can hardly refuse help to the bereaved.'

'She was recently bereaved?'

'One must assume so. My clients tend to be.' He allowed himself a quiet chuckle. 'I suppose she could have been asking for a friend.'

'Asking for a friend?'

The Abbot is noticing the drift into vagueness.

'Abbot, it was a brief phone call, as I remember, in which she was asking about cost, she was not asking about anything else – and it was not my business to ask.' Ephraim is as animated as he gets; but slows as he continues. 'An undertaker must always be aware of boundaries and not presume upon people. Do you understand? One must *never* presume upon people. I mean, one hears stories of undertakers pressing for business, when the bereaved are vulnerable, perhaps that's what they do at the Cooperative Funeral Services, who can say? But not here. We do not do that at Fennings.'

'Did you know Mrs Truelove?'

'Of course, I knew her. We handled the funeral of her husband a few years ago – Leonard, I believe. Or perhaps Arnold...no, that was their dog, I think. We buried him as well. Or was Leonard their dog? Mrs Fenning will know...'

'Apparently she was a former Sunday school teacher at St Botolph's in Lewes,' says Tamsin, cutting in. Johnson's text had arrived a few minutes ago. They'd found Mrs Truelove's 'Leaving book', after 37 years' service at the church; and Tamsin could have kissed Johnson all over – as long as it didn't involve any touching.

'Indeed,' says Ephraim recovering quickly from his canine equivocation. 'She was a Sunday School teacher there, quite a fierce one I'd imagine – no sitting quietly by blue Galilee with Mrs Truelove! Which is why the priest there, the Reverend Hand, took the funeral.'

'The Reverend Hand? He knew Mrs Truelove?'

16

~

'Look, Cathy, I really need your help.'

James Fairburn is smaller than she remembers him. People diminish in size when they no longer hold power over you, they fill less space, she feels this; though his hands remain huge.

'Is this why you're not behaving like a shit?'

He has been polite thus far, even taking off his shoes in the entrance, which he never used to do, knowing how she liked it. 'I don't want the street on my carpet,' she'd say. 'You don't know where my socks have been!' he'd say – though she'd had a fair idea. But today it is just his socks, smart casual from M&S.

'I've had police at the hospital for God's sake!'

'Injured?'

'If I'd had my way.'

'So what were they doing?'

She has made him coffee, prepared for the visit by his phone call. She has sat him in the side room, where she meets clients. She was unsure what power he still possessed, so the counselling room seemed best. James is in the client's chair, and yes, he looks smaller; and quite needy.

'They're asking questions about me – I mean, I'm a surgeon, for God's sake, and they're asking questions like I'm some cleaner from Lithuania!'

'Or a sturgeon, as Billy used to say.'

'Did he?'

'He always referred to you as a sturgeon after doing a school project on them.' She smiles at the memory. Most adult knowledge is discovered not through university studies but school projects undertaken by their children and Cathy had ended up knowing a great deal about sturgeon; though little about happiness.

'Look, this is serious.' He wants her to focus.

'It amused me that sturgeon are most active between dusk and dawn – which as I recall, rather mirrored your behaviour at the time, in bedrooms other than ours, of course.'

James is not amused and neither had Cathy been at the time. But time, like frost, makes for different scenery; and she now remembers these things with amusement and disdain. He has not been here, in her home, for ten years. 'It can't have been ten years!' he says when she mentions it. And Cathy doesn't know the man. Well, she knows him; perhaps she knows him better than ever; but she doesn't know what she was doing with him all those years ago. He seems a stranger. Were they really together? Did they really bring Billy into the world?

'And you fear reputational damage?'

'Look, I can't afford this, Cathy, I really can't. I need you to tell them.'

'Tell them what?'

'That I'm not a member of some paedophile ring. That's what they seem to think.'

'A paedophile ring?'

'I mean, do I look like a member of a paedophile ring?' he gesticulates in frustration. 'Really? I'm a surgeon, for God's sake!'

'Yes, I'd give up on the "surgeon" thing, James. It gets less impressive every time you mention it; less impressive and more insecure. Like Harold Shipman proclaiming, "I'm a doctor, for God's sake!"'

'There is no comparison.'

'At the end of the day, you're just a well-paid plumber. And as a recent biography makes plain, Bob Dylan is a complete shit apparently, a liar of the first order. There's no connection between talent and virtue. So while you *are* a surgeon, what you do with the rest of your life, who knows? I never did.'

'Well, that's bloody helpful, that is! And what's Dylan got to do with anything? Never liked him anyway.' She smiles. 'Are you taking pleasure in this or something?'

She had never seen him vulnerable. The alpha male who had swept her off her feet, and given her a vicarious sense of worth, was now a different shape, a different being in the client's seat.

'I'm just saying how it is, James. The police won't care that you're a surgeon. It may even excite them. Children have brought down bigger fish than you. Any particular children or young people you're worried about?'

'Of course not, of course not – no one can touch me.'

'I do think Billy was abused.'

James is silent.

'That's ridiculous.'

'What's ridiculous?'

'The idea of it.'

'It was about the time that you moved out, as I think back. I'm not saying it was you.'

'You can't say it was me!'

'I've never said it was you.'

'Did you say this to the police?'

'I voiced my concerns – but not about you especially.'

'You voiced your concerns!' So, *Cathy* was the source! He rages for a moment, and she remembers his rages and can't help but flinch; old body reactions kick in. 'No wonder they're up my backside with questions!' He has taken control for a moment, suddenly in charge. Cathy feels the panic and focuses on the client's chair. No going back.

'Not the best analogy,' she says, gathering herself. 'I'm not the whistle blower here. And if you shout again, I will ask you to leave.' It's what she would say to a client, and this is the difference now: she can ask him to leave and the control, momentarily seized, is gone.

'I just need some sort of statement from you, Cathy – as Billy's mother, as my ex-wife, and in your professional capacity as a – therapist.'

The word still sticks in his throat and he's rude about the breed among his colleagues; never misses a chance. "How many therapists does it take to change a light bulb? Only one – but it has to *want* to be changed!" People enjoyed that one. 'As if *I* could blame failure on my patient not wanting to be well!' he'd say, post-op. 'I mean, what an utter cop-out! But it's what the therapists do. They blame their failure on the patient! Well, in my book, that's not science – that's hokum!'

But now he needed a therapist. Perhaps a therapist could be useful for once in their ridiculous lives – if the therapist spoke up for him.

'You know I've never met a woman like you, Cathy,' he says, aiming for the bull's eye.

And she can't deny the power of the words; and the desire for them to be true. Somehow, he can still reach her, she notices this. But then he looks at her, to see if it has worked, it is there in his eyes, shifty, hang dog, clever... checking to see if the stunt has succeeded, like it always bloody used to.

You are a desperate man, thinks Cathy – more desperate than I thought. 'There's probably not much more to say,' she says. 'I'm just not sure what you're so frightened of.'

Though, of course, she does know. And he leaves without saying a word.

17

'I'm like a cold in February, Ernest – I keep coming back.'
The abbot has been sent to see the vicar; and so here
he is again in the thin-walled vicarage, four doors down
from the real thing and a century away from a time when vicars
had power and status. The Reverend Hand is busy enough in
the parish; but not important in the area, as if clergy have now
been sealed inside their religious bubble, measuring their lives
by Sunday attendance, parishioners' crises and the lost festivals
of Christmas and Easter. As for Pentecost, forget it; it's all
Valentine's Day and Halloween these days. And you certainly
don't want the vicar at those.

'I won't keep you long. We just need to ask you about Mrs
Truelove.'

'Mrs Truelove?' He guides Peter to sit down in his gloomy
study, the shelves full of books and icons. He seeks refuge
behind his desk; his last sanctuary, now the outer walls have
been breached.

'She was a Sunday school teacher here, I believe?'

'She was indeed...for thirty-seven years, remarkable in
its way.' He shakes his head in brief wonder. 'You don't find
people like her anymore. Everything's a life-style choice
these days rather than a commitment. Do you find that,

abbot? People take something on and they "see if they like it". In the old days, there was commitment whether you liked it or not. And you stuck at it; you did things until it was a physical impossibility to carry on.' The abbot nods; he will allow the melancholic rant. 'I, of course, only knew her in the fag end of her time here. She was a little stern... but some people like *stern*.'

'Did you like *stern*?'

'I always felt rather judged by her, to be honest. She reminded me of my old teacher, Nellie Willis. She'd stand behind me, and she wouldn't say anything but I could *feel* her judgement. I don't know what darkness she saw in me, but whatever it was, she didn't like it...awful woman. And Mrs Truelove was the same in a way. But there we are, takes all sorts, I suppose – though even as I say that, I don't think it's true. There are some sorts the world really doesn't need.'

'It wasn't that you'd done anything wrong?'

'I beg your pardon?'

'You said you felt judged by Mrs Truelove. I was just wondering if she had any particular crime in mind?'

'I can't help the parish gossip, abbot. We're all at the mercy of that odious little fellow.'

'She has been murdered.'

'*What?*' Ernest Hand stares at him, shock and fear in his eyes. 'Mrs Truelove murdered?'

'Strangled. Do you know anything about that?'

'Why should I know anything about it?'

'You knew both Billy and Mrs Truelove, whose deaths were twenty-four hours apart. It's a swine of a coincidence for you.'

His hands play odd games on his desk, as he searches for a response. 'I'm sure many people know them both.'

The abbot nods again. 'I'm sure they did.'

'I'd help if I could!'

'That's probably enough for now, Ernest. Unless you have anything else to tell us; anything which might prove helpful to the investigation? You must see a great deal...'

'Oh, I *do* see a great deal...but perhaps I don't always understand it. We don't always understand what we see, do we?'

'Understanding can arrive late. Is there anything in particular you don't understand?'

'I don't understand why Mrs Truelove was killed...another bloody mystery alongside all the other bloody and meaningless mysteries. And here ends the lesson.'

He rises, bringing the meeting to an end, like he did sometimes at the PCC, when he was irritated and just wanted everyone gone. He'd suddenly rise and strike a pose by the window, arms behind his back, suddenly distant.

'So keep safe, Ernest.' The reverend doesn't appear to hear and the abbot makes his way to the study door, and then turns. 'I don't know why, but I'm worried for you.'

'Could you show yourself out?' He is sweating a little. 'You should know the way by now.'

He looks vulnerable by the window, this is Peter's thought.

18

'Such a difficult lady,' says Sandra, putting the phone down. She mistakenly assumes interest from Tamsin. 'She only wants the gold tooth from her husband's mouth, all of a sudden! She wants to have a ring made – and wants us to remove it from the corpse! As if we're qualified to remove a tooth whilst retaining facial integrity! Anything could go wrong! Ephraim said he wouldn't be doing it, he was very clear, "I am not a dentist to the dead," he said – but the lady wasn't pleased.'

'And Ralph?' asks Tamsin.

'I mean, I'll wash their hair, the ladies I mean, put it in rollers, smarten them up for display – but remove a tooth?'

'A hairdresser to the dead. That's a particular calling.' Tamsin feels sick.

'We like to please, always. And if that means...'

'And Ralph?'

'Ralph?' She's still with the hairdressing. 'Well, he's still in his room probably. Always in his room, that boy! Would you like me to fetch him?'

'No, we'll talk first, just you and me.' Tamsin puts her small bag on the desk.

Sandra jumps up in terror.

'Oh, you can't put it there!' Sandra darts forward and grabs the bag as if an unexploded bomb. 'Not there.' Tamsin watches aghast. She hates others touching her bag; a serious breach of personal space. 'It's leaning on Doris – and we like to keep her in the clear.'

'I'm sorry?' says Tamsin.

'In the box there – that's Doris.' She points to the light wood casket on the desk.

'You mean, that's someone's ashes on the desk?'

She fails to wrestle the incredulity from her voice.

'Their cremated remains, yes.' Sandra is busy nodding to confirm her own words. 'Doris used to work here until last year, valued member of our staff, until the Big C got her – very sad. But her husband isn't sure what to do, and he doesn't want her lonely while he makes up his mind; and he says how happy she was here, in this very office, so we keep her company for now, no harm done. I'm sure it won't be forever, but to be honest, it's been six months now and it's nice to have someone to talk to...because men don't talk, really.'

And Doris does? thinks Tamsin, before saying 'Quite' as she can't think of anything else to say. Every office has its quirks, but a previous employee's remains on the work desk? *Truly, the biscuit has been taken,* as one of her colleagues would have put it. Though she's now concerned for her bag, wondering if Doris has spilled a little. She picks it up, reclaiming it from the dead and all seems well; there is no sign of Doris anywhere. She sits down, places the bag safely at her feet and seeks normality. She speaks with herself, *it's just another interview, focus on that, Tamsin,* though she can't help feeling there are now three in the room, as if Sandra has acquired an ally; as if Doris is watching them – and none too pleased with Tamsin messing the place up.

'So you and me will talk first, Sandra; and then I'll meet with Ralph.'

'Would you like me to sit in?'

'Sit in where?'

'When you meet with Ralph... I can sit in, if it would help.' She's nodding again.

'I don't think that will be necessary,' says Tamsin, as if to an idiot.

'Sometimes young people speak more freely if their mother's in the room – they say that, you know.'

'No one on *this* planet, Sandra. Maybe they say it in other galaxies, but not in this one.' Tamsin is pained by the fact that she needs Sandra; that Sandra has a significant story to tell in this investigation. She will need to be nice to her, in some manner. 'I am glad, of course, you had such a warm relationship with your own mother,' she adds, attempting to re-build smashed bridges.

'Well, you know, no one's perfect.'

'I find that too. So what can you tell us about Billy, Sandra – or Mrs Truelove?'

'Mrs Truelove?' Sandra is a-fidget. She has finally sat down but has not stopped moving. She'd prefer to be busying herself with something, not trapped in a chair. Her skin is shiny, a seemingly constant sheen of sweat. Though does anxiety have a glow of its own?

'Oh, hadn't you heard? We did tell your husband.'

'Well, I've been out all day at Eastbourne Crem. Gypsy funeral, and they know how to do it, that crowd – proper grief and fireworks with them lot. Have you ever attended a gypsy funeral?' Tamsin fails to reply. 'Wonderful horses...which are expensive, I grant you, but they don't mind, you see, they don't mind – because that's how it is with them. Proper send-off. I mean, I'm not calling the people of Stormhaven cheapskates, but the gypsies know how to do it...'

'Mrs Truelove – she was strangled.' Tamsin leaves a pause. 'Someone else knew how to do it as well...how to kill, I mean.'

Horror fills her eyes; genuine horror.

'Mrs Truelove was...?'

'I don't imagine her funeral will be quite as grand; maybe no horses.'

'Horses are pricey, I won't pretend otherwise.'

'And she had less than £4000 in her account. A lot of it seems to have gone to a village in Africa, some water project.'

Tamsin watches Sandra doing her deathly maths.

'We could do it for less than £4000,' she says. 'With a little left over. I think we could settle on £3600, with one limousine. And that would include doctor's fees. Mr Fenning can talk about the coffin with you. It may not be the finest...'

'I'm not here to arrange her funeral, Sandra.'

'Oh?' Is she stupid?

'I'm here to find out why she died. I did introduce myself as a Detective Inspector.'

'You did, yes.'

'It's why I will be talking to Ralph.'

'Of course, yes, all over the place this morning, me.' She's nodding again.

'And you knew her, of course. You'd arranged the funeral of her husband.'

'Arnold.'

'Lionel.'

'Lionel, yes, Lionel, never forget a name. I mean, his dog was Arnold, lovely red setter.'

'Do you remember anything else?'

'What like?'

'Anything.'

'The Rev Hand took the service, I know that; and I was the funeral director that day. Two of the mourners were late – and I wouldn't allow them in until they started to sing "Abide with me", I remember that as well. The Reverend Hand doesn't like latecomers interrupting proceedings, particularly his opening words – he places great store on his opening words and makes them wait until a song; which is also what they do at the Devonshire Theatre in Eastbourne, so it must be all right. I mean, they don't have a hymn there, obviously, that wouldn't work, but they wait until there's a pause, a new scene. Lovely theatre, the Devonshire. Have you been?'

'And Lionel's funeral?'

'It had rained a little in the morning, because there was some spray on the car when we arrived at the crem, and I asked Billy to wipe it down during the service, so it was clean when they came out, because you can't come out to a dirty limousine, absolutely no way. And it was a big coffin because Mrs Truelove was a large lady. Otherwise, I don't remember anything...'

'She rang this number the afternoon before she died.' Sandra fixes on her. 'It was her last call. You don't know anything about that, I suppose – Mr Fenning didn't mention it?'

'No, no.' She shakes her head quite violently. 'No mention. But he has been busy; busy time of year, with the flu...'

'Young Billy dies, and then twenty-four hours later, Mrs Truelove dies...and we're wondering if there's a connection. Can you think of a connection, Sandra? Apart from the fact that both the victims were known to you; and that the two deaths occurred about half a mile from each other, along the seafront.'

'I still think he killed himself,' she says nodding. 'Billy, I mean – and I know you say otherwise, but I have a sense and sometimes it's just as it seems. Never a happy boy, Billy, and I mean Splash Point – it is a bit famous for that.'

'Famous for what?'

'Famous for people killing their selves – not everyone goes to Beachy Head. You can park very near Splash Point, like a few yards away, so it's handy, no long walk. I mean, it's very sad, of course, no one likes to see it...'

'But all work for the undertaker.'

'If there's a death, we know about it, that's how it is; and if there's a suicide, we certainly know about it, not happy at all, those meetings – the meetings with the family, who all feel terrible, of course they do, wondering what they could have done, and I have to tell them, "You could not have done *any*thing"...whether it's true or not true, that's what I have to say, Ephraim told me that, and who am I to judge? It probably isn't true, but then who knows, perhaps it is, and that's what you say anyway, as Mr Fenning taught me, that's what you are to say, that's the line to take...and when the waves are a bit wild, as often they are here in Stormhaven, Splash Point – well, it'd be a very quick death, smashed in moments against the rocks; I sometimes reassure them in that way...a mess, mind, but quick, I'd say. Not that I'd choose it, wouldn't be my way, but I remember the last one... I remember the last one very well, because Billy knew the family.'

Tamsin wakes from a bad verbal dream. 'I'm sorry? Billy knew the family of the last suicide at Splash Point?'

'Well, he knew Mr Hallington, because of the football, he's his football coach – or *was* his football coach. He enjoyed his football, Billy.'

'Mr Hallington is still alive.'

'Yes, but his father isn't.'

'Mr Hallington's father?'

'It was his father who killed himself at Splash Point. That's what I'm saying.'

'When was this?'

Sandra sucks air between her teeth to indicate thought. 'About six months past. I've never seen a man so broke and in bits as young Mr Hallington. And angry, very angry. Sometimes people joke a bit at funerals, and sometimes there's only, well, you know – despair.' She shakes her head as she speaks, as if to exorcise the memory. 'That's all there was at Mr Hallington's funeral. Despair. And anger.'

～

'So Ralph, you were friends with Billy, weren't you?'

'Yes.'

'Good friends?'

'I suppose.'

Tamsin has forgotten how to speak with an eighteen-year-old boy; or perhaps she never knew. They are meeting in his bedroom, which somehow seems wrong, but maybe Ralph feels safe here and it is the only way to escape his mother. Tamsin sits awkwardly on his bed and Ralph sits on his chair turned away from the games console on his desk. He gazes at her in awe, this is Tamsin's feeling, as if an angel – or sex object, the two are one – has arrived in his room and he can't quite believe it and doesn't know what to do and words fail him. She pulls her black skirt nearer her knees and wonders if an open question will be better rewarded than her two closed attempts so far.

'So what do you think about Billy's death?'

'Well, it happens, I suppose.'

Was this meant to sound wise? Was he trying to impress her? She would need to let him know what it is she finds impressive; that always helps. *Strawberry lensing, Tamsin; some puffing up, as with a tired cushion.*

'But you're clever, Ralph, anyone can see that. I bet you're a pretty smart gamer.' She nods at the console and Ralph smiles the smile of a master. 'Yes, you have intelligent eyes – you'd no doubt make a great cop. But maybe we're not good enough for you.' His face blushes with joy and his eyes begin to water. 'So what's your take on it?'

'Well...' He looks troubled now. Has she gone too far?

'I mean, in a way, Ralph, it's your last gift to your friend; your final gift to your mate, Billy – to help us find his murderer.'

'I suppose it could be.'

Keep up the momentum.

'Did you play games together?' She looks at the console.

'We did, yeh.'

'And you see everything, I know you do. Did you know Mr Hallington?'

'He came into our school. But, I mean, I didn't play football, so I wasn't, like, one of his boys.'

'One of his boys? How did you get to be one of his boys?'

'Well, be good at football, I suppose. I was a better gamer than Billy, way better gamer... but he was a better footballer.'

'So Billy was one of his boys?'

'Yeh – I mean, he liked him and that. He trusted him.'

'Billy trusted Mr Hallington?'

'I think he went round to his house sometimes, which is a bit weird, to go round to a teacher's house, like, I would *never* do that – but I suppose he wasn't exactly a teacher.'

'Not exactly a teacher, no, as you say...more a sports coach. You don't miss anything.' Ralph is looking awkward again, but she doesn't want to lose him. He's a quiet gold mine, and Tamsin has forgotten she's on his bed with her skirt riding up her thigh a little. 'So he went round to his house – because he trusted him.'

'I don't think I can talk anymore, Detective Inspector.'

He is shaking a little. He looks overwhelmed, his face blushing again.

'That's OK, Ralph. We can speak again, can't we?'

'Yes, I'd like that.'

'But tell me, do you think Billy was murdered?'

He looks at her, as if weighing things up. He has never seen such beauty, and he smiles inside, a sort-of spring, because he isn't gay, though his father says this sometimes, as if it's bad; but he isn't gay, now he knows for absolute sure, this is heaven and he can't remember the question.

'I'm sorry?'

'I was just wondering – and don't worry, I am leaving.' She stands up and moves towards the door. 'But I was just wondering if you think Billy was murdered?'

'Oh, I know he was murdered, yes.' He gazes at her again. 'I know he was murdered.'

It was like a love-letter.

'We'll speak again, Ralph. You've been brilliant.'

When the Detective Inspector left, he hung his 'DO NOT DISTURB' sign on the door – not that his mother would take any notice. She'd come in and say, 'What is it that I am not meant to be disturbing?'

19

'So what have we learned today?' Tamsin sits forward on the comfy chair at Peter's. It is the end of the day, but no end to the cold and she cradles a glass of red in her hand – wine she brought herself, for peace of mind.

'I do have wine,' he'd said. 'The cellar isn't large, I grant you...'

'No quality control, abbot, so why would I risk it?' Peter nods. 'There are some things.'

'Lidl's wine has won a number of awards.'

There is pity in her laugh which becomes a piteous question. 'And your point is?'

'That evidence must stand a long time in the rain before prejudice will notice.'

Some say it's the worst weather ever; the coldest since records began. There are older folk who disagree and declare, '1963 was worse, much worse'. But water pipes are bursting, daffodils dying and the forecasts say *The Beast* is hardly begun, from Russia without any love. Though the abbot and Tamsin do not speak of the weather tonight, they take a break; for murder trumps weather, even in England, and the abbot gets the murder ball rolling. 'So Hallington's father killed himself at Splash Point?''

'That's what Sandra said.' If in doubt, name the source – then even if the information proves false, you remain standing; you do not sink with it.

'He seems a – well – decent man.'

'A decent man who, according to Ralph, invites young men home.'

'In the old days, whenever those were, it might have been regarded as kindness, a sign of commitment to the young people. We'd be sat here celebrating his worth, "just the sort of fellow this place needs!" Instead, we insinuate seedy intent.'

Tamsin sips her wine and knows that, whatever the deficiencies in the hospitality, she does feel at home here; or as home as she ever feels. She'd even caught herself relaxing while the abbot was in the kitchen, which was not something she does. Tamsin has struggled with home, with the idea of home, looking but never finding. 'Are you going home?' a colleague had once said and she'd heard herself replying, 'I'm going back to my flat, yes,' which sounded similar, though not the same at all.

'Ralph was not one of Hallington's in-crowd,' she says, 'not being sporty – a life spent behind a console, as far as I can see, hiding from his parents.'

'And the coffins.'

'But Billy *was* invited and he went along; he trusted Hallington apparently.'

'So maybe a decent man...'

'In your estimation...'

'But harried and chased – and maybe ultimately destroyed – by the testimony of James Fairburn.'

'There is talk among the boys as well.'

'Talk?'

'We have statements, though nothing specific...similar to Ralph's, in a way.'

'Which said nothing at all about Hallington.'

'There's no smoke without fire.' Tamsin sits back, feeling exhausted. She doesn't fancy the fifty-minute drive to Hove tonight, with the icy roads. There's talk of it dropping to minus eight.

'Sometimes there's just smoke, Tamsin. Sometimes people are picked on and there's nothing they can do. It's as if they've been chosen, but they've no idea why they've been chosen. At my public school...'

'Sorebottom Hall, yes, we know...'

'We had everyone down as a molester, all of the staff...even married members of staff...in fact, *particularly* them.'

'Using their wives as cover?'

'Of course, open and shut case. Family picture on desk? Classic diversionary manoeuvre: *paedophile!* Has anyone come forward and actually claimed abuse by Hallington?'

'No, they haven't; and not for want of a toe-rag solicitor trying. He's a rat, that man; no, really. Spends his life trying to build cases that don't exist, harassing the weak and the vulnerable, always trying to get the police involved, the press involved and the CPS...causing untold misery.'

'You have a moral cause? Someone wake me up...'

'He had one of my colleagues in his sights last year. And while I don't like to defend fellow police officers...'

'God forbid...'

'There comes a point...'

Peter had now heard it all: Tamsin defending a member of her own police team, who, for her own sense of worth, she must routinely demean or destroy.

'And then there's Fairburn,' he says.

'Alpha male-stroke-little boy...and I don't mean that as it sounds. He seemed to prefer female nurses in his younger days, though who he prefers now?'

'Can a man kill his son?' asks Peter, to no one in particular.

'Anyone can kill anyone, if they need to; if they are unhappy enough, if they are scared enough. No human is far from feral. '

'A father in Nevada killed his 14-year-old boy when he found out he was gay, I remember that one. He shot him dead.

Somewhere in his mind he thought he'd rather have a dead son than a gay one.'

'Well, there you go – answering your own question.'

'Stormhaven isn't Nevada.'

'No – it's got more charity shops.'

'Fathers generally kill their children to get at the mother – a sense of control lost, so they try to reclaim it with the massacre of innocence. But I don't see that dynamic here.'

'What if his son could destroy his career? What if he knew something that would bring his father's plane crashing to the ground in flames?'

'Very poetic.'

'Cathy said nothing came before his reputation. What if Billy threatened his reputation in some way?'

The abbot ponders his whisky. 'It's unlikely Billy would do that. Not impossible, but unlikely. Most, in that situation, destroy themselves rather than their parent...standard response. To take on their parent is beyond their strength, so they opt for taking on themselves. Self-punishment and self-hate – these are more normal survival options for the young.'

'But we don't think he did, do we? We don't think he turned in on himself in the end. With the death of Mrs Truelove, we think someone else turned on Billy.'

There is silence again...safe silence as the wind blows and the wood burner burns. Here is a solidarity she has never experienced in the police station. Peter slowly recites the facts, inspecting each.

'Mrs Truelove, formerly of Hardwicke House, was known to both Fenning and Hand – Fenning via his business, Hand via the church. Her last phone call was to Fenning, the afternoon before she died. He says she was ringing for advice about funeral costs. It's possible. While the Reverend Hand knew her as a Sunday School teacher at St Botolph's and took the funeral of her late husband Lionel.'

'Sandra looks constantly guilty,' adds Tamsin. 'It must be exhausting being inside Sandra; while Ralph, well – he knows something about someone. He was very clear it was murder. I'll need to speak to him again.'

'Remember to dress appropriately; and perhaps meet somewhere other than his bedroom? We wouldn't want any unpleasant accidents. Who knows what's going through his mind.'

'I will handle the witness.'

'In his dreams.'

'He does know something.'

'And finally there's Ephraim, keeping order and calm when all around is chaos. Is that our list of suspects complete?'

'If we're finally excluding Billy.'

'We are. This is murder.'

'So that's your final word on the subject,' she says. 'You believe Billy?'

The abbot pauses.

'I do, yes.' There, he'd said it; he was leaping down from the fence; you can't stay there forever. 'I believe our single witness. There is something rotten here, Tamsin, I think so. It reminds me of the dead badger on the cycle path to Newhaven.'

'Obviously.'

'It's been there for weeks, the smell of rotting flesh, quite the worst...and there's something rotten here.'

The abbot, helped by the whisky, feels engaged. He eases himself away from the individual conversations, comprised of trash and treasure, diamonds and dung; and allows a sense of the symphony. Inside him, there's a melting of the stories into one, which must occur; the different instruments become a single tune. You have to *feel* an investigation; and be held by it. It is never a mere set of jigsaw pieces. It is a picture, a shifting composition, a living picture and the picture draws you in and draws you on. It is the knowledge of deep breathing and elusive *nous* – an unknown and unknowable guidance.

'And the note?' Tamsin appears too tired to think.

'The note tells us, if we believe Billy, that the Reverend Ernest Hand is either the killer – or the gateway to the killer. We are to ask him.'

'And you have asked him.'

'Yes, and he doesn't wish to be the gateway. He's elusive. Maybe he's frightened. Maybe he's the killer – but I don't think so. He seemed in genuine shock when he heard Billy was dead.'

'This must be the first fire that actually makes a room colder,' says Tamsin, worried again for her health. Her left arm, away from the fire, feels numb.

'Do you want a blanket?'

'I want some heat.'

Peter adds more dead wood, though his mind is still on the case, like a washing machine on a slow cycle, churning.

'But there's also a path to Ephraim Fenning,' he says as he throws on the last log. He'll need to get back to the beach, which never fails to deliver. "The furniture from *The Titanic*," as one fisherman called it, when he saw Peter collecting. "The deck chairs they couldn't re-arrange!"'

Meanwhile, Tamsin looks ill. 'I think I'll stay here tonight. Is that OK?'

'That's fine,' says Peter, before disappointment can leak into his mind. He views all guests as invasion; though the invader must *feel* welcome. 'It's no problem at all.'

'I just feel tired and even if it is a bit like camping...'

'It's nothing like camping.'

'You'll be telling me there's hot water next.'

'Have you ever been camping?'

'Why would I want to go camping?'

'This is what they call a "character" cottage on Stormhaven's unspoilt sea front featuring a delightful spare bedroom with outstanding coastal views, which I know madam will enjoy hugely. But I will need to make up the bed with clean sheets.'

'Whose been sleeping in it?' says Tamsin, with tabloid shock.

'It's over three years since you last stayed. They could probably do with replacing.'

'You mean they haven't been washed since?'

'It's possible.' And then suddenly she's holding her chest.

'I'm not well,' she says, getting up. 'I'm really not well.' She stumbles forward and Peter moves to steady her.

'You need a rest. It's going to be all right. A good night's sleep.'

'But I am going to catch this bastard.' She chokes.

'And I'm going to help you, Tamsin. Tomorrow, we speak with Mrs Truelove's neighbour...and with Hallington.' But Tamsin isn't listening, too dizzy, and almost falling again. What is this? 'You sit here while I find some sheets. We'll give the murderer one more night of peace, just one – before we step out into the cold, smash down their door and drag them screaming into the sunlight.'

Part Two

20

'Well, I have to say, I thought she was joking at first.'
'And why was that, Mrs Sykes?' *Mrs Sykes is drunk.*

'Call me Theresa, please – no graces left to stand on, me. All trampled into the dirt.'

Theresa, a peroxide blond in her late fifties, drinks a Martini for elevenses and seems glad of the attention presently bestowed; a visitor, any visitor, breaks up the day. She wears tight-jeans and should probably be on the arm of a gangster, lounging by the pool in their plush Brighton hideaway. Instead, she's alone in a flat in Hardwicke House, a 1980s' block, short on charm though big on view. She has the look of someone for whom something has gone very wrong, this is Peter's sense, and the options are endless. Maybe Mr Sykes is in gaol for some gold bullion heist, all assets seized; or maybe he has a new and younger moll by the pool these days. Or maybe he was simply a waster, discarded along the way by Theresa, who can't be doing with all that – yet never quite replaced. Or perhaps she was happily married to a librarian, who died too early, before they lived their dreams. *What brought you to now, Theresa?*

'I just thought it an unlikely time to see one,' she adds casually. 'And she's not as young as she was, bless her. I mean, she's not young at all, now she's dead...' Theresa crosses herself in her confusion. 'Though who knows, maybe in death we start over, young again?' She likes this idea. 'I was named after St Theresa of Lisieux, though merry fuck knows who she was – excuse my French. I really ought to find out. But I doubt she had a martini for elevenses.'

When this elevenses had started, they don't know; possibly around 9.00am and her boundaries are down.

'So, what did Mrs Truelove actually see?'

This is the reason they are here...to discover from her neighbour what Mrs Truelove saw, which so disturbed her.

'Well,' says Theresa, knowing a moment when it arrives and eager to seize it. 'Mrs Truelove – I always called her that, never Dotty; she was a formal lady, and Dotty really didn't do her justice.'

'You were telling us what she saw,' says Peter.

'She saw a hearse.' She enjoys the reveal. 'Was that the answer you were expecting?'

'A hearse? And why was that strange? You see a few in Stormhaven.'

'But not at midnight. She claims she saw a hearse at midnight.'

A pleasing reaction, Theresa smiles...rabbit pulled from hat and audience applauding; but they seem to want more. 'She couldn't always sleep, she said, so she put the telly on; but it was rubbish; of course it was rubbish and so she turned down the sound and went and sat at the window, looking out on the water, which you can't actually see at night, but which you can hear. It's always talking, the sea, noisy or quiet but never silent, it always has something to say. And she was thinking about her life, she said, a meditation or something. She did that sort of thing.'

'And she saw a hearse drive by?'

'That's what she said.'

'At midnight.'

'There or thereabouts.'

'Which direction was it going in?'

'She didn't say. I should have asked, shouldn't I?'

'And she was sure it *was* a hearse? It was dark.'

'Well, that's what I asked, I did ask that – I mean, I didn't want to sound like I didn't believe her, because obviously the first thought is that she's a batty old lady, who is medicated halfway to eternity. But she said, "Oh yes, I'm quite sure, Theresa – I know a hearse when I see one. It's heightened awareness at my age." And Mrs Truelove wasn't a batty old lady, not in any respect; it wasn't as if she'd lost her marbles, not at all. Sharp as a razor, she was. Called the PM "an attention-seeking buffoon" the other day.'

Tamsin is looking out the window. The seafront road is about seventy yards away, across a thin band of shingle. Theresa sighs and takes another sip of martini.

'You're sure you won't?' Peter declines but finds it strange to be so close to the seventies again, the seventies in a glass, the smell of the seventies, different days, a return in time to both embarrassment and comfort. 'Funny thing,' she says, as if reading his mind. She touches the bottle affectionately. 'I never grew out of this. I mean, there isn't much left of *then* but Martini remains, for me anyway, some dream still calling me on. Mad, eh? And not to everyone's taste, it isn't always in the shops now...' And then she's dancing and singing the song, the song on the advert, filmed on swanky yachts in the Med or swish Alpine hideaways for the young and the gorgeous, swaying a little with the bottle in her hand: 'Any time, any place, anywhere, there's a wonderful world you can share, it's the bright one, the right one – it's Martini.'

'And what did she do then, Theresa? You have a lovely voice, by the way.'

'Thank you.'

'Mrs Truelove, I mean. What did she do after she saw the hearse?'

Theresa focuses again. 'She asked me what she should do. She came and knocked on my door, the following morning, told me what had occurred and asked me what she should do, it had unsettled her... though I think she already knew. I mean, I think she'd already made up her mind, because you didn't really tell Mrs Truelove anything, she just wanted confirmation, and perhaps a little attention, bless her. It can be lonely here – I mean it's a lovely setting here, people say that, but it doesn't mean you know anyone or have company. A beautiful view doesn't stop you crying.' Was Mrs Truelove's story now merging with Theresa's? 'And anyway, I said I thought it was a good idea. Not that I believed it was a hearse, I really didn't. Who sees anything clearly at midnight – if you're not drunk, you're asleep. But I couldn't tell her that. And she would not have been drunk. Totally tea, Mrs Truelove.'

'Sorry, just to back track a little – you thought *what* was a good idea?' Tamsin sits unusually quiet in the corner as Peter patiently, like the tortoise, pursues the hare.

'She said she'd ring Mr Fenning, the undertaker, a very nice man, that was her plan – to ring up Mr Fenning and ask if it was one of his...the hearse, I mean. And if it wasn't one of his, what might be happening? Or who might it belong to? I said perhaps someone had stolen it. People will steal anything these days, no respect.'

Peter likes the implication that there were some things that *could* be stolen with respect, legitimate theft; and other things which were off limits, and morally wrong...like a hearse. Whether bishop or brigand, he thinks, everyone has a rule book – it's just that, unfortunately, no two rule books are the same.

'And this was the night of the death at Splash Point?'

'Well, we know that now, of course; we know that *now*. But we didn't then, we hadn't heard about the murder then. And yes, that *was* the same night the hearse went by, which is a bit weird, is it not?' A sparkle appears in Theresa's bored eyes, her life suddenly close to intrigue. She carries her Martini to the door to say goodbye, as a party host saying farewell to late leavers.

'You've been very helpful, Theresa.'

'Any time,' she says with almost unbearable sadness. Peter just manages to stop himself adding, *'any place, any where'.* 'Of course, I rang them myself as well.'

'Rang who?'

'Fennings. Just in case Mrs Truelove forgot – or changed her mind. Something to do, I suppose. How sad is that?'

'Who did you speak to?'

'Batty Sandra – sorry, but that's how she's known. It's not malicious.'

They leave Theresa and her Martini and step into the cold burn of the wind, a malign gale ripping across the sea front. They find some relief from the slaughter behind a beach hut.

'Hallington first?' says the abbot, 'or has Fenning jumped the queue?' He's buttoning up his duffle coat.

'We need to split. You take Hallington – but don't be too friendly. I think he draws you in.'

'He doesn't draw me in.'

'He didn't mention to us his interesting relationship with Splash Point. Why the hell not?'

'I could think of one or two reasons.'

'I told you he draws you in.'

'He doesn't draw me in.'

'And I deserve a shot at Fenning. What was his phone story? Mrs Truelove asking him about funeral costs? Hah!' Tamsin tightens her scarf and Peter digs his hands deep into his coat – as good as new from the *Oxfam* shop in Broad Street, but never tested like this. And he must look for some better gloves next time; his hands hurt. 'So had Mrs Truelove somehow forgotten about the hearse at midnight, distracted by another matter? It's her final phone call on earth – and there seems some disagreement as to what it was actually about.'

21

Nick Hallington's bungalow, North Way.

'It's all right, I was just leaving,' she says and Peter is surprised. He wasn't expecting to find Cathy Carter in Hallington's hallway.

'Cathy?'

And she's surprised to see him and clearly in a hurry to leave. She exits without more ado.

'A friend?' asks the abbot.

'I'm not sure it's any of your business,' says Nick, with a smile to keep Peter and the world away. 'No offence, abbot. It's just that we're all allowed a private life, as I'm sure you'll agree. Do you want to come through?'

Cathy Carter here? Why?

It is a large bungalow surrounded by other large bungalows... in fact, bungalows as far as the eye can see on this former wartime army camp.

'Lovely home,' says Peter.

'Given to me by my father, to be near him... just in case you're wondering how someone who isn't incontinent comes to live in a bungalow. Tea? I can do tea.'

'Thank you, yes – and if you could leave the tea bag *in*.' The tea was always stewed in the monastery, he generally got to the urn last; and today he is happy to be reminded of the desert. Sometimes it almost comes and rescues him, returning him to eternity. 'And one sugar, if that's all right.'

'One spoon of white death – should I call the Samaritans now?'

Peter looks round; these bungalows are expensive. Some of them have Audis outside, Mercedes even....cars that cost more than Abbot Peter has earned in his entire life; though it's a home which somehow seeks a character; which in some manner, echoes its owner. There is an absence about Nick, something not there; so, who is this man? No photos of foreign trips, weddings or children; and the pictures on the walls, they're space-fillers – not cherished but bought to fill a gap. And a red rug ill-matched with the yellow paint on the walls; blue curtains that relate to nothing else, a gas fire that feels too small, some fake sunflowers on the window sill...there is something unfinished about it all. And then there's Cathy Carter.

Hallington returns with the tea.

'Thank you,' says Peter, 'though I should just say, Mr Hallington, that your relationship with Cathy Carter *is* now our business.' He hadn't wished to say so before, in case Hallington spat in his tea; common revenge in the hospitality sector. 'Do you understand that?' Hallington offers only a stare, silent, angry; the honeymoon is over. It may never have begun. And he's a darker, more troubled man than he was behind his work desk; surrounded by the sweaty debris of sport, he possessed more charm. His skin is pale and dark bags sit beneath his eyes, almost like make-up. And maybe the silence is meant to intimidate; people use it in this way. But Peter knows silence, knows it well, it holds no fears. He drinks a little of his tea, glad of the sweetness and heat. 'We have interviewed both you and Cathy, you see, in what we believe is a murder investigation. The victim is Cathy's son and also – and this is the thing – a young man you knew, who you took some interest in – so your relationship is very much our business.' Hallington sneers, as if what has been said is quite ridiculous. 'That's what murder does – it ends life, crucifies the bereaved and blows a big hole in privacy.'

'Not a good morning,' says Hallington, staring at Peter. 'So if you can hurry up.'

'What's not good?'

'I've been suspended by the council.'

'I am very sorry to hear it.' And he is.

'Only just heard; so I don't need your visit.'

'Cathy comforting you, was she?' Again, the silence and the stare. 'I can always come back if this is a bad time. I only have one question – well, two questions now. But they can wait a few hours. Would you like me to return later?'

'By which time I'll probably be drunk and disorderly.'

'I can feel the lace curtains of North Way twitching.'

'Don't be a pompous prick, abbot. Bungalows not your thing?'

'We all need the disorderly sometimes.'

He stares again. 'It just comes and finds me. And when it does, there really are no rules at all.'

Possibly a threat; almost certainly, the man's rage barely held in his skin; such anarchy inside him, looking for release.

And Peter is back at Henry House, back at the therapy centre, Mind Gains, a previous case. As a publicity stunt, and a stupid one, they'd organised their own 'Feast of Fools' – an echo of the old Roman practice when once a year, all social norms were subverted for a night, all hierarchies dismantled and the chaos overseen by the elected Lord of Misrule, a dangerous figure who could do or order *anything*. It had been an evening that ended in considerable darkness.

'And then you become the Lord of Misrule, Nick?'

'Human boundaries are a rickety fence, abbot; easily trampled down by the mob within. A little alcohol and who knows what comes out to play? So what are your questions?' He sits forward, focusing. 'Let's get this over. I may even answer them, though I can't promise anything.'

'The first you might guess, I've asked it already: what is your relationship with Cathy Carter?'

Hallington sighs. 'She's my therapist, though I don't see her so often now. No need.'

'But you had a session this morning? You didn't mention it on the phone to me.'

'Do I have to?'

'It's just that if I was agreeing to meet someone, I wouldn't have it coincide with a visit from my therapist. I'd put some distance between them.'

'She just dropped in; it wasn't arranged.'

'An informal visit from your therapist?' What could be less likely?

'She's aware of some of the shit flying around at the moment.'

'A paid visit?'

'No.'

The abbot nods. He'll leave it there, he decides to leave it there – and then he doesn't. 'I should just say, Nick, the therapist/ friend thing...it never works.' Hallington's face mocks the intervention, declares it of no interest. 'Transference is at the heart of therapy; but it destroys friendships.'

'No offence, abbot' – that long-distance smile again – 'but I don't really do your categories, all right? Not interested. People are forever making boundaries that don't exist.'

'Whereas difficult memories do. Like Splash Point.' The abbot watches Nick's eyes widen in surprise and then settle again. He breathes deeply.

'Is this your second question?' Peter nods.

'Were you close to your father?'

'Of course.'

'His death must have been terrible.'

'Something like that.' The words are a wall going up.

'Who let him down, do you think?'

'How do you mean?'

'Well, so often with suicide, for those left behind, there's the sense of 'if only'...you know, if only someone had done better; if only *I* had done better. Who do you blame for what happened?'

'How do you mean, who do I blame? Why do you think I blame anyone?'

'People usually do. Perhaps you blame yourself? You do seem given to self-punishment.'

'Are you here on police business? Because you seem to have wandered.'

'It is important we understand the forces at work in a situation, the transactions taking place. It's important we are accurate about those. That's all I'm trying to understand.'

'You have to give up blame,' says Hallington, suddenly speaking from beneath a halo, as though forgiveness is the most obvious thing in the world.

'Really?'

'You have to find a life beyond blame. That's what they say, isn't it, abbot, in the self-help books? A life beyond blame. You can't be carrying it around; it turns you into a demon.'

He is telling the abbot, looking straight at him and smiling.

'And you've done that?' says Peter, innocently. 'Given up on the blame? It's quite an achievement for the Lord of Misrule. I mean, it's one thing for the professionals to recommend it, but it's another thing actually to...'

'Like I say, I'm for compassion. It's why I do what I do. I don't get angry.'

Peter ponders the furious figure before him. Nick's body bristles; his chest hair, full above his shirt, seems to sweat and writhe.

'I suppose if you did blame someone, whoever that was, they'd need to be careful.'

'That's true. And that's exactly why I started seeing a therapist.'

'And you chose Cathy Carter.'

'I did, yes.'

'There must be a number of therapists in Stormhaven.'

'Maybe.'

'But you pick Cathy Carter, ex-wife of the man who, with his allegations, is presently trying to destroy you. And mother of the young man who so tragically died.'

'She hasn't been with Fairburn for years. And no one knows him better either; so perhaps she's a wise choice. Nothing surprises her about Fairburn. He may be everyone else's hero – "Surgeon Superman" – but he's some way from being hers, I can tell you. Have you heard what he did?'

'So why didn't you mention it when we spoke? Splash Point and its significance for you. It was always going to come out.'

'I speak about it with Cathy. And it has sod all to do with any murder inquiry.'

He hadn't been there at the end, when his father ended his life; he hadn't said goodbye. He'd only heard what witnesses had told him. They'd all seen his dad, but hadn't suspected anything; and why would they? An old man stands holding the railings, he keeps himself to himself – why would anyone be concerned? He wasn't joining in the banter of the terror-seekers; just standing on the concrete promenade, feeling the thunder and roar of the high winds and wild waves. And he was safe... quite safe, until he put one foot on the lower rail, heaved himself up and toppled forward, falling over and down, head over heels, swallowed immediately, swallowed and smashed against the rocks, blood spilling in the foam for a moment, just a moment, pinky white, like a strawberry shake...the terror-seekers stunned.

'It's just the coincidence of geography,' says Peter, putting his cup down on the table and getting up to leave. 'You must understand that coincidence of place has to be noted. Two deaths, one place. Sometimes geography speaks. And, of course, some say – and they have their reasons – that nothing is coincidence.' They shake hands, standing. 'But I'm grateful for your time on this difficult day, Mr Hallington; and I do hope for good news from the Council.' The abbot walks through the hallway, turning only at the door. 'It sounds to me like you've found a good therapist in Cathy Carter.'

Hallington smiles, some joyless triumph breaking through.

'I think she needs one more than I do.' He then closes the door behind the abbot and picks up the hallway phone.

22

Fennings, the Undertakers.

'Ralph, I don't think we need you here,' says his father with tight-jawed cheeriness. 'As in, please go away!' He speaks with an insistent smile.

The large frame of Ralph remains in the doorway; he's not picking up the signals; or perhaps he *is* picking them up and choosing to ignore them. In truth, he has recently discovered the joy of ignoring signals; it's the first experience of power at home, and one to be treasured. Though he has other power as well, and one day he'll use it to bring his father down; though more in his dreams. He couldn't do it, he knows that.

'Just making sure you're all right, father.'

'I am quite all right thank you, Ralph, quite all right; so if you could just peel your eyes away from the Detective Inspector and go to your room, that would be good for us all, I think.'

He doesn't move.

'You want me here when it comes to cleaning the cars,' says Ralph. 'I can't be here quick enough then...whatever the time of day.'

'Our cars are cleaned after every funeral,' explains Ephraim happily, as if embarking on a sales pitch. 'As soon as they return, inside and out.' Ralph stares at him and then turns towards Tamsin.

'I'll be in my room, if I'm needed. I mean, you can come to my room if you need to speak privately.'

'I'll see how we go,' says Tamsin. 'Is there new information?'

Ralph's face suggests there might be. 'Have you got any more cleaning for me to do, father?'

'We have a funeral tomorrow,' he says. 'We'll need you then, Ralph.' And to Tamsin: 'He is a good cleaner, does a decent valeting job. And well paid for it, mind!'

'Minimum wage.'

'Living wage, I think you'll find, Ralph. And free accommodation, which is most favourable maths in my book.'

Finally, the boy leaves and Ephraim shakes his head, an embarrassed smile, as across the corridor Ralph's bedroom door is closed.

'A young lad, I'm afraid, Detective-Inspector, but I hope that's no crime. He can stare for England, of course; but what's behind the stare, the Lord only knows.'

'I've come about the phone call,' says Tamsin, pleased to be free of Ralph's eyes; glad to be underway. Like the dogs let loose and the fox in sight, she feels the energy of the chase, the acceleration of pace, when all else in life is forgotten.

'Oh, hello, hello, hello!' says Sandra, arriving from the kitchen. Tamsin feels the pain of another interruption. 'Sorry, didn't know you were back! Is there anything *I* can do, Detective-Inspector? Anything you'd like to say to us both? We have no secrets from each other.' She looks at Ephraim in search of agreement. 'Marriages can't have secrets!'

'Nothing you can do, dear,' says Ephraim, 'we're just having a quiet word – but do please mind Reception.'

'I've only been out a moment.'

'But it's not good to leave it *vacant,* dear. "How we're received is what we believe" – a constant guide in this business.' This is an aside to Tamsin, though its true target still loiters by the door. Sandra doesn't wish to leave them alone; she wants to hear what's being said.

'Well, the bell will ring if anyone comes in...' she says.

'Mr Davis is dropping by with his wife's teeth. He'll be along with them shortly.'

'They've been found?' This is good news.

'Yes, the care home located them in the end – though why it took quite so long, I'll never know. I did say to them they could not have gone far. I mean, how far can false teeth go? And he'll be here shortly, so if you could just...'

'Well, it's a mercy. She doesn't look her best without them,' says Sandra. 'Mr Ash postponed the viewing. You can't have a viewing without the teeth.'

'But he can re-arrange it now,' says Ephraim briskly. 'Mr Ash can re-arrange it now, all right? Would you tell him that, dear?' And then to Tamsin: 'Our business manager, he works in the other office. He is called Mr Ash, which can cause some mirth. And I believe we have all wished to seal him in an urn and toss him in the sea at some point.'

But Sandra is still with Mrs Davis and her teeth: 'I mean, let's be honest, she won't be a picture *with* them...'

'But better, I think, dear, better... the teeth will help.' And then to Tamsin. 'She was hit by a car, poor dear – a car driving much too fast in Sutton Road. I mean, a good innings, a decent age – but that's no way to go, is it?' And then again to Sandra: 'And we do need to confirm the funeral music with Mr Davis. I wonder if you could do that, my love? Could you do that when he calls in? He does need to decide on the exit music and we need to know today, you tell him that – or the printers will be grumbling. He was choosing, I think, between "Love Me Tender", the Elvis Presley version and "Abide with me" – or "the FA cup song", as he calls it.'

'Well, I can do that, of course I can,' says Sandra – "Love me tender" is such a lovely song... I know the chords.'

'Sandra is learning the guitar,' says Ephraim, while Tamsin is losing the will to live and worried an impromptu performance might break out. Sandra is fishing for it, there's no question of that; she would like to play 'Love me tender'. But Ephraim doesn't offer encouragement and the moment passes.

'If you need anything, just shout,' says Sandra, leaving reluctantly. 'And I'll come right on in. I won't be doing anything that can't be interrupted. I mean, is anything in particular the trouble?'

'Nothing in particular,' says Tamsin. She's getting really irritated by the family's insistent availability. First Ralph and now Sandra – it's as if they're terrified of Fenning being left alone with her. Perhaps they are. 'Just routine,' she adds.

'Well, if it's just routine...'

'Just routine, yes.'

'Terrible business,' she says shaking her head. 'Whether suicide or murder – and who can say? But if it's just routine...'

The silence demands her departure and the door finally closes. Some sort of eternity has passed since they began their conversation; it's as if Tamsin and Ephraim must start again.

'If there's anything I can do to help, Detective-Inspector. I believe I told the abbot everything I know of this appalling matter...'

'It's the phone call, Mr Fenning. It keeps popping its head up above the parapet. I mean, I'm sure you can clear the matter up for us...but it does *need* to be cleared up.'

'Any phone call in particular?'

'I believe the abbot mentioned the phone call from Mrs Truelove.' Ephraim nods. 'Her last phone call, in fact, the one she made before she died. Memorable in that way, at least.'

'Well, I believe he *did* mention that, yes.'

'You told the abbot she was ringing about funeral costs.'

'Funeral costs, yes. I think that was it, though memory can sometimes prove vague. Is there a problem?'

'It's just that it doesn't tally with what her neighbour says.'

'Oh?'

'Yes, her neighbour says she was ringing you about something entirely different – about seeing a hearse driving along the seafront at midnight and thinking it a little odd. Does that ring any bells, Mr Fenning?'

'I don't think so.'

'Well, do think hard because this is important, Mr Fenning – and you know that we'll turn Stormhaven upside down to get to the truth of this...*upside down*...which may include listening in on the call itself, should you force us down that path.'

Mr Fenning sits at the table nodding his head, as if in deep agreement with her proposition.

'I have, of course, lied, Detective-Inspector – and I'm not proud of it.' He pauses and somehow looks pleased with himself. 'No one is proud of a lie. But I did lie, I withheld the truth, to protect dear Billy, if you must know – and it appears you must, of course you must. I just didn't wish for this to be the last memory of him.' He shakes his head.

'What happened, Mr Fenning?'

'Well, there isn't a polite way to put this, but he was drunk, or so I imagine – and he took the hearse out for – what I believe is called – a "joy ride".'

'A joy ride in a hearse...at midnight?'

'What gets into them?' He shakes his head again. 'Some call it hormones, but I do wonder. Lads without dads...'

'Yet seven hours later his body was found at Splash Point?'

'Indeed. It makes no sense, does it? It certainly makes no sense to me. I mean, he returned the car, and I – well, cleared up the mess – the bottle of vodka, his cigarettes.'

'That's how you knew it was Billy?'

'He always said he could drive, but didn't possess a licence. So I said to him, "Well, take your test and get a licence, young man, and then you *can* drive." I was offering the boy a job, a leg-up. But Billy didn't like work, and he didn't like rules, they frustrated him. Lived in his own world, I'm afraid – and one well furnished with illusion. But what got into him that night, heaven only knows.'

'So where did you find the car?'

'I found the car back here in the morning. I rise early, and noticed it oddly parked. We are very precise where the cars are parked, needs must; it had clearly been taken out, and when I looked inside – well, I did not wish for it to be the final memory of young Billy, the final disgrace. And so, yes, I cleared up quickly, and spoke an untruth...'

'You lied...'

'I wasn't strictly honest, which is the worst of sins, *mea culpa*, I stand exposed. Mrs Truelove deserves better than that...and so does Billy...because he was a good boy. '

Again, Mr Fenning starts nodding.

'Can anyone confirm your story?'

'They certainly cannot!' he says as one on a moral crusade. He regards the lack of confirmation as a trophy. 'I was most discreet – you must remember, both Sandra and Ralph were very fond of the boy, most fond – in their different ways. He was like a son to Sandra, and a brother to Ralph.'

'So you wished them kept in the dark?'

'I wished them free from pain and distress, yes – I see no manner of sharp practice in that.'

'And you are the only witness to your story, Mr Fenning – the story that disconnects you, rather conveniently, from the death of Mrs Truelove?'

'By the grace of God I am, yes.' He smiles: 'The only witness. And for the sake of Billy, I would have it no other way.'

23

Hove, late.

Tamsin arrives home and glad to be so. She is fifteen miles from Stormhaven, but in quite another world. In a recent national survey, Hove came top in 'the most sought-after coastal location' category – with house prices to prove it. It's not Brighton but 'Hove, actually.'

She has called off her meeting with Peter. She doesn't feel well enough. Energy leaked from her as soon as she left Fenning's bleak parlour; enough to make anyone ill. Did she believe him? Belief or disbelief can wait another day – and when was that ever so? Whatever virus is passing through is leaving her drained and she needs only to be alone, to lie down, to get to bed, without even a glass of wine. She takes off her coat, removes her shoes, which is too much effort – the bending down and the pulling; and then she falls on the sofa, as instructed by Peter.

'Just collapse,' he'd said, 'and think of nothing until the morning. All will be well.'

But nothing's well at the moment.

The doorbell rings; the last thing she needs. It's probably Terry from upstairs, a pilot for Ryanair and due back from Amsterdam today. He'll be wanting some milk – or possibly chocolate, as if there isn't enough of the stuff at the airport. He does like to chat about nothing very much; cheery but distant neighbours. They pass on the stairs, share a drink at Christmas, laugh in the hallway; and then retire to their upmarket flats without knowing much of the other's story. There are some who find strangers the best place to spill and reveal – but Tamsin is not among them. Tamsin tells nothing, dodging questions like sniper fire, because information is power and why should she want to give that to anyone? And probably Terry prefers it this way; prefers the safe game of neighbourly banter which goes nowhere but itself. She knows he'll understand, living with jet lag as he does; so she pulls herself up from the sofa, work enough, and wrapped in her yoga blanket – her one concession to the wellbeing movement – she moves towards the door to both greet and dismiss.

Abort the greeting, it's James Fairburn. She has opened the door, and he's standing there, mad-eyed and uncomfortable. Tamsin feels as though she's been punched.

'I had a nurse speak to me today,' he says. He just starts talking. 'She says people have been asking about me.'

'You shouldn't be here, Mr Fairburn.' Tamsin is trying to gather herself; her guard is too low. She could do with Terry right now.

'You don't understand. Can I come in, by the way? I just need to sort this out.'

'No, you can't come in.'

'People have been going round the hospital, asking about me.' He's trying to be reasonable. 'The police, I mean – and I'm a bloody surgeon, for God's sake! I can't have people asking about me! How do you think that looks? It was a nurse who told me. A nurse told *me*, a surgeon, that the police were asking questions!'

'It's routine, Mr Fairburn. Now, if you don't mind...'

'You don't deny it then?' He is glowing with fury and Tamsin's head hurts. His turbulence cascades around her, he has too much power here. She's feeling inside for her police persona, for personal protection; she searches for disdain and mockery, for a caustic put-down.

'Why would I deny the normal procedures of a police inquiry?' She needs to keep her calm, and see him off the premises; she has no other aim and no other concern. She needs to get rid of him, ring Peter. 'It's routine, it's called a murder investigation and you're a suspect... and now I advise you to leave, before I make a formal complaint.'

Tamsin begins to close the door.

'It's not routine in my world,' he says, pushing the door back open. 'Can I come in?'

'No, you can't come in!' Who the hell does he think he is? But how her head hurts; she shouldn't have shouted. But she's worried; she needs to ring the abbot. 'And how did you find my address?'

'Do any of us have any secrets now, Inspector? You seem to want to know all of mine.'

'You'd better leave.' Her heart is pounding, her chest compressing; she's holding back the door from opening further.

'I'm not leaving,' he says, a belligerent child in the grip of a rage he has no power over, his large hands holding the door and the chest pain returns, it's crushing her, a tightening terror at this invasion... and a rage of her own, it arrives late, but so much rage in her now – rage that her place of safety, her sanctuary, is treated in this way, invaded, made unsafe! And now he's pushing again, pushing the door further open, wedging first his foot and then his body in the gap, Tamsin cannot contain his force and she's reaching out to strike him, to claw him, but now he's through, he's in the hallway and she's falling backwards.

'I'm not leaving until we've talked this through,' he says. 'It's a citizen's right.'

But Tamsin is past talking, she's somewhere else, another land, falling backwards into nothing.

~

It's Sergeant Banville who brings rumour of trouble.

Peter remembers him; the policeman who would be Pope at Splash Point; the man who'd waded into the freezing water with Peter, pulling him towards the shore, as he in turn pulled Mary. And when Peter had run for his clothes on that freezing shoreline, it had been Sergeant Banville trying to blow life back into the smashed and lifeless corpse.

And he was an unusual copper on the phone, as well; no hostility towards the abbot, passive or active. Maybe shared experience forms a bond, some secret tie, unspoken and unseen, like an underground stream beneath the rattle and rush above. In a crisis, and in the cold, they'd both done the decent thing.

'I know you're working on the case with the DI Shah,' he says over the phone, 'and I can't get hold of her.'

'She wasn't well last night; I sent her home. She may have everything switched off.' Though he didn't believe that for a moment. 'And how are you, Banville? I was told you were taken to hospital. Warmed up yet?'

'Routine,' he says. 'A quick check over, a form signed, a legal box ticked. It means I can't sue the police.'

'Of the covering of backs, there is no end. But you wanted to speak to the DI?'

'I did, yes, about the Billy Carter case. A young woman has come forward and made a rather interesting statement, which she should definitely hear about.'

'I did tell her to collapse.'

'It's unlike her, though, abbot...she doesn't like to stop working, not from what I've seen.'

'No.'

'And I can't imagine her phone off. I just cannot imagine that. She never turns her phone off. Whenever you want abuse, and whatever the time of day, you can ring the DI.'

Banville used to work in Dorchester, where maybe a monk was less offensive. The ancient town of Lewes is offended instantly. The large Cistercian monastery had been overrun in the 13th century, and physically dismantled during the reformation. Fiercely protestant, Lewes had been no place for any religious order since; and certainly nothing Roman. It burned an effigy of the Pope every bonfire night with blood-curdling relish. So a monk helping the police was not a good idea, not in anyone's book. Apart from Banville's, it seems.

'You say a young woman has come forward? I'd be interested to know what she said.'

'We took her statement yesterday and let her go. We didn't think much of it, to be honest. But then PC Willsher said the vicar she spoke of was involved in an ongoing inquiry, concerning a possible murder at Splash Point. He'd had to shadow him a couple of weeks back, all secret squirrel-like! Which is why I wanted to speak with the DI.'

'And the vicar in question is the Rev. Ernest Hand.'

'That's right, sir.'

'Well, I'm sorry you've got the monkey and not the organ grinder, sergeant; but I would very much like to speak with the young woman; and I'd like to speak with her straightaway. Might that be possible?

'I don't see a reason why not.'

'So if you could give me her number, that would be kind' – and then, as an afterthought. 'And perhaps a female officer to accompany me?'

~

And so it is – one phone call and a bus ride later – that he sits in the home of Geraldine Spoony, a 21-year-old still living with her parents; and in the same room she's had since she was three. Peter is on his own, without a female officer.

'Like that's possible!' the desk sergeant had cheerily declared, much amused at the idea. 'That's a good one, that is! As if anyone can find a spare police woman these days!'

'Doesn't stop you trying, Sarge.'

And Geraldine, made up like the dead, wears glasses and a vacant look. She tells him she works 'in recruitment'.

'That sounds incredibly important,' says Peter, setting the truth bar low.

'It's just head-hunting, really,' says Geraldine, glad to be able to explain. 'And I mean, the *money*.'

'The money's good?'

'I went to Thailand last year. Oh my God! And I'm going to Canada this year. I don't see many of my friends doing that sort of thing.'

She is suddenly happy, animated. Even a death mask can come to life.

'So what do you do in recruitment? You must explain the inner secrets.'

'It's common sense really.' She sits forward. 'You just find out what a company wants, what sort of a person they need and then you match their needs to the geezers you have on your books...or perhaps to geezers not on your books. I mean, I'll call cold, I don't mind calling cold. I'll call anyone and ask if they've ever thought of moving job. And some people haven't thought of it, it hasn't crossed their mind – but when you give them the chance, they think '*Why not?*' I do whatever it takes to find the right guy.'

'You sound very skilled.'

He watches her relax, just as he'd watched her tense at the sight of a monk in her hall way.

'You a monk then?'

'I was. Now I help the police.'

'Why do you do that?'

'It's possible I'm good at it.'

'I don't like the church much.' *She hates it.*

And it had been tricky at first, Geraldine hiding behind a sullen face and sulky pose. But now she's relaxing, a slow melting, as she speaks about her greatest achievement, her life in recruitment. Who wouldn't be glad of the chance to talk about that? Her family aren't interested, they don't think it's a proper job, whereas this monk does. He even asks questions which her friends never do.

'And when you *find* the right guy, when you manage to place him in the company, then you get your commission, I suppose?' She nods knowingly. 'I hear these things are all about the commission.'

'That's right, yeh! Otherwise, why do it? The pay's shit but the commissions are good – once my boss and team manager have taken their slice.'

'Sounds like its working very well for you, Geraldine, the world at your feet, Thailand, Canada – and so young.'

And ripe for the quarter life crisis, thinks Peter, he sees it often: folk in their mid-twenties who have found a job, found a flat, found a partner, and yes, found Thailand for their holidays. They have everything they ever wanted, everything they ever dreamed of. So why do they feel so awful, so empty? Money was the gateway to Elysium, they all agreed, but now they have it, they find themselves still some way away. And their partner's a disappointment. They become dispirited, listless, depressed. 'Perhaps I just need a bit more money,' they say. 'Yeh, I need to start looking round for a job that pays more, then I'll be fine.' The answer was always round the next corner.

This is why young westerners had stumbled their way to the desert, to St James-the-Less, stepping into the hot absence of the desert in search of something other than cash, gym membership and crazy Thailand nights.

'What are you looking for here?' the abbot would ask.

'I don't know,' they'd say.

'And that's a good place to start. It's OK not to know.'

It was always a great step forward when people could give up having to know.

'There has to be more than this, I know that! I just want to be happy!' they say.

'Well, there's nothing here,' he replies and they look worried. They always looked worried when he mentioned "nothing". 'A great deal of nothing, in fact. The desert is famous for offering nothing. But if you make a friend of nothing, maybe some thing will appear. "From no thing, some thing," as our Eastern friends remind us.' They would nod blankly, feeling only the tightening cord of despair. 'And when it's enough just to be alive, then you've come home,' the abbot adds.

'I mean, I wouldn't want to do it all my life,' says Geraldine, dragging him away from the desert and back to his chill Stormhaven present. 'No way.'

'Sometimes we do things because we have to, it's how we survive. But it doesn't mean we *always* have to. Not one adventure but many; I think so.'

Peter looks out the window and thinks of a head teacher who is oppressed by her job. She comes to see him four times a year; he is her "safe place", as she calls it. But daily she says to herself on her journey to school, "I don't have to do this." And somehow, the knowledge that she has a choice in the matter gives her strength to carry on. It seems important for Geraldine as well.

'I want to be out by the time I'm thirty.'

'And then a fresh adventure?' It was a bit early to retire.

'I suppose. But I'll have my money sorted then.'

Why did people still equate having their money sorted with having their life sorted?

'I'm sixty-five and mine still isn't sorted. And I do know you didn't speak with the police yesterday about the benefits of the recruitment game.' It's as though she's been hit. Time to focus; he leaves silence for her recovery.

'No, I didn't.' She avoids his eyes; she's closing down again, a return in time to the secretive little girl she must have been all those years ago, holding the confusion inside. Peter had read her statement.

'Can you tell me what you *did* speak with the police about?'

'I gave a statement to them, it's all there, you can read it. I told them everything – they said I could go.'

'I know, and I'm sorry – but could you also tell *me*? It's irritating for you, repeating the same things; and difficult things...things you don't wish to repeat, who would? But it would help because I'm investigating a case which coincides a little with your statement and I think what you have to say could be important...very important.'

A written transcript by the witness is no substitute for seeing the whites of their eyes; and he has questions of his own.

'I just thought it's time someone knew,' she says, shifting her large frame on the sofa. He sees both energy and lethargy before him, both compassion and a deep desire for oblivion. She'll take things up for a while – running, diet, yoga, snorkelling, whatever – pursue them with a passion and then drop them; exhausting fight, then crash and burn. But today, he needs her energy – the energy of recall, of accurate remembering... he needs in Geraldine the energy of the hunt rather than lazy cover-up.

'Time someone knew what?'

'What he done... I mean, it's not right, is it? It's not right, there's no way it's right.' And now her eyes are watering and she looks in her bag for some tissues. Peter looks out the window to the big Tesco's by the river.

'How old were you when these things happened?'

'I don't know, nine or ten – I was in the choir.'

'At St Botolph's?' She nods. 'Did you enjoy it? The church, I mean.'

'I was an altar girl as well – that's a bloody joke, eh? "Altar girl with benefits." But the benefits weren't mine.' Peter remains silent. She has been harassed enough by people in robes, and Peter feels trapped in his own. It would be better if Tamsin were doing this, but she's not answering the phone. 'He used to give classes, about what to do and how to behave around the altar on a Sunday. Fucking 'ell! Well, that's what he said they were... *classes*. But I was the only one who came, I was often alone... and he had me change out of my clothes. He said it was OK because it was God's house; and then I'd put on the stupid altar robes. But in between? He said we'd all stand naked before God one day, and to do it now prepared us for that.' Peter doesn't speak. 'And sometimes he'd hold me when I was naked, he'd hold me close to him, I could feel him, you know.' 'He'd say "This is how God holds you. Do you like God holding you?" I didn't really think it was bad or nothing, not at the time...I

181

mean, I thought it was a bit weird, but church is weird...I didn't think it was bad – you don't, do you?'

'Everything is normal when we're young. That doesn't mean it's good – but it's normal. Normal can be very bad. I think this was very bad.'

'I mean, others talked about it as well; he did it to others, I know he did – but it was like it was a joke. And he was always very nice to us, so I sort-of forgot about it really and just got on with things. You do forget.'

'When you have to.'

'But I stopped going as soon as I could; and my mum got upset, because she liked the church – from a distance, she never came 'erself! So I told her what happened, because why shouldn't she know, she sent me there, saying what a nice man he was, and all that. "It's good for kids," she said, though I just think they wanted me out the house. I came home early one day and they were upstairs in the bedroom, so I knew why they wanted me at church.'

'But she was angry?'

'Yeh, when I told her about the Reverend Hand, she was as angry as I'd seen her, called him a pervert and all sorts, and she tried to tell people, she did her best. I mean, I didn't tell her much, not the full story – your mother doesn't need to know. But I don't think anyone believed her, because he was very popular, the reverend, everyone liked 'im. Even the bishop.'

'The bishop?'

'So what can you do?'

'What bishop?'

'I don't know, but I had seen him before; he'd been to our church in his monk's outfit, a bit like yours, as it goes.' Peter dies inside. *That* bishop. 'Did you know 'im?'

'Before my time. But yes, I have heard.'

'Well, he wore the same clothes...the Bishop of Sussex, was it?'

'Something like that. He left a terrible legacy. People like you whose stories weren't believed.' And this was the only church

Geraldine knew. For the first time in his life, Peter is tempted to burn his clothes and start all over again.

'Anyway, he turned up and spoke to my mum – the bishop, I mean – and I don't know what he said, but he was very charming and all that, she couldn't believe him coming to our house, and in his monk's outfit, said he had a lovely smile, very humble – and she calmed down after that and just said that it was best that I just leave the church, and the less said the better. He basically called me a liar, I think.'

Peter's rage simmers but it's not why he's here. He's not trying to bring a man down, though he'd like to; but trying to see how everything connects, where everything belongs.

'So, as you say, you forgot about it.'

'Yeh, I forgot about it.'

'For twelve years, you decided to do nothing about the vicar abusing you, until yesterday you suddenly thought, *"I can't keep quiet anymore."'*

'Well, I hadn't completely forgotten about it...'

'It was always there inside you, hidden away somewhere, I understand. The body stores these things.'

'Yeh.' She nods.

'Until yesterday.'

'I suppose.'

'So what happened yesterday?'

'Well, nothing really.'

'Were you at work?'

'No, I was at home...home all day. I've got a couple of days off for extra driving lessons. Got my test next week and I can't afford not to pass. It's my third attempt. I badly need to pass.'

'Then good luck.' He smiles. 'I imagine that will be a big day for you.'

'Just a bit.'

'So as you say, you're sitting at home, and you suddenly think -*"I'm going to the police."'*

'*She* said I ought to. It wasn't my idea.'

'Who said you ought to? Your mum?'

'My mum's friend – I mean, she'd always known about it... one of the few to believe me, I think. She said I definitely ought to report it, that the matter shouldn't be left any longer.'

'And this happened yesterday.' She nods. She's wondering where this is going. 'So how did that unfold with your mum's friend? Did *you* start talking about it? Was it on your mind?'

'No, I think it sort-of came up. I mean, I never talk about it. Why would I want to talk about it?'

'You wouldn't, no. So how did it come up?'

'I dunno!' Geraldine is frustrated – she's having to think too hard, and she can't really remember. It wasn't as hard at the police station, no endless bloody questions there. But he needs her energy, he holds her gaze. 'No, *she* brought it up!' says Geraldine triumphantly. 'I remember now.'

'Your mum's friend?'

'Yes, she said how terrible it was, all these stories you read about in the papers, the things people do to children – she said it was a disgrace...especially the priests.'

'And you agreed?'

'I sort-of said it was, yes – I mean, I try not to read about that sort of stuff myself. You've just got to get on with it. I mean, what's the point of complaining? People do what they do.'

'Until someone stops them; and your mum's friend, she said you ought to stop him.'

'She just said I ought to tell the police what happened to me.'

'Out of the blue, she just said that?'

'That it was about time, she said; and that if I didn't want to do it for myself, I should do it for all the other children who went to that church.' Peter nods. 'I didn't want to – but she said she'd drive me if I was up to it, you know, to the police station. It's hardly very far, and then it would all be over...and I could move on.'

'And you agreed?'

'I suppose so...I mean, she's right, isn't she? And, you know, she's been a good friend to my mum.'

'So she came with you to the police station?'

'She drove me, yeh...though not in the hearse, thank God! That would have been weird!'

'Not in the hearse? Why do you say that?'

'Well, she's an undertaker... or a "funeral arranger" as she calls herself! I don't know how you do that job, really I don't – I mean, apparently, you can make a bit extra on the memorial stones and the pre-arranged funerals, but even so, the pay's crap. And dead people all day long!'

'And what's the name of your mum's friend?'

'Oh, she hasn't done anything wrong!' There's panic in her voice.

'Absolutely not! No, I'm here in admiration. She's obviously taking very great care of you, like a good friend should...to be applauded.'

'She's always been a good friend to us.' Geraldine smiles as she contemplates the friendship down the years. 'Bit nutty, obviously – but who isn't?'

'And what's the name of this wonderful woman?'

'Sandra.'

~

The vicar of St Botolph's puts down the phone, and one thing is clear: he'll have to pay him a visit.

He may even be behind all these shenanigans; Ernest is beginning to wonder. He's still shaken by this morning's call, of course. Who wouldn't be? Some police sergeant doing his best to be civil; not the monk, thank God, someone else. But telling him – no 'informing' him – that an accusation had been made against him, in a written statement, and that in the light of this, they'd like to interview him under caution...*under caution?* He's only a bloody vicar!

And he'd said that he didn't know what they were talking about, because, well – he didn't know what they were talking about. It surely wasn't...? And they said that they quite understood; but that they would need to speak with him about the allegation, if only to clear things up; the sergeant felt that might be all that was necessary. And was it possible for him to get over to the police station this afternoon? I mean, talk about crucifixion! Here he was, stuck in this thin-walled hovel, playing the 'care game' for all and sundry, kindly framing everyone's life but his own, jumping to everyone's tune – yet somehow in everyone's sights, a sitting target for the mad and the bad, the disaffected and disgruntled and nowhere to hide. Everyone knows where the vicar lives; which can, at times, be fatal.

He'd known a priest near Bexhill, old college friend, Ralston. He was murdered in his vicarage – stabbed to death in his hallway, after letting the visitor in, with the promise of a sandwich and some tea. He'd always give a sandwich and some tea to the travellers – it was the vicarage, after all. He didn't know the man, he'd never set eyes on him, but apparently – as it transpired in the court case – the murderer had been abused by a priest as a child, somewhere up north. He just wanted to get his own back; and any priest would do. His actual plan had been to *crucify* Stephen, rather than stab him. But the plan broke down, as his statement declared, 'because I left my nails in Eastbourne.'

This was the trouble with the priesthood: you're open to everyone's projections and everyone's madness; and while some elevate you too high, with 'nothing's too good for Father', others, well – there's no telling what they imagine or will do. And the other stuff, which may not have been wise, it was a long time ago.

But Ernest would need to get to Stormhaven before doing anything else; before even his visit to the police. And as he stands in the hallway, he feels cold, as though the sun has retreated behind the cloud, as though favour has been withdrawn. There is a sense, it creeps through him, that he is being hung out to dry in a bitter wind. But two can play at that game, sir.

He postpones his pastoral visit to Mrs Mates – an inappropriate name for such a bitter and lonely woman. She'll not notice his absence, let alone mind. More often than not, she thinks he's her son; who, sadly, she has no time for. And occasionally, it does happen, Ernest allows himself to wonder about the point of it all. He wonders what benefit accrues to anyone in this painful transaction? Neither of them leaves the meeting happier – so why? Why does he do it? It is a dangerous thought, however; a short step away from questioning the point of anything, which is not a path he wishes to go down right now. He may never get back. So today Mrs Mates can wait. Instead, the Reverend Hand will get himself down to the station and onto the Stormhaven train.

Something, or rather some*one*, needs attention...

~

'What do you mean, she's in hospital?'

It's the Lewes nick on the phone; one of the support staff is ringing, confusion reigns.

'That's all we know, abbot.'

'Which hospital?'

'The *Royal Sussex* in Brighton. Make sure you take a map with you. You can wander round that place for hours.'

He is gazing through his study window. A hunched walker plods like a ploughman, making for the sea with a shivering dog.

'But you don't know *why* she's in hospital, what she's doing there?'

'She just told them to tell us where she was. So that's what I am doing.'

'And thank you; appreciated.' But so many questions. 'Is she visiting someone?'

She hadn't mentioned a visit last night. And why would she be letting them know that she was?

'Don't think she's visiting anyone; I think she's hurt, abbot. Or ill. Probably hurt.'

'Why do you say that?'

'When they rang, it was like she couldn't speak for herself, she was unable to. She might have been attacked. That's what it sounded like to me, but they weren't saying.'

'*Attacked* – where?'

'Like I say, it wasn't a long conversation – they were busy. "Information-sharing".'

'Without the information.'

'Hospitals don't like speaking with police. They think their healing hands are above that sort of thing – until, of course, they have some nutter on the premises, when they're suddenly on the phone, demanding help on bended knee. "Send someone now, officer! – no, yesterday!"'

'I'll get over there. And thank you for the tip-off.'

And so the forty minute bus journey to Brighton, getting off at Paston Place, then a steep walk up the hill to the *Royal Sussex*, something of a building site, but carrying on as best it can, troubled staff scurrying along the polished corridors; exhausted staff having a smoke outside, the all-weather brigade; and they need to be today. It's amazing the fags stay lit. But nothing comes between a smoker and their cigarette, not even a Siberian winter.

It had been a journey beside the sea. It is calm today; no troubled conscience, no obvious worries or regrets. The sea comes in and the sea goes out, blessing and killing, killing and blessing – 'teach us to care and not to care', as Eliot said. And sometimes it has the answer, the big horizon, its full expanse stretching away like an empty canvass on which to paint his one precious life; though in Peter's mind, it is peopled today with the ghosts of others – Billy Carter, Mary Houseman, Dorothy Truelove. Their faces haunt the bus ride sky.

And in the solitude of the upper deck, he returns to the odd triangle of accusation. Rev. Hand pointing to Fairburn; Fairburn pointing to Hallington and Hallington pointing back to Hand; rats in a bag, fighting and biting, not all could live. And then a single line, Cathy to Hallington, Hallington to Cathy...what sort of line was that? A surprising connection and Hallington's smug smile, when they'd talked of the relationship. Did he feel he was out of his league with someone like Cathy? Did there always have to be a league?

And Hand knows something, thinks Peter, as the Rampion wind farm comes clear into view, almost ethereal; one hundred and sixteen turbines, eight miles offshore, but somehow nearer – Hand knows something, but he won't say what; and Ralph knows something, and he won't say what, while Ephraim Fenning, Stormhaven's *Man of the Year 2016,* (against strong opposition) lies about a hearse. But did he then lie again? Tamsin hadn't been sure, which was unusual and a sign she wasn't well. She was always sure, even if she wasn't always right.

Consider: Ephraim's story that it was Billy driving the hearse along the seafront, drunk. Consider also: the idea of Ephraim keeping his mouth shut out of kindness. It was possible. But why would Billy do that? It didn't sound like Billy at all. And would Ephraim have invented a story to protect the boy's good name, when really, *his* was the only good name in town? Perhaps there is some hidden goodness in the man. But it's well hidden, some way from view. And it does look like the hearse cost Mrs Truelove her life – though how and why? Who didn't want questions about the hearse? Surely only an undertaker? And Fenning was the only one who knew, according to his own telling of the tale; so this didn't look good for him.

And then there's 'batty' Sandra. Sandra Fenning chooses this particular moment to visit Geraldine, to tell her to expose Hand. Suddenly, after years of silence, it becomes a most pressing matter, with Geraldine hustled into her car by Sandra, 'terrified I would change my mind!'

And all started, all set in motion, like a tick-tock on a bomb, by the note in Billy Carter's bedroom, '*He's done bad things to me...*' Testis unus.

'Could you come this way?' says the nurse. 'You can see the surgeon now.'

'The surgeon?' He hadn't expected that. 'Is she OK?'

'I'm sure he will tell you.'

'And your take?'

She smiles. 'I don't have one. I'm only a nurse.'

Instant rapport. 'Of course. What could you possibly know? But speaking from your deep ignorance?'

'A bit touch and go, from what I understand. She wasn't well, heart stuff; everything hastily arranged. But the surgeon will tell you more – because surgeons know everything.'

'I wake up jealous every day.'

There is something understood between them as she sets off at pace down the corridor, her shoes clicking on the shiny lino; and the abbot follows, keen to keep up with such medical speed, disturbed by events and anxious about Tamsin.

Hand has decided he'll see Hallington first; speak with him face to face. God knows, he hates conflict, absolutely not his thing at all; but this whole business needs quietening down and he needs to be sure. He needs to find some sort of footing in this swirling mire of accusation.

'The sword of accusation hangs over me,' the reverend had said over the phone.

'Join the club, mate,' said Hallington. 'It's when you learn who your friends are. I've seen lepers with more friends than me.'

'Though I'm rather wondering if you put it there, Nick. The sword, I mean.'

'Why would *I* put it there, Ernest? Are you going mad?' He's dismissive, which riles the reverend.

'Well, you do have form, Hallington – sending the police rather ingloriously to my door after the death of Billy.'

Hallington laughs. 'I think they would have been at your door without me, Ernest. The boy did leave a note.'

They had been an odd couple, meeting pitch-side in Stormhaven on cold winter nights. Ernest taking an interest in his young people's sporting progress; a world he'd never known as a child. But he'd enjoyed it. He loved to shout and to holler for his crew, a slightly eccentric member of the crowd, who clearly knew nothing about the game. He would cheer at inappropriate moments – like when Billy broke an opponent's leg with an 'unfortunate' tackle.

'Splendid!' he'd shouted.

And, of course, it was boys and girls playing these days. 'They all play football now, reverend,' said Hallington. 'It's a different game, but the same rules, if you know what I mean.' Parents tended to love or loathe Hand; for some, he was a pervert, because all vicars are; while for others, he was just what a vicar should be – entertaining, fun and out there in the world, rather than hiding behind the altar or shouting 'Sin!' from the pulpit. And for the record, Ernest Hand never shouted 'Sin!' from the pulpit. He didn't like the word at all.

And that's where he'd met Nick Hallington – because he'd just had to tell the man what an excellent job he was doing with the young people. And he *was*, the hardest job in the world: life alongside the unlovable young, and worse, their awful parents. How the human ego invests in its offspring! And how repulsive it makes them!

'I don't know how you put up with it all,' he'd say.

'Oh, you get used to it,' said Hallington. And occasionally, Ernest had gone back to his place afterwards, with some of the young people, which was all rather intoxicating, despite the absence of alcohol, which would have been a serious mistake. He'd had to watch himself or who knows what would have come out of his mouth! Ernest did 'spill' sometimes, with no sense of edit. He'd endured accusations of being 'inappropriate' all his life; but 'inappropriate' could be most entertaining, as some told him – and he liked to entertain.

But there's a time for everything, and a time for every purpose under heaven: a time to be born, a time to die; a time to plant, and a time to pluck up that which is planted; a time to kill, and a time to heal; a time to break down, and a time to build up; a time to weep and he had wept – metaphorically, perhaps – as the young people had left St Botolph's, flown the nest, leaving an emptiness in the place. It wasn't the same, not like it used to be, not for Ernest. Perhaps he'd loved that crowd in some way, but he wasn't interested now, not with all the new guide lines, child protection initiatives and all the accusations they bring. Oh, he could do without all that! These days, he just couldn't rustle up the energy to go and watch them kicking a ball around. What was the point? Someone was sure to be pointing an accusing finger. And he always had the internet, which was all perfectly harmless.

So he hadn't seen Nick for a while, apart from that odd 'coffee morning' with him and Fenning at *The Plough*. He knew Fairburn was making his life hell, of course, always on Hallington's back; but Nick somehow seemed oblivious to it all and laughed him off.

'If I bowed to every parental demand, James, I'd have a first eleven of twenty-three.'

'But Billy is obviously your best striker,' says Fairburn.

'And your "obviously" is my "sometimes",' says Hallington.

'And your "sometimes" is my "bollocks".'

And while, on occasion, James could see the funny side, the occasion was rare; and he'd get angry on the touch line and Ernest would have to calm him down, play the jester.

'It's all right for you, you don't have any children, you gay bastard,' Fairburn would say. And Ernest would roll his eyes, and take it as a joke, and it was a joke obviously – James had a sense of humour. And Ernest wasn't gay, he didn't think so, though who can ever really say? He just knew he needed to be careful. 'Not everything and everyone can be labelled,' he'd say.

'Apart from a gay.'

James even came along to some services at St Botolph's when Cathy threw him out – or when *he* stormed out, "unable to take any more of her nonsense", whichever version you believed. But he couldn't manage more than a few weeks' attendance. 'Sorry, Doggy,' he'd said – he called Ernest "Doggy" because of the dog collar. 'Can't quite manage the religion thing. Not my bag.'

And so it is that Ernest now stands on Lewes platform, awaiting the Stormhaven train. He's had a delightful coffee in the station cafe, and an interesting chat with a hitch hiker from Cumbria, who's walking the South Downs Way. Whether by accident or design, he misses the first train, delaying the inevitable – and Ernest does like to delay the inevitable. But he needs to go now, he really must; and he watches the carriages wobble slowly towards him, emerging from the tunnel, easing slowly alongside the platform. It's a nineteen minute journey to Stormhaven, so time for a chapter of his book – a look back at the glory days of Hollywood.

Standing close by – perhaps too close to the platform edge – is a figure in a red hoodie. They too are watching both the reverend and the approaching train. Here is someone who knows better than Ernest that the inevitable must not only be delayed... it must never happen at all.

~

'A heart attack?' says the abbot.

The surgeon nods with calm authority. 'Fortunately, I was able to attend to her quickly. A theatre was made available, pulled a few strings, and we got her in and straight down to business. It's all about early response with heart attacks.'

'And how is she?'

The medic's face is ambivalent, professionally so.

'She's stable at the moment, that we *can* say, heart rate steady...not strong, but steady.'

James Fairburn is a different figure from the haunted man in his lonely Rodmell mansion. In work scrubs, he is no normal human being at all, no angry divorcee, no insecure touchline terror; but a superhero with remarkable powers.

'You're optimistic?'

'No surgeon says that, abbot – not unless they're a fool. The human body is not a machine; it doesn't always behave as it should, moves from strong to weak in an instant. Life is fragile, abbot, we only *pretend* control, any of us.' Peter wonders if this is from a lecture he gives to students. It feels manicured; lacks spontaneity. 'And so if I say I'm optimistic, or if I say I'm hopeful – you take me at my word, imagine everything's fine! And then any sign of a dip in the patient and you're be back here with your smart-arse lawyer to complain that I said she was well! That her care must somehow have been deficient, that a mistake must have been made!'

Where to start with this nonsense? 'I've never taken the words of authority seriously,' says Peter. 'And certainly not those of a doctor. I merely asked for your sense of things. But I understand your defensive response. In the family of the psyche, it is the ego who screams the loudest.'

'I'm professional, abbot – not defensive. Why would I be defensive?' *We can only imagine.* 'And she wasn't well; that was very clear once we'd opened her up. I'm only surprised you hadn't seen the signs.'

'Signs of what?'

'Her heart condition.'

'We don't live together.'

'But you *work* together and she was some way down the path of ill-health. It was like looking inside a stress factory! If Carlsberg did stressed hearts...' He smiles at his comedy, but within his smile is also accusation. 'She must have been suffering tiredness at least...unusual fatigue, nausea and dizziness, I'd imagine.'

'Possibly.' Is the abbot to blame for Tamsin's appalling self-care? It appears so.

'And some serious chest pains.'

'She didn't mention...'

'Women often describe chest pain as pressure or tightness; it's not unusual. And it may be because women are different from men – and not just in the obvious way, that they have fantastic tits!' *Let me out.* 'Shall we walk and talk, abbot? I need to be somewhere.' Peter finds himself scuttling along in his majestic wake, the apprentice behind the master. 'No, they tend to have blockages not only in their main arteries, which men do, but also in the smaller arteries that supply blood to the heart.' The abbot's own heart is busy, just about keeping up.

'It's a condition called small vessel heart disease or coronary microvascular disease...and that's Tamsin, I'm afraid.'

'I have been encouraging her to see a doctor.'

'Who's defensive now?' says Fairburn with '*Got you!*' relish. He is still smarting from the abbot's 'defensive' jibe – no judgement forgotten, imagined or otherwise.

'She did say she wanted to get home early last night. I said that would be a very good idea – an early night.'

Was he being defensive again?

'Ah, the "early night" school of medicine! A school frequented by the hopeful – but not the informed. She has a stressful job, of course, no denying that – all that crime to sort out, all those murderers to snare and catch.' He nods at his own wisdom. 'But she's hardly the only one with work place challenges – and fortunately, we don't all collapse!'

The message is clear: James Fairburn also has a stressful job, but unlike her, he hasn't buckled, he's continuing to save the world and wants some applause for his night's work. *He really is quite a needy man.*

'I think we make our own stress,' says Peter, 'and mistakenly relate it to our jobs...though I would make an exception for those in bomb disposal and youth work. Now *those* are stressful jobs.'

'Well, if that's all, I'd better be...'

Fairburn, a medical Adonis, is looking down the corridor as though being called – and perhaps he is; everyone wants him here, you sense that. And you don't pay a surgeon to stand in the corridor talking. You pay them to cut you open and sort out your arteries or remove the tumour or the bullet. You pay him, scalpel in hand, to produce bloody and scientific magic, to give you back your life.

'Though this is all a bit of a coincidence,' says the abbot and Fairburn looks quizzical. 'I mean, that you should be on-hand to treat her.'

'Ah well, coincidence happens, abbot – as the law of averages dictates! We don't need to bring God into it.'

'I'm not aware I did.'

'And she's a very lucky girl, that synchronicity smiled on her, otherwise... ' He draws an imaginary knife across his throat. 'It would have been *kaput*! No, lucky I was with her...very lucky.'

'You were with her?'

'I've got to shoot to brief the care team, abbot; they can't start without me. But one thing before I do: I'm hoping this is the end of police harassment. Yes? I don't know if you have any say in the matter, it may be above your pay grade – and perhaps Tamsin was the driver in this whole wretched affair. But I've saved one of yours tonight, and that's no lie; I've saved my pursuer...like Jean Valjean in *Les Mis*, for God's sake! So perhaps we could call it quits. I don't want this to get nasty.'

'How could it get nasty?'

'Forget I said it.' His jaw locks with irritation.

'Can I see her?'

Cathy puts the photos in a pile, all but one.

It hasn't taken long to gather them together. She has never been obsessed by photos, as some are; as if their lives must be saved on film, every moment caught, every gathering organised into a group snap... as if it isn't real without one.

'We haven't taken a photo!' they say, in some existential terror that they may not exist without photographic evidence. Cathy, though, prefers the moment to the film; prefers the experience to some photo pinned like a dead butterfly in a book, or stored in the clouds, eternally out of context – as someone in a coffin, life-like but cold.

'I don't know what you've got against photos,' her friend said and Cathy told her she didn't have anything against photos, 'except that they are against life. If you take a photo of the moment, you have missed the moment. You weren't there.'

'Nonsense, Cath – utter nonsense. Take a photo and it's a memory you can return to, whenever you want. Otherwise you'd forget. I mean, the photo takes you back there.'

'But why do you want to go back there?'

'Well, it's nice, isn't it? On a cold winter's evening....'

'But why do you want to live in the past? That's what I'm saying. It doesn't exist anymore, it's gone. We only have the present...'

'You're nuts, Cath, you know that! Fucking insane, you are!'

So Cathy takes the photos out into the garden, with a bath ball, left over from Christmas. People always give her bath balls, but they make a mess in the bath and create scum round the edges, so why would you want one? Until now – because now, it's exactly what she needs, the bath ball is perfect; everything belongs in the end. She places the photos in a barbeque tray, and fills a bowl with water.

She's sitting in the garden, wrapped-up warm; frosty views across the golf course towards the sea. It is too beautiful. The flat may be small but the horizon is big and invites the remembering of those gone – the remembering of her son Billy, though sometimes she is distracted by the robin, hopping with busy intent...and perhaps the robin is Billy, because he too liked to hop. Who knows what would have become of his life on earth, had it been granted more than nineteen years? But he did like to hop, to try things...the drowning was an end to his trying. Tears fill her eyes; sadness and rage spill.

'I'm sorry I wasn't there for you, Billy.' She knows guilt, she could predict it, she could see it coming, she could even explain it – but she cannot be free of it. The head knows but the body won't follow. 'I would have been there, if I could. I would have been...' Terrible tears, quite uncontrollable...and then the robin flies into a tree and looks down at her. The robin looks down, just for a moment, before it flies off...the robin flies away, disappearing behind the neighbour's roof.

'Goodbye dear Billy, goodbye dear heart.' The tears break out again, blurring the sky, smudging everything but her grief. 'For all that has been, thank you.' She pauses. 'Thank you' – she says it again and again, until she calms. 'And for all that shall be, yes.'

And now is the moment. She breathes deep and pouring fuel onto the photos, she lights the match, she sets them alight, Billy's face burns, a lost past burns; a busy, consuming flame, smoke in the air cascading skywards, images curling and destroyed, until only charred scraps remain. She then places the bath ball in the bowl of water, releasing it to fragrant death, it fizzes wonderfully, diminishing by the second, sweet smells, merging with the water, both its death and its life – and she says it again,

'For all that has been, thank you. You will never die in me, Billy, never. And for all that shall be, for you and for me – *yes!*'

Her phone rings; it's Hallington. She doesn't answer, she's watching the robin. The bird has returned, perched on the woodpile, brisk in manner, watching her, though only briefly – everything is brief with this bird, then swooping so close she almost falls off her chair... and recovering her balance, Cathy begins to laugh.

The robin is gone. And the phone is ringing again.

~

'The thing is, the case is quite far advanced, Chief Inspector.'

The abbot is fighting for his life; or rather, for the life of his investigation, which is in danger of being dumped on. The impression of unstoppable momentum must be given.

'Well, *how* far?' says Wonder, feeling panic in his soul. He has a high profile case on his hands. There have been two murders in twenty-four hours on Stormhaven's seafront, which, whatever you say about it – and people do – everyone knows. Everyone's been there – cheap family holidays, days in the rain, walks along the Seven Sisters, they all know the sea front. And they so also know about the murders, colossal interest; *BBC News South East,* always short of a story, seem to have a camp there. 'Waves of Despair!' was one headline. 'The High Tide of Murder' another. And so it's no time to lose your lead detective, leaving – well, leaving 'a bloody monk' to take the strain. If Geoffrey Sitwell hears of this, and he will hear of it, because he's a shit-stirrer, Wonder will be handing a gun to his own assassin while wearing a target on his heart. It could even be the end of the *Trusted Citizen* scheme.

'An outsider coming in is going to struggle,' says Peter. And more pressingly, *he* will struggle with some needy idiot being parachuted in to take control. 'I believe they'll slow things down before they speed things up. And we can't afford a slowing down at this particular moment.'

Though Peter knows it's less about things slowed down and more about hasty removals. Tamsin invited him in; but the invitation will not be extended by another. In the absence of Tamsin – cut, wired and patched in hospital – he is vulnerable.

'You know the killer, abbot?'

And *there's* a line the Chief Inspector never imagined saying, because it was true, he hadn't always been keen, as he'd made clear to DI Shah a few years back.

'We can't be seen as a uniformed branch of the church, Tamsin.'

'Have you forgotten the Christmas party?'

He had tried to forget but failed; and now he blushes again. The Police Christmas party had been no church outing; but an appalling drink-fuelled free-for-all, from which various sergeants – and relationships – were still recovering. Most awkward had been Wonder's clumsy hit on Tamsin; about which his wife must never hear. The daily embarrassment is punishment enough, surely?

'It's all about perception, Shah. We can't be seen to be favouring Christianity over other religions; that's what I'm saying.' He has gathered himself again. 'It's professional suicide these days – perception is everything, you know it is!'

'And substance is secondary?' She borrows the line from the abbot; any weapon to hand.

'Identity politics, Tamsin, you know the score – it bows to race, gender and ethnicity. What it doesn't bow to is bloody Christianity, and that's a fact! Another reason, as if I needed another, that I do not sit comfortably with the abbot being involved in the investigations.'

'I'm a non-believer, Chief Inspector, not an evangelist. I am not here on behalf of God. So find me an imam or a rabbi with investigative skills, find me a Buddhist Sherlock or an atheist Miss Marple – and I'll drop the abbot immediately, for the sake of balance.'

'It's not funny, Tamsin.'

'I don't remember laughing. But I do remember the abbot getting results, which is what I like to get...and what I do get: results. He helps me get results.'

The Chief Inspector scratches his bald head; the less the hair, the more the itch. Another mystery.

'Well, he needs to carry on getting results, that's all I can say, he needs to carry on, because he's a liability for us...a bloody liability.'

He has to admit, though, as he sits with the abbot now, his loyalties have shifted over the years. He must be getting old because he even finds himself thinking of Skegness and when did he last do that? 'I took part in a Beach Mission once – in Skegness,' he says to Peter, like a man casting a line. 'Yes, it was run by the, er, – Scripture Union,' he says, wistfully.

'A beach mission?' says Peter, surprised at this digression. 'Is it the sand that needs saving or the deck chairs?' He has an investigation to save. He'd prefer not to go to Skegness.

'Don't be an arse. A mission *on* a beach – not *to* it. Can you imagine that, abbot?' The abbot shakes his head. 'Me – leading a beach mission, eh?'

'Traumatic memories for everyone concerned.'

'I was thinner then, of course. But they're bloody good memories, actually! Ever done one of those?'

'Ever done one of what?'

'A beach mission, for God's sake. Have you ever done one?'

'I was twenty-five years in the desert. It's like a beach – in a way.'

'Wasn't everyone's cup of tea, of course, you'd always get a few comments from folk.'

'I can imagine their gist.'

'But the kids loved it, they really did...good days they were in Skeggy!' He wonders where the years have gone and more pressingly, where that young man has gone – the one who took custard pies in the face and even had to lead a bible study one night. Ye Gods! How did he bluster his way through that malarkey? 'Long time ago, of course, though like yesterday. Strange thing, time.'

'And the truth is, we're closing in, Chief Inspector; we're closing in on the killer.' *Let's get away from the beach.* Peter doesn't yet know the identity of the killer; but he does wish to communicate forward energy in the investigation; energy which should not be disturbed.

'Well, clearly we'll have to get you a new case lead. There's DI Geoffrey Sitwell, who might... '

'He's always a possibility.' *He'd be a disaster, he'd heard all about him from Tamsin.* 'Or perhaps someone more capable – like your self?'

'I mean, Tamsin won't be back for a while, will she?' The Chief Inspector is just checking.

'No, she won't...not for a while.'

'Have you seen her yet?'

'I can see her this afternoon, when I hope she'll be able to talk. There's much I still don't know. I'm told she is lucky to be alive.'

'But she is going to live, isn't she, abbot?' A note of genuine concern is in his voice; really quite touching.

'The surgeon was optimistic. Told me so himself.'

'Who'd have thought of a stunner like her having a heart attack, eh?'

'It's not only the ugly at risk,' says Peter and Wonder closes like a crab.

'All right, all right – we're not on camera now. She is a stunner.'

'And also my niece.' Wonder grunts in vague affirmation. 'My interest is in justice for those murdered, Chief Inspector; but the recovery of my only relation on earth would be also be nice.'

The Chief does sometimes forget they are related. Tamsin is so devoid of sentimental attachment, that family ties seem somehow impossible.

'Well, I'll leave you in peace for now, abbot; but keep me informed. You bloody well keep me informed.'

'Of course, Chief Inspector. And how about Sergeant Banville, sir, as my link man, my support?'

'The "Dinosaur from Dorchester"?

'And also your best officer.'

'No offence to the boy, just banter.' He nods his head in agreement with himself. 'Saved by the fish and chips!' he says heartily.

'I'm sorry?'

'In Skeggy...the fish and chips. Now they were something!' He smiles at the memory. 'No fish and chips like the Skeggy sort and good days in their way, abbot... more innocent, eh? I think so, more innocent. We all slept on the floor of the church hall...and slept surprisingly well. I've never slept as well since.'

'Children are exhausting.'

'I was in charge of the drama, I remember now.' Wonder is relaxing, his belly extends in remembrance. 'Which involved a lot of over-acting, fluffed lines and playing the part of a donkey's bottom.'

'So ideal preparation for the police.'

'The world was a younger place then.'

'Or perhaps we were just younger. We start out so fresh but can dry up along the way. And Sergeant Banville?'

But Wonder is still at the beach, it's all flooding back, as if a crack in the dam has suddenly become a hole, unrestrained memories smashing, crashing through. He's remembering the jam sandwich lunches the team would share – cost was always an issue – followed by a piece of fruit. The bananas went first; you had to be quick to get one of them; and then an afternoon of beach football or other mad games. But he'd been a lithe young fellow in those days with the energy of a shooting star. And everyone loved him, *he'd* been the star in a way; and he'd never stopped until he got back home at the end of the week and collapsed on his parents' sofa. Different days, no question of that; and he'd have to go home today and see if he had any photos...be a bloody shame if he didn't. 'What about him?'

'I just wondered if I could have Sergeant Banville on a seventy-two hour secondment to the investigation...until the new case lead is sorted? That would be very helpful.' Seventy-two hours would be enough.

'It's where I saw my first tattoo – in Skegness.'

'Really?' It is not a word of encouragement.

'It was exotic then, of course, something for sailors and the South Pacific...different days, eh? All our yesterdays!'

Though today, the abbot does need to be getting on. He has an appointment with Tamsin.

$$\sim$$

'The suicide of a murderer perhaps?' she says, as though grasping at familiar words, some old autocue inside her head. She is raised up in her hospital bed; and recovering her colour.

'He was pushed,' says the abbot.

'It would make sense.' She hasn't heard him. She's still with the autocue. 'Good honest Christian guilt – for good honest Christian depravity.' She enjoys saying that...her first real pleasure since waking up in the hospital, confused and unsettled. She had been told of the heart attack by a nurse, which she couldn't believe, because it was ridiculous. And then of the operation, which felt surreal, as if she needed an operation? But the gradual realisation, as she lay alone in her room, that this *was* real – this was real life and she's stunned, she can't believe it's happening. She should be on the case. And while she doesn't know what case it is she should be on, she knows she shouldn't be here.

And then prior memories surface, the struggle at her door, a man pushing her over; but they make no sense, she doesn't know where they come from, they may be a dream, hard to say right now, with reality such a shifting thing. *Focus on what's before you.* And before her is the abbot.

'He was pushed,' he repeats. He sits in the visitor's chair, which is clean but not designed for humans. Making comfort impossible, it almost demands the visitor leaves soon. Perhaps he could get one for his front room.

'More likely the suicide of paedophile,' says Tamsin. There is something about needing to be right; and particularly now. If she puts the abbot down, she's back in charge, so it's obviously a suicide and she's taking back control. 'What with everything closing in on the bastard. I never trusted him. So he goes down to Lewes station and jumps, preferring death to the cameras.'

She feels tired, her head separate from her body; but the suicide of a paedophile does make sense. And this was the general opinion at Lewes station, where witnesses to the death had found themselves much in demand. Interest was heightened by the fact that it was a reverend who was spliced by the train, "a man of the cloth" – not hung, but certainly drawn and quartered, the brakes too slow, the wheels unkind. There was no undertaker on earth who could make Ernest look pretty after that.

'He was pushed,' he says, for the third time of asking. He doesn't wish to argue with the invalid, but nonsense must be named.

'How do you know he was pushed?'

'You look pale.'

'I just don't have make-up. It's not a medical condition.'

Until now, Peter hadn't realised she wore make-up; it was the only Tamsin he knew. Yet here was someone different. And he thought of Cassian, the doorkeeper in the monastery, who hadn't realised his uncle was a drunk, until one year, at a family funeral, he met him sober. Tamsin is frailer without the magic brush, as if her strength is painted on; and younger, in a way.

'There are two witnesses who think they saw someone in a red track suit, with the hood up, nudge him forward.'

'They *think* they saw someone *nudge* him?' The abbot nods. 'Oh, well *there's* water-tight testimony. I don't see any problems with that! No wriggle room for the defence lawyer there! Case closed!' She pauses for a moment, made tired by her talking. 'A bit of pushing when the train arrives and suddenly they're all murderers. When were you last on the Victoria line?'

'You seem to be recovering,' says Peter, sitting beside her. He has come to see how she is. But news of the death of Rev. Ernest Hand at Lewes station has gate-crashed the visit. He'd heard from Banville on his bus journey to Brighton.

'Is there CCTV on the platform?' asks Tamsin.

'No...or none that is helpful. Banville checked that.'

'Banville?'

'He's a sergeant who's helping me. We met him at Splash Point during the reconstruction. He was the one in the sea with me.' Tamsin nods in a non-committal way. 'He's helping me until you're back on the case.'

'"The Dinosaur from Dorchester" takes my place?'

She doesn't go along with that sort of talk herself, she doesn't join in. But she hears it in the canteen and in the stairwells, where people imagine themselves unheard. Why does anyone think they are unheard in a stairwell? It's a loud speaker system.

'No one takes your place.'

'And as you and I know, abbot, I won't be back on this case.' She's waking up slowly.

'You're on it now. Why else am I here? You don't imagine I'm concerned for your wellbeing?'

'Wonder will bring in some stuffed shirt to take-over, probably Geoffrey Shitwell. There's not an ounce of him you can trust.' Peter was working hard to delay his arrival, but knew she was right. Wonder would have to cover himself. 'And he won't listen to any progress that's been made on the case – and why? Because it was progress made without him, and therefore constitutes a threat.' Tamsin accurately describes both Sitwell and herself. 'So he'll rip it all up and start again, he'll be back at Splash Point for a second reconstruction, all suspects will be re-interviewed, he'll waste everybody's time, so that it's *his* case and no one else's case, happy as a clam at high tide... it's how things work, you must know that.' The abbot did know that. 'And you'll be washing up at home.'

'Indeed.' The abbot quite liked washing up. 'The good news is: you're definitely on the mend.'

She sighs, exhausted again. 'So no grapes?'

'The NHS hates grapes; the nurse took my bag of seedless. "They just rot," she said. So no more grapes; and no bread to the ducks. That's not a kindness either, apparently. All the old certainties of life have been removed. So what happened?'

'I like grapes – and the food here is appalling.' And then, with only the slightest pause, 'How do you mean, "what happened?"'

'The heart attack…I'm told it was a heart attack.' Tamsin doesn't like the idea, she's quiet. 'I mean, where were you? How did you get to be here? I sent you home. Did you get home?'

'I did, yes.'

'Did you rest?'

'I began to rest – and then he turned up at my door.'

'Who turned up?'

'Fairburn. James Fairburn.' And now she's remembering; she's seeing him. 'It was James Fairburn! He came round to my flat!' She's breathless.

'It's all right, it's all right.' Peter is leaning forward, calming her with his hand. 'Fairburn – round at yours?' She nods. 'How did he do that? I mean, *why* did he do that?'

'He got hold of my address, Facebook probably sold it to him…used my upstairs neighbour to gain entry… and pushed his way in.'

'He pushed his way into your flat?' Peter wishes he'd known this earlier.

'Are you auditioning for the part of a parrot?' A faint smile drifts across her face, but she doesn't want to be telling this story, she feels stupid and doesn't want it dragged out of her. She doesn't want clarifying questions from the audience, because she isn't the hero, she's the victim, and she never wants to be the victim… she just wants it over with. But the abbot is thinking of the hospital god in his scrubs, the wonderful surgeon with the precious scent of respect, and a bank balance to match. He's seeing him as he forces his way through a woman's front door, pushing her aside in some kind of a rage. 'I don't really remember, abbot, but I was tired; I just felt this terrible pain in my arm...'

'Fairburn was your surgeon, Tamsin.' She looks surprised.

'Fairburn?'

She dies again.

'He must have seen you fall, called the ambulance...and then operated on you.'

'I feel sick. The man's a creep. To think he had his hands...'

'The important thing is that you're well.'

But she doesn't feel well, not now. She feels vulnerable, she feels stymied; denied control and in the hands of powerful others...in the hands of nurses, doctors, consultants, the creep Fairburn. She has no control in this situation, and this is oblivion for her; an empty abyss she is falling into. She senses the onset of panic, it's coming back; her breathing shortens.

'Are you all right?' Peter reaches towards her.

'You need to go, abbot.'

'I can't do that.'

'Just go – *please, just go.*'

'I won't go until...'

'I just need you to go! You're not wanted!' He sees demand and desperation in her eyes.

'OK, I'll go,' he says getting up slowly, knocking over his chair. He picks it up; he's disturbed by the venom of the dismissal. 'Just stay calm, Tamsin....some deep breaths. I'll be back, it's going to be all right. It's all going to be all right.'

'Just go.'

She's still again; staring at the ceiling as he leaves. He looks back from the door, but they don't connect, not in any way at all. He closes the door behind him, he's walking down the corridor looking for a nurse; he needs someone to keep an eye on Tamsin – I mean, someone must be doing that anyway, he thinks, it must be someone's job, though the epidemic, and the cold, has left everywhere short-staffed. And while there was strength in her dismissal, there was panic as well, she needs medical attention, she needs watching over – and then his phone rings. It's Banville.

'You'll never guess who pushed the reverend in front of the train!' he says, with friendly delight. For Banville, the joy of the hunt transcends the private tragedy.

'You'll need to hold for a moment, Banville.' He is still with Tamsin, in his mind at least; he needs to find a nurse. And when five minutes later he has done so, and when he has named his concerns for his niece – 'Are you family?' had been the nurses' first question – he returns to the call. 'I'm sorry,' he says, 'just something I had to do. So you have news.'

'I do have news, abbot.'

'So tell me,' he says, deciding on the stairs rather than the lift. He doesn't like lifts.

'You might be surprised.'

'Stop being a drama queen, sergeant – this isn't *Strictly Come Dancing.*' He was recently forced to watch an episode, when a neighbour's TV broke down. They'd come round in a state, almost suicidal, and implored him to turn it on. Fair enough, but never again, really – never *ever* again. A twenty minute show, crammed into an hour and a half; oh, and the hysteria! The human race is not at its best when carried on that particular tide. And the extended pause before the result is announced – a pause in which he could have done something useful...the abbot is still in recovery.

'I didn't imagine you watched that, sir.'

'Without CCTV on the station, Banville, how on earth can you know who killed the Reverend Hand?'

By the time Peter reaches the fresh air, Banville has gone up in his estimation; and the abbot is thinking about Geraldine again.

~

Tamsin feels calm; as calm as she can manage for she is never calm, but she has settled.

Calm is control and she feels more in control. The breathing has helped, the deepening of her breathing; and it is a relief to be alone. She wishes for no more hospital visits...from anyone. Visits and visitors are a judgement on her, this is the truth. Their very presence by her bed is a judgement, whether they intend it or not; their intentions make no difference. The sense is particularly strong now, the powerlessness of the patient, to which the visitor is a witness. They are a witness to her weakness, to her humiliation, laid so limp and low, unable to pursue the investigation, unable to achieve anything. This is not how she wishes to be known by the outside world. She wishes to be known by her success; while within, it is simply the end of everything, to which she must become numb.

But slowly she is feeling better; there is energy again. With the abbot's departure – she had not wished to be rude, but there we are – panic gives way to something approaching peace. Slowly, consciousness returns, neural pathways connect and she takes stock of her situation, easing into her new reality. She has had a heart attack, she's recovering in a hospital bed, she's allowed visitors, so she must be OK; she must be on the mend. She has seen the abbot, talked about the case, felt energy in her blood and more strength will arrive. She just needs time.

And then the footsteps. She hears footsteps and they pause outside her door and she doesn't like the pause. She wonders if the abbot is coming back. Perhaps he forgot something; but it isn't the abbot, she knows it isn't the abbot, those are not his feet and fear rises inside her; a hot sweat of fear on the back of the neck. She tells herself to stop being ridiculous, calls herself to order, tries again to breathe. *You're in a hospital for God's sake! You're safe!'* Again, the footsteps on the corridor floor; she hopes they pass and journey on, perhaps a cleaner. But no cleaner wears shoes like that, and they don't pass but stop outside her door, as if looking round. They're shifty steps, men's steps, men's shoes and again she hopes it is the abbot, it could be the abbot.

A moment of silence, her heart shouldn't beat this hard, her drip-wired body alert, waiting – and then the handle turns, the door slowly opens... and James Fairburn appears. He closes the door behind him and smiles.

~

Banville explains everything. They sit at a window table in a small coffee shop in Church Street. Sun spills in, local art on the wall, home-made cakes; but there's been too much murder for Peter to feel the joy.

'She saw it all as clear as day, abbot, clear as day – in fact, I'm not sure she'll ever forget it. They got help in Dorchester, the train drivers; though why so many people wanted to end it there, I could never understand. It's a very historical city – Thomas Hardy country.'

'That may be the clue.'

'And she's a nice woman, very pleasant – still in shock obviously.'

'Obviously.'

'And she will need help because, I mean, well – seeing the body fall in front of you, seeing the face, the final look of terror... that'll be waking her up in thirty years' time, I'd reckon.'

'You did well to speak with her. So, what did she actually...?'

'I just hope my interview didn't make things worse.'

'I'm sure you handled it kindly, Sergeant. And kindness is never mistimed.'

They both drink ginger ale. The abbot had ordered one for himself and Banville said he hadn't had a ginger ale for a long time – "not since my last picnic with Enid Blyton!"- and promptly followed suit. He is an engaging young man with thick black curly hair, eager for action and ever eager to please.

'So you spoke with her?' Peter encourages him to focus.

'I spoke with her, yes, because I asked myself the question: if there was no relevant CCTV on the station – which I can hardly believe in this day and age – then who'd have the best view of the scene? And I was thinking, well, the incoming driver would have the best view, wouldn't they? I mean, they've got a bloody front seat, excuse my French.'

'It's all about asking the right questions.' *Though do feel free to get on with it now.*

'I had a mind to apply to C.I.D., actually.' He nods, as if agreeing with himself. 'I did, yeh. I mean, I talked to the Chief Inspector about it a while back.'

'And I'm sure you were heard.' Out of kindness, he'd refrain from including the "Dinosaur from Dorchester" narrative.

'They call me "The Dinosaur from Dorchester", says Banville. 'That's what they call me back at the nick. I know they do.' His voice breaks a little and his face is suddenly sad, like a disappointed child. 'They like to think they're a branch of the Mets down here, which is a joke. It's bloody Lewes, for God's sake!'

'I wouldn't let them define you, Banville. But before eternity is spent, you must tell me what the train driver saw. Or rather, *who* she saw?'

'So how is my patient?' The surgeon is brisk and professional.

She feels her heart pumping, panic rising like sick; she pushes it down, brutally. The SAS compartmentalise, that's how they survive; they'd had one of them down for a training day, with tales of survival and endurance. The young men had loved it, the older ones felt inadequate, and so curdled. She didn't realise she'd been listening.

'I'm fine,' she says. Don't give him anything. He raises his eyebrows jokily.

'I've seen you look better, to be honest.'

'And no thanks to you.'

She is intimidated again, like at the door of her home, her last memory of this man; that pressing figure at her door, a man she couldn't keep out.

'Well, if you are fine – and we can't be sure yet – it's all thanks to me, you know. I was your surgeon last night. There's nowhere my hands haven't been inside you.'

She feels ill. 'The abbot told me...just so long as you don't expect gratitude.'

'I saved your life, Detective Inspector.' Tamsin shakes her head with a withering smile. 'My hands are forever in your heart, you might say. Slightly surprised you had one, to be honest! I was half-expecting a hole there.'

'Are you going now? I'd like you to go. I've been told to rest.'

'Lucky we got to you in time, Tamsin.' He glances out the window, westwards across Brighton.

'This is all down to you, and you know it. So if you've come to apologise...'

He smiles. 'All I know is that I came round to yours to ask about the case and you had a heart attack when you opened the door to me. The right man in the right place at the right time, I'd say. It's a great story for some newspaper or other!'

'Or you could tell them what really happened...as I will.'

'If you survive, which is a bit touch and go. And anyway, Testis unus, testis nullus, Detective Inspector. It means...'

'I know what it means.'

He nods equably and sits down.

'God, these chairs are uncomfortable.'

Tamsin is listening for sounds in the corridor. She wants someone else in the room with her – desperately.

'So, how's the case going? You can tell me, we're alone now. Quite alone.' Tamsin doesn't respond. There is nothing healing about this surgeon, whatever the skill in his hands. Cathy had called him 'a plumber' and that's exactly what he is...a plumber but not a healer. 'It's strange, isn't it, how power shifts,' he says. 'A day or so ago, you had my life in your police hands. You could order whatever you wished, and ask whatever you wished. You could send your lackeys round to the hospital to ask crooked questions – and I was absolutely powerless. And yet today – well, what a turnaround! Who'd have thought it? It's as if I planned it, though I assure you I didn't. But here you are full of wires and drips and a rather large and scary scar across your chest, and it's *you* who is quite powerless – and me who can do anything. Anything I like. Who'd have thought it? So now, out of the two of us, who might benefit from offering an apology?'

⌒

'It could be the title of a thriller that, "What the train driver saw!" I love thrillers, abbot, do you like thrillers?

'And the driver?' says Peter, impatience ill-disguised.

'She saw it all, like I said – she saw what happened. She was looking along the platform as the train pulled in, natural really, and she saw the figure in a red hoodie, caught her eye for some reason, perhaps a sixth sense – and then she saw the priest, next to them – well, in front of them, and then suddenly, she sees the woman pushing the priest in front of the train, pushing him onto the track, 'Oh my God!' she heard herself saying, and it's quite deliberate, she's certain of that, the push, I mean, and she's jamming on the breaks, but way too late, he's falling forward, he can't stop himself, falling in front of her and...'

'And she recognised the person – the figure in the red hoodie? She knew them?'

'Oh yes, she knew them! Well, they were hard to forget, because they'd buried her mother. I mean, it was the undertaker, she'd met them a few times, they'd been very helpful – though she hadn't been wearing a red hoodie then obviously.'

'It was a woman?'

'Oh yeh, it was a woman. She knew her. She says everyone knows her. Sandra Fenning.

⌒

Undertaking is not your average business. Peter is reminded again as he sits in Reception – glad to be warm, glad to be alive but a man walking knowingly into risk. 'It's a risk to get out of bed in the morning,' people say. But it's more of a risk to do what he now proposes.

He can see the world outside, through the large shop-front window; but knows also, he left it behind at the door. Whatever is happening out there on the street; whatever empires rise and fall, there's no sense of them here. It could be the 21st century – or the 17th. And who currently inhabits No. 10 or vies for power in Argentina – these things are of no consequence. For death arrives here; and all else dissolves.

Here is another world, only thinly related to normal; a world of particular calm, one might almost say a tomb – a sealed-in place, a zone where you don't have to say why you're here, for they know this already; their demeanour respectful and appropriate. In the High Street, no one can spot the bereaved; nothing marks them out. But in the undertakers, they are known before they speak; they need not explain. So tantrums will be allowed, as will indecision and tears; it's all part of the service. Changes of mind over the service sheet, uncertainties over the headstone, anger over the price of the coffin, foolishness over the flowers – such things are quite in order, madam, and handled with measured understanding.

'This is a most difficult time, madam. But rest assured you are in safe hands with Fennings. Your wishes are paramount.'

What the undertaker wishes for will be held in for later, until well out of view and some way from earshot. With the bereaved sent on their way, choicer language may be screamed and frustrations released.

'Mr Ludlow, bless him, is bothering the actual crap out of me!' Ephraim might mutter, before apologising to Sandra for his language.

'I can handle him next time, dear,' she says – but this will never happen. He will complain; but also keep control.

'I will manage Mr Ludlow, dear, it won't be a problem. But he does go on somewhat.'

Though all is quite calm in Reception today; piped music, anonymous as a lift, eases the strains of life away. It is so anonymous and so bland that Peter only notices it after five minutes of sitting there. It has somehow played without being heard; but Sandra is heard as she stumbles through the door, the bell rings, a rush of cold air, the strains of life in her shiny face; though hardly pleased to find the abbot waiting.

'Oh, it's you again.' She is sulky, like a teenager.

'I'm afraid so.'

'And I don't know what you're doing here. You seem to be *always* here!' She tries to laugh. 'You should be looking for the murderer rather than bothering us.'

The abbot stands up. 'I was hoping to meet your husband, Mrs Fenning – but if you yourself had a moment?'

She intensifies her bustle, busy with this and that; and then stops.

'Oh, well, I always have a moment, I hope!' She goes behind the desk to put down her bag.

'You certainly had a moment for Geraldine in her time of need.' The abbot cuts to the chase and mention of Geraldine has an effect. It both stops and starts her; brakes and acceleration, freeze and panic. There's terror there but there's always terror with Sandra, so what's new? Well, *Geraldine* is new – she might be the cause. Or is it the Reverend Hand, deceased on the rail tracks at Lewes? There are a couple of reasons to choose from. 'Which was very commendable, I'm sure,' adds Peter, not wishing to frighten her further.

'Poor girl, yes....well, one does what one can. You spoke with her then?'

The question is pointed; her face seems to point.

'I spoke with her, yes.' She remains safe behind the reception desk, and Peter returns to his seat beneath the poster advertising marble headstones – 'a lasting memorial, the ultimate in class'. 'She told me about your advice, of course.' Sandra is busy with paperwork, moving files around.

'I don't know about advising her, I don't know about that. I remember consoling her, poor girl.'

'Indeed. And advising her to go to the police – that's the advice I meant...after ten years of choosing not to; ten years of putting everything behind her.'

'Too long, much too long.' She speaks without looking up.

'You obviously felt it was the right moment and even offered to drive her to the police station. A very particular service.'

'Well...'

'I suppose some might say your advice was oddly-timed.'

'I don't know what you mean.'

'Given that you've known about the Reverend Hand for a long time now. Years, in fact. Some might comment on that, I suppose – the timing.'

'It was not *my* decision, abbot.' She's looking up now. 'It was never my decision for her to go to the police, no matter what some may comment – it was the *girl's* decision. Now if you have asked all of your stupid...'

'No, quite... I mean, I understand that, Sandra. I absolutely understand that. I'm not interested in "what some might say" – and neither should you be.' She nods in relief. 'We are grownups after all. How something looks from the outside is not always how it is on the inside. They can *speculate*, of course...'

'Oh, they do that all right!'

'But that's all it is, speculation; and frankly, if someone doesn't wish to report something, they can't be forced.'

'They certainly can't.'

Peter pauses again, nodding at Sandra's wisdom, as though profoundly helpful.

'And I presume you have heard the terrible news?'

She blushes. 'Terrible news? No, I don't think so. What news is that?' Her alto voice goes falsetto. 'Funny throat,' she says.

'That the Reverend Hand appears to have killed himself?'

'Oh, really?' Again, she loses control of her voice; the downward pressure to sound natural. 'Well, there's a thing; and there's a thing.' She moves more files. There's so much to do behind the desk. 'Hardly surprised, though, you can't be surprised,' she says, looking up. 'Suicide... well, you can't be surprised. I must tell Geraldine.'

'Oh, I think she knows.'

'You've told her?'

'I mean, we can't be sure it was suicide, of course. It's so difficult to be sure in these instances, as you will know, if they don't leave a note – and Ernest Hand didn't...which I think he would have done, don't you?' Sandra shrugs. 'He just had a ticket to Stormhaven in his hand, so he was coming here to see someone. Or that's how it appears. It would be helpful to know who he was coming to see... but who can tell us that, I wonder? It's a shame the dead can't speak.'

'Quite, quite – wouldn't get much sleep in this place if they were all a-chatter!' She likes her joke. 'So I suppose we'll never know, will we? But it'd make sense – the suicide, I mean, like you said, abbot...with what we know of the poor sod, it would make sense, wouldn't it?' She's nodding. 'Perhaps we'll never know for sure. Still, there are better men out there, I think so, abbot.' She starts re-ordering some more papers, so much paperwork. 'We'll not mourn Ernest Hand for too long, I shouldn't think so; there are better men than him.'

'Well, possibly, yes...but we will know, Sandra.'

'I'm sorry?'

'That's the good news that I bring. We *will* know what happened to the Reverend Ernest Hand. We'll know exactly what happened. I don't think you asked – but it all happened at Lewes station.'

'Oh?' She is shaking now.

'And we've been very lucky with witnesses.'

'At Lewes station? I don't know what a witness could see, really I don't. Must be hard to tell anything with all that pushing and shoving.'

Peter smiles sadly. 'Fortunately, Lewes is not Tokyo at rush hour; particularly not the Stormhaven line. But obviously, I wanted you to know of the death, Sandra, whether it's suicide – or something worse, perhaps.'

'You mean murder?'

'We can't rule it out.'

'Well, I need to go out.' She's coming out from behind the reception desk. The paperwork can wait.

'Of course, some fresh air...after the shock.'

Ephraim appears in the office doorway. Has he been listening?

'If I might just catch you before you go, Sandra? Would that be possible? You don't mind waiting a moment, abbot?'

'Not at all, I'll go through to the office. This space is for the bereaved. I don't wish to clutter it up.'

'Quite,' says Ephraim, 'how thoughtful... and I won't be a moment.' Ephraim follows Sandra out of the door onto the street. Peter goes through to the office, which like a church in a city, seems suddenly quiet; away from the anxious presence of Sandra. Though he will not mistake 'quiet' for 'safe', and he feels more vulnerable here, he notes this. He had held all the cards in his encounter with Sandra; but he holds fewer cards now, possibly none... and his battle plan is imperfectly formed, as all battle plans must be – for no one can predict enemy movements; especially true if you're not sure who the enemy is.

He looks around. His eyes note a record book not quite returned to its place; as though hastily shoved into place. The abbot looks closer. Down the spine it says *'Car Cleaning'* and inside, is the record of every time the car has been cleaned throughout the year. Here is an organised mind. Is such a book really necessary? Maybe it is, for the payments. And looking along the shelf, it is clear everything has its book. Record keeping at Fennings is hard copy only, and Peter glances inside the pages. It looks like Sandra or Ephraim have created the form, putting in the date and the funeral, followed by the time and Ralph's signature to indicate the cleaning work done. Flicking back, he finds Billy's signature there as well on occasion. Flicking forward again, he sees the funeral of Mrs Dowd, but turning the page, the date jumps a day. It's clear a page has been ripped out...meaning any cleaning done the day after the murder is not recorded, when every other cleaning is. This feels like panic, and therefore, revelation; in a methodical office, the book feels brusquely treated, not placed in an orderly fashion but *shoved*. He hears Ephraim re-entering the shop, and returns the book to the shelf. Is it possible that the missing page is in the bin? It is where haste would put it; and he has just seen what might be the missing page, scrumpled into a ball – when Ephraim enters.

'I'm so sorry for the delay,' he says, 'I just had to catch Sandra.'

'It must have been a trying morning.' He is irritated he didn't have time to reach the bin. He wants to get to the bin; but Ephraim's eyes are all over him.

'Obviously the news of the Reverend Hand's suicide is most upsetting, yes. Sandra is in pieces, of course; she cares too much, of course; it is almost a fault! I have just been comforting her but what can you do? We've known Ernest for a very long time, a marvellous man who takes a wonderful funeral, many have said so. I'd even said to him I hoped he'd take mine!'

Peter decides to go fishing. 'I heard he got a police caution early in his ministry. Do you know if that's true?' It was Banville's research which had discovered this. Tamsin must have been distracted or too unwell; it was an unusual mistake for her.

'Well, I didn't wish to mention it, abbot; but of course it's true, yes; poor old Ernest.' Fenning knows everything. 'It was when he was in his first curacy, near Worthing. One count of Gross Indecency – and they say the only reason he wasn't prosecuted was that he agreed to resign.'

'And did he?'

'Well, apparently so, that was a condition – but the dear Bishop of Chichester, wonderful man, forgave him his error, and appointed him to another parish almost immediately, after which Ernest didn't look back and enjoyed a most fruitful ministry, I believe. A marvellous gesture by the bishop, such a forgiving spirit. We have all done things of which we are not proud, have we not, abbot?'

'But a caution *is* an admission of guilt?'

'Oh yes, he had gone rather too far with one of the silly choir girls, he admitted that. He chose the honourable path and pleaded guilty. But a caution is viewed very differently from a prosecution – and the waters closed over the incident, like the waters of the Red Sea over the Egyptians, one might say, and he was able to carry on. So well done the bishop!'

'But he erred again at St Botolphs...with Geraldine.'

'Just another silly girl!'

'Who Sandra knows, I discover.'

'And we only have her word for it, the word of a child. Really!' *Oh good, he's getting exasperated.* 'Clearly, though, there was turmoil in the poor man to wish to end it in this way, leaping in front of a train! I would not myself leap in front of a train. Such a mess. And it's the suicides that are the worst, abbot – no funeral can hold the pain of these decisions. I couldn't help but hear a little of your conversation with Sandra.'

'Oh?'

'The camera above the door. And believe me, it was suicide.'

'You feel the need for a camera in Reception?'

'It's there to maintain high service standards, of course; to monitor performance, as I believe they say these days. But it is also there to protect us. Those in grief can behave in the most appalling ways, as if grief removes all rules of decency. We have had violence threatened over a service sheet correction. Tea?'

'That would be kind.'

'I would say "essential" on a cold day like this,' says Ephraim with a smile. 'Absolutely essential!' Peter hopes he will leave the room to go and make it. He would like to get to the bin; he needs that piece of paper. But the kettle is in the office, which Ephraim stands over as slowly it boils, only half turning for the tea bag and the milk. The work done, some milky tea is set before Peter, next to a large cactus in a pot.

'A gift from a dear customer after we buried her husband,' says Ephraim, noting the plant. 'She imagines, for some reason unknown, that we are collectors of cacti. Who knows how these ideas arrive in people's heads? My father was given Toblerone every Christmas for thirty years by a cousin, who misheard him. He had once said to her 'I have no such love for Toblerone' – but she heard only "so much love" instead!'

'Or perhaps she just didn't like him very much.'

Ephraim smiles angrily; a smile that precedes correction, like a teacher about to deal with a stupid answer. 'I think the former,' he says. He is not pleased at the idea of someone not liking his father. 'My father was something of a saint, and I don't believe his cousin was a vindictive woman. My family are not like that. But in the meantime, the cactus sits there waiting for deportation to some appropriate gulag. Now how can I help, abbot?'

Ralph appears in the room; he has heard voices, but his father would prefer him elsewhere.

'I am just speaking with the abbot, Ralph.'

'I heard about the Detective Inspector.' He is shocked. 'Wouldn't think a woman like that would have a heart attack.'

'We all need to look after ourselves, Ralph. You probably feel immortal, the young tend to!'

'Not those brought up by an undertaker.' Ralph hits back.

'The good news is, she's on the mend.' Peter intervenes. 'How did you hear, by the way? It's not well known.'

'My father told me!' he says, as if it's obvious.

'*Mea Culpa*, abbot,' says Ephraim. 'I'm afraid it goes with the job. We are told everything here in Stormhaven. It is as if we have a network of spies – quite unintended, of course. But everything is reported. Some call it gossip, but I prefer to think of it as people sharing their concerns. Wouldn't you say so, abbot? But it's very good news that she is on the mend. An intruder in her home, apparently.'

'I want to take her flowers,' says Ralph. 'Could I do that?'

Ephraim offers an indulgent smile; and then decides more is needed. He gets up to hug him and Ralph stiffens in the grasp.

'Such a sweet thought,' says his father, pulling away a little, though still holding him, at arm's length. 'But I think the flowers can wait, they really can. And in my experience, hospitals are not particularly keen on flowers, lovely though they are – medical reasons, no doubt, even if they can appear as horrid old killjoys. And now you must leave us for a moment, there's a good chap.' He pats him on the arm a couple of times, a form of dismissal.

Ralph looks at the abbot like a condemned man catching the eye of his wife in court...there's longing there. And then he's gone, back to his room. The door closes.

'Now where were we, abbot? Ah, trouble with your phone?'

'A little, I'm afraid.' Peter is having obvious difficulty.

'Call me old fashioned, and many have, but I can't be doing with those things; and your present struggle with technology only confirms me in my choice.'

'I have remembered to put it on silent,' he says, 'Not as easy as it sounds.'

'They are of the devil, abbot – or at least a close associate of the same.'

'I believe God uses them on occasion.'

Fenning shakes his head, he must sadly disagree. 'Now how can I help you? And how remiss of me not to offer you a biscuit with your tea.'

'All drunk, I'm afraid.' Peter points to his empty cup. 'I was thirsty.'

'There are worse things in life than addiction to tea!' says Ephraim happily. He seems suddenly cheered, removes the cup and after washing it, returns it to the tray by the kettle. 'So what brings you here, abbot? And if it's to talk about Billy again, I simply do not wish to do that, really not – I cannot tell you of my grief. Yet neither can I cry; I find myself quite unable to do so. I must put my own feelings aside and stay strong for Sandra and Ralph who miss him quite as much as I. Have you ever lain in a coffin, abbot?'

It is not a question oft asked.

'I used to sit with the skulls in the desert,' he replies. 'The skulls of those who had passed before us at St James. They were stored in the tower, and I'd go there sometimes and speak with them. I suppose it's a related activity.'

'Fascinating...I can imagine doing the same. Oh that the dead could speak more clearly! The things we would learn!'

'Indeed. It would be good to hear Billy's story. He'd speak with a very clear tongue.'

Ignoring him. 'I prefer the coffin as a meditation on the brevity of life... for it is so short, is it not? "The lyf so short, the craft so long to lerne" as Chaucer put it.'

'A tragedy that Billy had so little time to learn.'

'Indeed, indeed. And sadly we don't have long either, abbot, I must be elsewhere – so come with me, you must try one for size, you must absolutely try one – it will do your soul good.'

'Try what?'

'A coffin, abbot, a coffin! And we can talk. Yes?'

'Well, why not?'

'Most excellent.' Ephraim leads the abbot through to the back and into the coffin parlour, where various caskets lie empty, some lined, some bare. 'My father was a carpenter, of course, who made coffins as a side-line; until his side-line became his sole work. And so a builder who made occasional coffins, became an undertaker, who occasionally built. I don't think he was particularly pleased. It was him who gave us the Latin motto you see in Reception.'

'"Numquam Mori" – yes, I did wonder what it meant.'

'"Never say die." It was his little joke – he had a certain contempt for the people of Stormhaven. "They'll never know," he said. But I dropped the building completely; it was never for me.' He looks down at the coffin at his feet. 'Now this one is desperately cheap,' he says. 'We can do better for you, when there is need. But it's the right length and will give you an idea for now.' The abbot hesitates. 'Forgive me, but I can measure people for a coffin just by looking at them. It's a gift I have, if gift it is – and I measured you a long time ago. What a terrible admission! But it's my first thought on meeting someone: "Which coffin will take you?" So hop in, abbot, why don't you?'

Peter steps inside and lowers himself carefully down into the casing, which is some way from solid; clearly a money-saver but then every coffin is just firewood in the end.

'You can spend £15000 on a coffin if you wish to. Some do. Or you can spend £200 and get the one you lie in. I don't think the dead are too bothered, frankly – though that's not a line I use, as you might imagine. There's a very decent profit margin on high-end coffins...oh, and you can't take your phone with you!' says Ephraim with a smile, as the abbot is caught fumbling again. 'The screaming and wailing in hell, I suspect, will be less about the fire – and more about the loss of people's phones.'

'Maybe I am still in awe, having come to them late,' says Peter, now settled into the coffin's confines. 'But he's not called a smart phone for nothing. He is a very clever little fellow.'

'Quite so, quite so – but "clever" should never be mistaken for "desirable", abbot. Now let the dying begin!'

~

She can hear him; he's appearing in a dream.

'So how does it feel, Detective-Inspector?' He's by her bed, smiling. But why's she in a bed? 'Oh God, I'm beginning to sound like my shit ex-wife and I never wish to sound like her.' Should she be polite? Maybe that would be good. 'She always wants to know how people feel, God rot her soul. The whole therapy thing is a complete fraud, you do know that?' She nods, there's a man by her bed, she must be polite; she thinks she knows him. 'I mean, I remove a tumour and it's gone. What does a therapist remove – apart from the money in your account?' Tamsin smiles, he likes that, perhaps he's a nice fellow. She likes his joke. 'Are you awake?'

'Yes, I'm awake.' It is best to be polite.

'The fact that I could pull out the drips that are keeping you alive, Tamsin – and never be suspected of a thing? How does that feel? A perfect setting for a perfect crime, don't you think? If I *was* a murderer.'

Tamsin is now wondering if it's a game. 'I could scream,' she says, because now she's unsettled and she'd like to wake up. She is trying to wake up.

'Not for long, I'd move quite fast. And at the inquest into your untimely death, I'd call it resuscitation, which can appear quite violent. "I was so desperate that she should live, your honour!"' He pauses again, she's smiling at him; she's being polite. 'There would, of course, be an inquest, but it would all be good for me. Sudden cardiac arrest, surgeon takes quick action – sadly you wouldn't recover and I'll sound so remorseful the coroner will love me. "I'm devastated – if only I could have done more!" I'll declare and they'll tell me I mustn't blame myself; and I'll tell them, "If only it was so easy!" Oh, I'm looking forward to that already.' He's talking a great deal, she can't hear him now, but she must hear him, if she wants to survive, she must smile. 'I seem to prefer praise to blame, Tamsin – but you couldn't manage that, could you? You have to blame, I imagine you always do; and unwisely, along the way, you chose me. I really don't like blame.'

'It's not personal, James.' Use his name, that's a good one. If you want to please someone, you use their name, everyone knows.

'No, it's an *attitude,* Detective Inspector – it's there inside you...the desire to bring others down. Does it make you feel better? The victim gets smaller, and – what? – you get bigger? Is that how it works?' He stands up, the man by her bed stands up, he's checking outside, a cheery word with a nurse, he may be good, he doesn't feel good, but best to be polite, that's her mother talking, always be polite to men, they're violent. And then returns, standing at the end of the bed. 'You really are the fly caught in the spider's web and you know how that always ends. The web is just too strong.'

'We must talk about the baked beans,' she says though why she says that, she doesn't know. Why mention baked beans? That's embarrassing. Now he'll think her stupid.

'Is that what she said?' He does not seem bothered by the baked beans. This is good, she hasn't upset him. 'Once again, Tamsin, *Testis unus, testis nullus* – one witness is no witness. I heard an interesting talk on that recently – but then the abbot would know, he was there, I remember him, sitting at the front, licking the speaker's arse.'

'The abbot will know, yes.' It is good to speak of Peter. Perhaps he will be along, that would be good, she's waiting for him, where is he? It would definitely be good.

'Will know what?'

'He sees people.' She smiles again. This man will like the abbot, she can tell.

'The vague suspicions of a religious relic; a has-been punching way above his weight. I'm terrified. Are *you* terrified?'

She doesn't think she's terrified, though she isn't sure, but she's hoping the abbot arrives, because she may never see him again, which will be sad but perhaps this man will find him for her. 'Perhaps you could find the abbot?'

'And perhaps I couldn't!' And now he smiles and removes her phone from her bed. 'You won't be needing this. And it may disrupt the heart monitor, which wouldn't be good.' She's not sure about this but may be it is for the best. He seems to know.

'I'll leave it on the chair for you.' He's leaving it on the chair for her, which is nice, though she can't reach it, and she would like to reach it. 'I do so love surgical gloves, Detective-Inspector – they're so bloody handy. Sorry, medical humour.'

This is a joke, so it is best to smile, to be polite, though she's still looking at the phone.

'Of course, they protect the surgeon as well as the patient. And sometimes they only protect the surgeon. Are you sure you're awake?'

A nurse arrives and the nice man leaves.

'Everything OK?' she asks when they're alone. 'You've got the nice Mr Fairburn looking after you! Lucky girl!'

~

'You need to ring to arrange a session, Nick. You know that.'

Hallington stands at her doorway in Chyngton Road, unannounced and unwelcome. She didn't answer his calls, she chose not to; her mind was elsewhere and now here he is. Cathy is not keen on letting him in. Boundaries matter and he looks rough and disorderly.

'I just need to speak with you, Cathy.'

'Have you been drinking?'

'No.' *He has been drinking.*

'Not sure you should be driving.'

'I'm not. I'm standing here talking to you.'

'OK. What would you like to say?'

'Can't I come in? Don't I at least deserve that?'

'Have you been drinking?'

'What if I have?'

'You always need to pre-arrange, Nick. And we don't meet here anymore, you know that.'

She now hires a room in town, behind the hairdressers, to meet with certain clients – those she does not want in her flat. She has a counselling room, but feels the need to separate work from home. Nick had not been happy with this; but for the last three sessions they'd met in town. Not that they had gone particularly well; there had been an increasing sense of distance; passive anger.

'You said you'd be there for me,' he says but the words sound phoney to Cathy, like a line borrowed from a soap. 'You said you'd never turn me away, as long as I needed you.'

'And I'm not turning you away, Nick. We can arrange a time to meet, but it isn't now, and it won't be here. I'm not turning you away, but...'

'But what?' Hallington is now pushing forward, like the Lord of Misrule, pushing himself against the door. His solid frame is an assault weapon, sudden and strong, forcing the door back, forcing Cathy back, and she stumbles.

'You need to leave, Nick,' she says, breathing hard and recovering her balance. Nick stands before her in the small hallway. He closes the door behind him. It clicks shut and Cathy feels fear.

'Is that what you said to my dad?'

'Your dad? What's your dad...?'

'Is that what you said to him?'

'I did everything I could for your father, Nick, you know that...'

'Like fuck you did, you bitch! He said you did *nothing*!'

Now the rage is out, unleashed in the hall, no longer passive but launched like a strike, like a missile, like a rocket.

'There was no helping your dad, Nick.' Cathy is thinking fast, or trying to think fast, and she never thinks fast, but words are just coming out. 'He was a very unhappy man, a depressive; and the accusations against you, he heard about them and he found them very difficult...'

'Oh, so it was *my* fault? His suicide was my bloody fault, was it?!'

'It wasn't your fault, Nick, I'm just talking about triggers. He felt ashamed...'

He walks towards her and the hallway feels small. 'Shall we sit down and talk about this, Cathy?' He is calm again, almost civil, like the insane are; gushingly civil. 'I think we should sit down and talk about this. So let's do that.' He takes hold of her upper arm and indicates that she should move; that she should lead the way into the front room and he follows her inside. 'It'll be like a therapy session, Cathy, only I'm the one asking the questions.'

She is struck by the thought. The clarity is overwhelming and rolls through her like a mad wave, turning everything over and upside down.

'Did *you* kill Billy?'

~

'Now you must humour me, abbot.'

Peter is comfortable in the coffin, peaceful even. He'd prefer it if Ephraim stopped talking, he'd like silence most of all, but the undertaker has taken warmly to the Master of Ceremonies role, which he does for a living. Daily, he hosts 'the death show' that is a funeral, handling the players with a bow, a nudge or quiet word in the ear, the ceremony must go on; and a ceremony is what Peter now finds himself in.

'You're going to imagine the dying process, abbot, and I'm going to help you. How does that sound?' Peter nods happily. 'Sandra runs away from it, poor girl, she really does...she doesn't like death at all, not for herself, I mean. The death of others, and she's as happy as Larry – loves the drama, loves standing at the centre of other people's needs. But her own death? She will scream at the thought; no, really. She wakes at night, you know, and I send her to the spare bedroom. I can't be doing with the hysteria.'

'We know in our heads we will die. But that doesn't mean we've acknowledged or accepted the truth.'

'Have you accepted your death, abbot?'

'Probably not. I asked the desert skulls to help me, but I'm not sure they did. I still feel a little immortal.'

Ephraim shakes his head with the kind smile of a forgiving parent, allowing the childish nonsense.

'Sandra doesn't understand how things are and how they must be, abbot; that death must follow life...for each of us. But I believe *you* do, abbot – you know how things are, and right now, things are not good, because I haven't been absolutely honest with you.' A naughty but loveable admission. 'But bear with me, and the investigation will benefit, truly it will. We are going to solve this case, you and I.' He looks down at Peter. 'It is a strange feeling, to lie in a coffin, is it not?'

'Focusing, I'd say.' Peter wonders if his life will start appearing before his eyes; but at present, he's aware only of the trapping space he inhabits; a walling in, not felt in death; but a pressing truth when alive. He is held by the cheap wood panels, perhaps more than he'd like to be.

'And now the challenge! To feel what it might be like for your heart to stop pumping, your brain to shut down and your body to cease working. Can you imagine that, abbot?'

'Not when I have a murderer to catch.'

'Indeed, indeed, so much to do! But how about we pause and enter the abyss? How about we trespass into the forbidden lands and imagine what happens to the body after death. If it is cremated, of course – would that be your choice?'

'I think so, yes.'

'We start there then, and it is the most popular way, for those who do not wish to rot. Once in the oven, and the intense heat, the body turns quickly to ash, becoming almost nothing... a small casket of dust. "Cremated remains", as we call them.'

'As you mentioned.'

'And you will be in one of these, abbot.' He points to a small urn on the shelf. 'You won't take up a great deal of space in the world; much less than presently. Scattered somewhere. Any particular choice?'

'Perhaps by a tree. I'd like to feed a tree.'

'How lovely, yes. But it's a different story if your body is buried, of course – and there's still time to change your mind.'

'Choices, choices.'

'It is a slower process but perhaps less hasty, more honourable, the carcass rotting slowly in the ground, in its own time. Have you ever imagined that?'

'I was once buried, a previous case...'

But Ephraim is not interested. This is his show; he needs no side-kick with independent thought; there's no requirement for that now.

'The bacteria inside your body – including the friendly bacteria of the stomach, which helped you digest food while you were alive – well, this changes now. It's all change, I'm afraid, because they start to feed on your flesh, which always strikes me as a little ungrateful. But there we are, the selfish gene and all that! And the early stages of the rotting are the most horrid, because at this time, as you can imagine, the corpse still resembles what you were when alive, abbot – although the decomposing flesh does produce rather ghastly odours and colours. Truly nasty, believe me – as the corpse of William the Conqueror proved. Did you know about that? A lesson to all undertakers, of course. He was allowed to lie for too long after his death, unrefrigerated obviously, the corpse became bloated, his bowels swollen – which caused him, God help us all – to burst open when they tried to force him into the sarcophagus. A quite appalling stench was released, which no amount of incense in the church could cover. You will not be surprised to hear that the rest of the ceremony was conducted in a great hurry, with courtiers' noses buried deep in their ample sleeves!' Ephraim enjoys the image, a playful smirk across his pale face. He remembers his history teacher Mr Wickson, who taught him the power of an anecdote at the right moment; and while he'd taught him nothing else – a rather moral soul, too prone to judgement – that was probably enough. He would often use an anecdote to calm a customer, or to give them time to recover themselves; or simply to seal a deal: 'Oliver Cromwell famously demanded that he be painted "warts and all" which is all very admirable, in its way. But in death, we at Fennings believe one should be presented at ones *best*. We will, of course, wash and blow dry your dead wife's hair.'

'The rotting cadaver, abbot – whether royal and common, no distinction in death – is actually dangerous to other human beings because of the risk of infection. However lauded in life, and however often bowed to, no one wants you when you're dead. Sorry! And then, after a while, and with the passing of time – as William's courtiers discovered – the belly explodes and the flesh just rots away. The skeleton remains, of course, held together by sinews – no longer so terrible to look at. "The thigh bone connected to the hip bone" as it says in *Ezekiel*, but not for long, as the sinews rot and the skeleton falls apart into a collection of disconnected bones. Rather like your skulls in the desert. Still with us, abbot?'

'Still with you...though feeling a little faint.'

Ephraim continues briskly. 'Depending on the immediate environment – and they do differ obviously, the humidity of the soil etcetera – the bones then break down into molecules which join the soil, feeding plants and animals. The circle of life, as they say – was that the name of the film? Never saw it myself, more for kiddies probably, but a good title. The circle of life...and that's it, that's your future role, abbot...a plant-feeder! Once we walked this earth, so hale and hearty, "strutted our stuff" is the phrase...but now we don't. "We" are gone, whatever or whoever "we" were – ashes to ashes, dust to dust, abbot – sorry to be the bearer of bad news.'

'I have contemplated my death, Ephraim.'

'But perhaps you did not imagine it quite so *imminent*.' The abbot looks quizzical. 'It does focus the mind, death's imminence...though your mind may be a little un-focused now, due to the tea you drank.'

Peter remembers the tea; and the residue round the side.

'So you are the killer, Ephraim?'

Ephraim smiles. 'I kill and I don't kill.'

'I think I'm too tired for riddles; I was never good at crosswords.'

'The funeral arranger is also the murder arranger. That captures it rather nicely, I think.'

'Very well done, Ephraim...even from here, I can see that's very clever. I underestimated you.'

'Bless you, I value your praise, really I do. And yes, never underestimate Ephraim! People have been doing it for years.' His sweating face beams down, intoxicated with praise. 'You were a very worthy runner-up in 2016, very worthy...and a worthy runner-up yet again today. But the podium is mine.'

'I was too slow for you.'

'I'm amazed you're still awake, frankly; really I am. Billy was out like a light, dear boy. You're clearly made of sterner stuff, abbot, your desert training, no doubt.'

'The tea was disgusting.'

'It did have rather a lot of powder in it.' He chortles at the memory. 'I should use a measuring spoon; but it's sometimes difficult to organise in the moment, with the victim watching. I'm sure you'll understand.' He'd used even more on the abbot than he had with Billy. 'And, of course, Nick Hallington will find Billy's murder very difficult to deny...poor Nick.'

'Poor Nick?'

'The tragic death of his father at Splash Point, another suicide...I arranged the funeral myself.' He seems lost in the memory of that sad day; the pathetic funeral of a man who couldn't cope. 'And now those difficult, *difficult* rumours about Nick and the Under 16's...there will be no case against me, with the poor reverend now gone. Such a tragedy – but believe me, I had nothing to do with it, not that one, really I didn't. That was all Sandra, my dear wife...she took his killing on herself. But he was going to betray me; and was foolish enough to let me know – so he had to go, I'm sure you can see that. And Hallington might not mind, you know. He actually might not mind Billy's murder on his card. Well, it *is* on his card, he is the killer, after all – and he might think it worth it...I mean, he got what he wanted, did he not?'

'And what did he want?' Peter sounds very weak. 'And could you speak up? I seem to...'

'An eye for an eye and all that. Can you hear me now?'

'What do you mean, "He got what he wanted"?'

'"She killed my father – I kill her son," he said, which has a certain symmetry to it, a sort of justice. I mean, this is not a world where justice has any part to play, not in my experience – it's dog eats dog, it's every man for himself, but...'

'Cathy killed Hallington's father?'

'As I say, Cathy, I'm the one asking the questions.'

Tense as an abused dog, Hallington is playing 'normal' – or as normal as he can in Cathy's front room. He doesn't have a plan; but he does have his rage, years of it, bloody years of it; and he has come here to sort this out, he won't be messed around. But what this sorting will look like, he has no idea. Fuelled by drink he'll do what he needs to do and by all means necessary; he won't be messed with.

'You want to watch me suffer?' says Cathy. She isn't yet scared; he still feels like a client. He's bringing his rage into the room, but there's nothing new there. Transference – Freud's shocking and reluctant discovery – is a key tool in the therapists healing armoury. It is the way in which the client, unknowingly, makes the therapist a figure from their past and dumps on them the rage they feel towards the family member. Freud saw little value in it, but therapists since have used the negative energy as a key part of healing. 'So who are you really angry with, Nick?'

'It's always questions with you lot, isn't it? Always bloody questions, you can't help yourselves. Try asking yourself some questions.'

'I'm just trying to understand what it is you want. But perhaps you don't know what you want. *I* don't know what you want. And I don't know what your father told you...'

'No, I said ask *yourself* a question, Cathy – not me, ask yourself one, you bitch!'

'And what question should I ask myself, Nick?'

This throws him for a moment, but he'll give it to her with both barrels, he'll come out shooting, he'll destroy her, this is different, this isn't therapy – this is war.

'Ask yourself why you didn't care. Ask yourself *that*. Ask yourself why you didn't fucking care!'

'The question is a waste of time, Nick, because I did care.'

'Wrong fucking answer.'

'But true.'

She hasn't seen Hallington like this before. Perhaps he was pretending in their sessions. And now, as she thinks about it, he almost certainly was. *Oh my God!* Was he just after *her*? Had he been playing her along all this time, summoning up the courage for the big day, the final reckoning? She needs to fight back; but is it worth the risk?

'He told me you didn't care – that's what he told me.' Hallington nods his head, as if in agreement with his own lines; as if in applause. 'He told me you didn't fucking care, so why tell me that you did? Want to piss me off or something? You don't want to know me when I'm pissed off!'

'I do want to know you, Nick. And I did everything I could for your father.' *Stay calm, Cathy, stay calm. Keep him as a client. Stay professional even though your guts are heaving.*

'You *liar*...now you're lying.'

'Do you know what he told me, Nick?' She chooses his first name again. 'Do you really want to know what he told me?' Hallington just stares. 'He told me *you* didn't care. That's what he told me – '

He lurches forward; her hands move up to defend herself. He knocks them away and he's grasping her neck. She digs her hands deep into the sofa, then knees him in the groin – and he's rolling back, yelping.

'I'm sorry,' he says, getting up from the floor. He is shaking his head. 'Never strike a woman, I never strike a woman. That isn't me. I would never do that.' He's breathless as he sits back down on his chair; he sweats a great deal, the smell hits her.

'You just did, Nick. You attacked me. You struck a woman. Is this how you want to be?'

He is sheepish for a moment.

'You need to behave, Cathy, you need to behave.' He's leaning towards her again. 'You need to fucking behave – and he didn't tell you that, did he?'

'What about *you*, Nick?'

'What do you mean, what about me?'

'Do you need to behave?'

'You're dead, you know that.'

'Think about what you learned in therapy, Nick.'

'I learned jack shit in therapy. I was taking the piss.'

'No. You learned to notice your feelings rather than be kidnapped by them.'

'No, I just enjoyed watching you suffer three times a week, it was bloody worth it...well worth it. Remember how I kept mentioning Billy, how I missed him. I watched your face... you just wanted to tell me to shut up about it sometimes, I know you did...made me laugh, that did, you bitch. An eye for an eye and a tooth for a fucking tooth.'

'If your anger left you now, Nick, what would be left? You need to think about that.'

'More anger...more bloody anger! Does that answer your question? My anger could last twenty years, thirty years! I've got warehouses of the shit.'

'I just want to tell you something, Nick – and this is for your sake, not mine.' Nick looks puzzled. For the first time, he feels some power removed, authority draining away. He wants it back, he wants the power back.

'What do you want to tell me, bitch?'

'I want to tell you, that if you attack me again, I will kill you. That's all.'

'Kill me?' He laughs at the thought, a repressed snigger.

'I don't want to kill you.' She speaks slowly and deliberately. 'I wish a long and happy life for you. But if you attack me again, Nick, I will kill you. So that's a choice.'

'I think you might be forgetting something.' His body expands again, the sweat glistening on his chest hair; his muscles, grown in the gym, move like lazy rats beneath cloth. 'I could have killed you five minutes ago...you won't be so lucky next time.'

'So let's not have a next time. Depart in peace.'

'Depart in peace? It's that easy, is it? Depart in peace? Do you understand *nothing?* '

'Sometimes when we surf the wave of anger, it's high for a while and then we find the wave weakens...and when it weakens, then it's time to take stock, to pack away our board and go home. The wave has weakened now. Make the most of it, Nick. Go home.'

'You haven't apologised for your lie.'

'What lie?'

'Your lie about my dad. He never said I didn't care; he wouldn't say that.'

'Do you really think I'd make that up? Do you really think that helps me in this situation?'

The silence that follows is a terrifying quiet, a threatening absence of noise. It is like the quiet of the volcano before larva bursts and flows, before some thing, no thing... no words between the stillness and the charge across the room...such immediate snarling force, Hallington comes at Cathy.

~

'Did you not know, abbot?' *If hubris could kill, Ephraim would be taking his own funeral.* 'Nick knows it. He firmly believes Cathy killed his father. She didn't actually put the knife in, obviously; but the man needed help and there she failed. Or so he believes. You do seem a little bit behind the rest of us, abbot; quite some way in fact. You must die in the dark, it comes to us all.' Peter remains trapped in the coffin, Ephraim Fenning standing over him, a looming figure. 'How was the tea?'

'It was too milky.'

'Too milky? I like it milky myself, more comforting, I find.' *Still hungry for is mother.* 'And now you must sleep.'

'I believe I shall.' The abbot closes his eyes, only to open them again. 'But before I do' – and now he whispers, barely able to talk – 'Please help me to understand, Mr Fenning, because you are so clever, please help me to understand...' Ephraim bends down, he leans in to listen to the fading sentence, his aftershave mixed with delighted sweat. He's smiling.

'What exactly would you like to understand, Peter?'

His face exudes benign victory, as the abbot's fist smashes upwards, catching the bottom of the chin and a little of Fenning's soft neck, sending him falling back and choking, the abbot's tense body splintering the cheap ply, it knocks the undertaker back, coughing and tumbling in shock and surprise – and the abbot is up, gathering his habit and out of the coffin, violent resurrection, death postponed...and Fenning cannot believe his eyes.

'But –'

'I didn't drink it, Fenning,' he says, kicking the undertaker hard in the thigh, a dead leg, to stop him rising; and then he's on top of him, such extreme energy in his body, as if it's been saved there all his life for this moment. His hands are round the undertaker's neck, and then, fearful he may kill him, he pulls back, grabs his left arm and flicks the undertaker over onto his front, forcing his arm up behind his back. 'Like I said, it was too milky. The cactus might be feeling a little drowsy – but I'm not. If only you'd thought to ask how I liked it.'

'You're hurting!' screams Fenning. 'Are you a madman or something?' He is still choking, his thinning hair all over the place, and the abbot is aware of Ralph. He has appeared in the doorway, watching; though maybe he has been there all this while, Peter can't be sure. But this could ruin everything.

'Get him, Ralph!' shouts his father; though his voice is damaged. 'Deal with him! He'll destroy us! All of us. He has come to destroy us.'

And Ralph, like an obedient dog, moves slowly forward.

~

Cathy sees Hallington coming, in slow-motion, in fast-motion, across the room. She's ready for impact, ready for the assault and she's ready and not ready, you're never ready – the wind knocked out of her, the first hit, no going back, he's holding her down, pinning her shoulders so the right hand must work, it's the last chance for life, feeling the pain, nauseous pain, lifting her arm, the right hand must work, she must stop the beast, she must stop the beast, bloody hell, this man murdered Billy! –

~

Ralph stops two yards from the struggling adults on the floor.

'Get him, Ralph!' Ephraim squeals, trying to wrench is arm free. 'He will destroy us, I tell you; everything we've built, your mother and I!' Peter half-turns in anticipation, expecting trouble, he cannot fight them both, and the large frame of Ralph is moving towards him, with uncertain eyes. It will be hard not to obey his father...and then he stops, and stands over them both. He bends down and he's crying... he's beginning to sob and he can't speak.

'We don't need a cry baby, Ralph; we need a man, a proper man. Man-up for God's sake!'

But Ralph wipes the tears from his eyes with his sleeve, and gently places his hand on his father's head. It seems to still him for a moment, in shock – 'What are you doing, boy?' – and Ralph talks quietly.

'*You* destroyed us, dad. He's not destroying us...you destroyed us. You did that all by yourself... when you raped Billy.' And then he is crying again; he withdraws his hand and turns away. He rises, moves towards the door and looking back briefly, as if he cannot bear this scene – he walks out.

'Call the police, Ralph,' says Peter quietly. 'Please call the police.' But he hears no reply and has questions of his own. 'Now what were you saying about Hallington, Ephraim? What was the deal between you? You will tell me.'

He forces Ephraim's arm further up his back, the undertaker squeals.

'*Testis unus, testis nullus*, abbot – one witness is no witness, I saw you at the talk, most interesting...and you remain a most deluded fool, unable to see what is before your eyes. Now be a good man and refrain from this obscene violence. Ralph needs help.'

24

The abbot is safe in his study, and at the heart of his safety, the solitude – the fact that he is alone. There is no peace to compare with this. Sometimes people would ask him if he's lonely having left the monastery community to live by himself on the seafront. 'You must get a bit lonely, abbot; I'd imagine you must. Miss the hubbub and all that.' But they imagine wrong. They imagine for themselves, but not for Peter. 'Loneliness is being unhappily alone,' he would say. 'Solitude is being happily alone. And of the two, I know a great deal more about the second.'

It is dark outside, a wonderful dark; the darkness of absence; and he's enveloped in an electric blanket, which continues to be the best Christmas present he has ever received. There is a whisky and ginger beside him...and memories.

He remembers a picture of Charles Dickens at his writing desk; he once had the print, with a gathering of his characters in the air around him, an assembly of the tragic and the joyful, the harsh and the hurt. And it feels like that tonight, as the dust settles on the Splash Point murder of Billy Carter – a death which became another, and then another... and then another still. It was a hungry death, this is what Banville called it, 'a hungry death, abbot,' and he was right – a death which couldn't be sated.

He'd never known Billy; though in a manner, he knows him well and he is surely the star of this story; though a star who left the stage almost before the curtain lifted; before the play had even begun. The star who wasn't there – and yet remained there throughout the show. But before going, before the first act, he had left a note in his bedroom. Was it meant to be seen? Who can say? It was the scribbled note of one witness, *testis unus*... and in many ways, an unreliable voice. He was a dreamer, after all; though with hindsight, it had been the truest voice, with Billy the truest witness. And the note made all the difference.

Billy died at the age of nineteen without finding a fixed address in himself or the world, preferring the young comfort of impossible dreams. Had he lived, he might not have been happy: who is, in this world? But he would have known happiness; he would have had the *chance* to grow joy, had he not been so harshly pincered by the rage and guilt of others; trapped in a moment, in a coincidence of depravity, when it suited the critical two that he should die. He had been tortured on that cold quay only that his mother might suffer for the rest of her life; and that Ephraim's secret might stay hid. His death had been a means to other people's ends.

As Peter had discovered from Ephraim, Billy had told Hallington about Ephraim's abuse. He had had to tell someone; he needed a witness and Hallington listened to his story and sat on it, until the moment came when the knowledge served him; when he could use it to twist Ephraim's sad little arm. It was Ephraim who lured Billy to the garage, who drugged his tea after the funeral. But from there, it was Hallington – Hallington who wished to be the big 'I Am', driving the hearse through the night, 'feeling like the cock of the walk' as he'd boasted to Cathy. 'The cock of the fucking walk! And your little boy in the back!'

Mrs Truelove was also Hallington's work – tipped off by Ephraim, of course. Ephraim didn't himself like the violence; he found it rather distasteful. He was angry that her death was deemed necessary, 'not an unpleasant woman, Mrs Truelove;

a busy-body but not an unpleasant woman.' And all because of Hallington's insistence on the hearse. 'The hearse was quite unnecessary; really it was'.

But that was Hallington for you. He didn't like other people's rules. He needed a show, needed the power, needed the vengeance; there wasn't room enough in the world for his vengeance. Did he also want to nail Fenning, should anything go wrong? The hearse would rather lead things back to him.

They were busy trying to nail each other, thinks Peter, as he looks out into cold darkness. He is enjoying his whisky. It slows him, softens his perceptions, which can start out with a granite edge, critical and hard like a machete. Though he is soft towards Cathy. He likes her style; a rather brave and impressive soul. And Chief Inspector Wonder doesn't think she'll be charged.

'You can use reasonable force to protect yourself or others, if a crime is taking place inside your home.' He'd explained this to Peter. 'And there's absolutely no question that a crime was taking place, no question at all – there is clear evidence of assault. So the victim can protect themselves in the heat of the moment; which includes using an object as a weapon.'

'Even a knife?'

'Yes, if that's what is to hand. I confess, I'm not quite sure how it was to hand; unless their cutlery arrangements are unusual. Clearly not a woman to mess with.'

And the knife *had* been to hand, because she didn't clean very thoroughly; or, at least, not down inside the sofa, where everything remains for years; and sometimes for generations. And so the blade had remained. It had stayed there since her married days, when a weapon had needed to be there. It had sat there, year after year, quiet amid the padding, until discovered in terror, grasped in the fight and used during an assault.

'There's no clear definition of "reasonable force", that's the thing, abbot – it depends on the circumstances.' Wonder was now sounding very like a policeman. 'If you only do what you honestly think is necessary at the time, then that's within the law. And Cathy was being attacked, no question of that; and attacked violently, marks all over her body. What else could she do? There can be no charge.'

Hallington would not be greatly mourned, having died from wounds to the neck. If you die insanely assaulting a woman, the mourners will compromised, awkward in their grief. 'He has been through a difficult time,' they will say. 'That's not the Nick Hallington I know.' Every tyrant is grieved by someone and Nick would be mourned, mourned in some manner – because while everyone else was leaving youth work, and going into HR or Brand Consultancy, he'd stayed. He'd stayed to get kicked and abused by both parents and young people alike, until his own grief, guilt and rage fused in madness of the most terrible kind. Unfortunately for Hallington, Cathy had lived with a man equally intent on control, long before she knew him – and she'd learned to be prepared. So Cathy would need a new sofa, for the old one was too soaked in the youth worker's blood to continue. And no doubt when it arrived, there'd be a knife tucked down the side somewhere...

Or maybe she'd decide, from here on, no knives.

Peter gets up from his desk. He turns off the heater and taking his whisky, goes through to the front room, perfectly sized for one. He's waiting for the phone call; it's the uninvited guest in the room, the sick elephant in the corner, the waiting and the wondering. He places a couple more logs in the burner; it can't have enough fuel tonight. He pulls the chair a little nearer the flaming window and wonders if Sandra and Ephraim, twenty-eight years married, now share a prison. They'll be on remand in Lewes gaol and a shared cell seems unlikely – though a catch-up might benefit them both.

Overtaken by events, he'd hardly thought of Tamsin; but he thinks of her now; and she's safe and in quite the best place; though she doesn't want to see him.

~

Tamsin is awake after an unsettling dream, a man by her bed, and while the dream is gone, the unsettled feeling remains, one of extreme vulnerability. Dreams can do this.

She has seen no one for a while, the corridors quiet, eerily so. Occasional steps, occasional voices. But the present epidemic is straining the service – doctors diverted by need, nurses drafted into ICU, shifts altered, A&E awash with people who shouldn't be there but have nowhere else to go. So the Detective Inspector can wait – she's in recovery, she'll be checked on later, she can really be no one's priority; though that is not quite true.

Because James Fairburn, Rodmell's feted surgeon, has finished his shift, found himself a fresh pair of surgical gloves and has unfinished business to attend to.

Healing work, he says to himself as he strides down the corridor...healing for him, at least.

~

The abbot now has a fair picture of events.

Banville, his new hero, had followed Sandra when she left the abbot, and, after a brief visit to the bank, she was picked up in Newhaven, waiting to board the ferry, with a sizeable slice of the company funds in her pocket. What she was planning to do was hard to fathom and maybe she didn't know either. 'I was just planning an adventure,' she told police. 'No harm in an adventure, is there?' But she had known there was trouble after hearing of Billy's death. 'Of course I knew,' she said, almost triumphantly. 'I knew something wasn't right!' She is suddenly talkative, the can opened, like a fizzy drink hissing.

She remembered Ralph cleaning the hearse at seven that morning, the morning after, while Ephraim hovered. It had been cleaned the evening before, so why cleaned again now? What had happened in between? There hadn't been a midnight funeral, she knew that much! And Ephraim never changed a routine; a change of routine was a blasphemy. And so her anxious energy, (not her words) was turned towards deflection and cover-up, though for who, she hadn't been sure – for Ephraim...*for Ralph*? She had listened in on the phone call between Ephraim and Ernest. Ernest was coming over to talk to Ephraim; he was going to expose him and take the consequences; he was going to break the circle of silence. 'I can't live with myself anymore!' he'd said. And while Sandra was not in favour of things done so long ago – it hadn't been right, she knew that – it was long ago and a different time. Things were different then. So Sandra had quietly left the office to Ephraim, taken a train to Lewes and ensured that the reverend wouldn't have to live with himself anymore; an act of kindness, in a way.

'I was doing him a favour really. That's the long and short of it...doing him a favour, I was. What sort of a life did he have ahead of him?'

Ephraim had not known about his wife's train trip to Lewes. He had known only that Billy couldn't live; that if he was speaking of things he shouldn't speak of, things which were not helpful to anyone – and to Hallington, of all people! – then he would have to go, it would be better that he die. Billy had told Ernest as well, a while ago; but Ephraim knew too much about the dirty old reverend to feel threatened by *that*...until the phone call.

And it was sad about Billy; it gave Ephraim no pleasure, absolutely not. But he was Stormhaven's *Man of the Year* and a much-loved member of the community, serving the bereaved with meticulous care, 'managing the deceased' was the technical name – not something which could be said of young Billy Carter, who had always been a questionable influence on Ralph. And he, Mr Fenning, was not one to be taken down by someone like Billy. 'One must protect purity, abbot, one must always protect purity and protect it well – it cannot be dragged into the mud by guttersnipes. Do you believe we must protect purity? I'd imagine you would.'

'Imagine starting again, Ephraim. It's your only hope.'

~

The flu epidemic is a bonus. Not for those gasping on ventilators obviously; but maybe there needs to be a cull occasionally? There are a lot of people in Brighton, and many of them unsatisfactory; this is Fairburn's view as he makes his way along quiet corridors, away from the front line of the ICU, the hospital now a perfect setting for murder games by a concerned surgeon. And he is concerned – concerned at the way she'd attacked him and his reputation, for there is no inbetween, he *is* his reputation, so he can hardly forget it, hardly release it from his head, it is all he knows, the rage and the shame, the shame and the rage – no therapist can get rid of those.

His father had been a disappointing man; a doctor who preferred his patients to his family; and seemed always to be hiding when at home, avoiding wife and children, a distant and irrelevant figure. He forgave his patients everything and his family nothing. His patients could abuse their bodies in whatever way they chose; and he'd always find a kindly pill or doctor's note. But his family? They never did right, they were always to blame. So Fairburn had taken charge early in life, and the more he did, the more his father retreated. His patients still loved him; but his family ignored him. In his home, growing up, James was in charge, almost a dictator; and he was in charge again now.

'It's not personal,' she had said, as people do. 'It's not personal. We're simply pursuing inquiries.'

But Tamsin's death would be personal because he'd been personally hurt. And it was almost a gift, from start to finish – her collapse in her flat, his oversight of everything since, a distracted hospital, Tamsin wired up and vulnerable – this really was the time; he'd never get another chance like this. 'A time to kill and a time to heal,' said Ecclesiastes.

True. And this was the time to kill.

~

Peter sips his whisky and smiles at the memory. "A bloody good job, mate." Those had been Wonder's words. He'd actually said that! "'A bloody good job, mate!" The whole wretched crew nicked or dead, which suits me very well... very bloody well. A nest of vipers, that lot, eh?'

'One viper attracts another,' says Peter. 'Our company reveals us.' Though he'd been quick to deflect the praise, sending it like an arrow towards Banville, who had shown him how to record a conversation on his phone.

'Banville?'

'A diamond from Dorchester, if I may say so, Chief Inspector. I mean, where to begin? He instantly thought to speak with the train driver... effortlessly IT literate... and a helpful spirit, which cannot be over-praised. I couldn't have done it without him. If he's a dinosaur, then it's we humans who should become extinct.'

Down the years, the abbot had received nothing but hostility from the Wonder. He had been made to feel, at best, an irritation, and at worst, a downright charlatan, with Tamsin as the medium for his dis-favour.

'He always wants you off the case,' as she once encouragingly explained. 'I think it's the habit.'

'Well, it *is* the habit, we know that.'

'It is the habit, yes. It's definitely the habit. Do you really have to carry on wearing it?'

And he knew the jokes about getting back to 'good old 13th century policing'.

But like a break in the clouds when the sun shines through, Wonder has softened. And the hospital said they'd ring as soon as they knew anything about Tamsin – but since when did hospitals ever have time to ring? That any hospital worked at all, on any given day, was an entire, if expensive, miracle. Given the numbers of staff off with stress, (and the other staff waiting their turn,) they didn't need him pestering them for news, especially with the flu thing. The *Royal Sussex* had a queue right now, and he was right at the end of it... though he wished to pester them, because he did want to know. And he wanted news of life tonight, and not death.

Though what Ralph wanted, who could say? He remembered Ralph's terrible choice among the coffins, between a stranger and his father – not a choice a young man should have to make. He had chosen the stranger; though really, he'd simply been choosing the truth, which must, in the end, have its day, even in families. At what cost for the boy, though? Ephraim would face a judge in court, and not a forgiving one, with both child rape and conspiracy to murder on his card. But he had faced his harshest judgement already – the judgement of his son, when he bent down and said quietly in his father's ear, 'It was you who destroyed us.' And Ralph, as well as Ephraim, would have to live with that.

'I'm not saying you did the right thing, Ralph,' the abbot had said the day after the arrest. 'I mean, I'm *glad* you did what you did, I am a beneficiary. But you did what you *had* to do, that's all I can say. If you could have done anything different, then you would have.'

'I did what I had to do.' Ralph nodded in agreement as he spoke and seemed relieved.

'I couldn't have blamed you if you'd struck me down. And I thought you would, to be honest. But you didn't, because your truth wouldn't allow it...you could do no other.'

Ralph was breathing deeply.

'It felt all right,' he said, as if to reassure himself.

'It may not always feel so.'

'I'm so relieved!' The words burst out, like an exhalation of air and he started to cry. He could barely speak, his throat constricting, as if trying to silence him. But he wouldn't be denied. 'And is that allowed? Is it OK that it felt all right?'

How it would now go for Ralph and Cathy, the abbot didn't know; and the offer had come as a surprise. But in a rather business-like manner, Cathy had offered him a home in

Chyngton Road – or at least a bedroom, while he sorted things out. The Fennings had lived above the shop in Stormhaven and now there was no shop, its future uncertain, there was also no home. And Ralph had jumped at the chance, in a restrained sort of way; but feeling more joy within than he showed, because he'd always envied Billy his mother. You knew where you stood with Mrs Carter, you could talk with her – about *anything*. Literally, anything.

'You don't know what you've got there,' he'd say to Billy; and Billy just laughed at him.

'You don't fancy her, do you Ralph? That's gross!'

'I don't fancy her!'

'That's gross, Ralph. She's my mother!'

'I *don't* fancy her!'

He hid in his room and played his games because his father was a paedo and his mother an anxiety ball. He hoped he wouldn't always have to hide in his room. And what a great view from his bedroom window, across Stormhaven's famous cliff top golf course! Not a headstone or hearse in sight!

He'd had enough of coffins. He wasn't going back.

~

'It's going to be a cardiac arrest, by the way. Will that suit?' Fairburn smiles at Tamsin.

She heard him coming. She heard the footsteps, his expensive shoes clicking their way down the corridor, until pausing at the door. He didn't knock – he was a consultant.

'Cathy was right about one thing. I mean, she was wrong about most things but right about this. It is my father who is the trigger; and you are just like my father.'

'I'm a woman.' This is like her dream and for a moment, she wonders if she's back there. But this is real, surely?

He smiles. 'You are a woman, Tamsin; and despite your behaviour, I'd still have you. There's so little gratification in the world; it must be taken and enjoyed.' He smiles again and sits down in the visitor's chair. 'And wives don't like that, of course. They don't understand. But in the end, man or woman, I would need to kill you. To honour his memory, so to speak – the memory of a disappointing man who was better off dead. And we certainly were. He only had blame, you see, that's all he could do; which meant all *we* had was shame. And that's your game exactly. Blame and shame, you don't care, you really don't. So maybe this sacrifice is for the best, to give it a positive gloss; for maybe that will then be that, I'll be free; free to start again. That would be good. You die – that others might live. I've always felt there was something in that whole Good Friday thing. But someone *does* have to die.'

'Why does anyone have to die? Your father is dead.'

'But not forgotten.'

'It's over for God's sake!'

'*Over?* You're very stupid, Tamsin. But I'm decided – a cardiac arrest it is, that will be simplest. I came in when I heard you struggling – did all I could, but – well...and I'll be gutted, as you can imagine. "I only wish I could have done more," I'll say. I'll be a bloody hero in my failure; and while you won't be smelling so good – decay truly stinks – I'll be smelling of roses! And really, that's all I ever wanted – to smell of roses. Now I'll make this as quick as I can -'

⁓

The doorbell rings and Peter is surprised; the east wind is murdering the seafront, a howling freeze, it's no time to be out. But just in case it's an angel, Peter crosses to the door and opens it a little; and there, wrapped for the arctic, is the cold body of the Chief Inspector.

'Room for a small one?' says Wonder, who isn't small at all. 'A bit parky and I don't mind admitting!'

'Come in,' says Peter, if only to get the door closed; and with the Inspector inside, the space is suddenly filled. 'You probably don't want me to take your coat.'

'Tamsin did say it was always cold here.'

'Yet she keeps coming back.'

'Is she OK?'

'I haven't heard.'

'She's not answering her phone. It's probably been taken away from her, which is all for the good.'

'She's not answering?' Sudden fear; a force through his body. *Let go of my phone? I wouldn't do that for anyone or anything.*

'No.'

'Where's your car, Chief Inspector?'

25

~

'We need to see her,' says Wonder on arrival. 'This is now a police investigation,' though it wasn't – more of a hunch, really; but a hunch that was scraping his nerves.

'It may be nothing,' Peter had said in the car, and then they'd received the text. The Chief Inspector parked in a vacant ambulance bay, someone wouldn't be pleased. 'Police!' he shouted to anyone listening, and they were soon past reception, Wonder waving his card and aftershave around, like he was Head of Drama back in Skegness. He may be enjoying it.

Peter's moving at speed down the corridor. But towards what? The last time he saw her, he'd been dismissed from her room, a barrier placed between them, a high wall, declaring no more visits. And now the text; she needs to see Peter. 'No one else will do. Quick! Quick!'

And to be honest, no one else will do for Peter either; he knows that he needs Tamsin alive; the possibility of her loss has made this clear. He had not invited her into his life, by no means; and neither had he gone out looking. Indeed, he had done quite the opposite, closing his door to relationship at every opportunity down the years. Tamsin had just arrived at his front door one morning; and never quite gone away.

Everyone needs a family, a place where they belong in some manner. Peter had left his adopted parents at the first opportunity and been relieved to do so; but he had never found a new family – though may be the dry stones of the monastery wall were something like that down the years. Robert Frost said that home is the place 'that when you have to go there, they have to let you in'. And although he had never visited her in Hove, and probably never would, he knew that he could...*if he had to.*

He needs her alive, he knows this now as he sits in the corridor waiting for matron. Is this really necessary? He has the focus of the insane, with only one thing on his mind. And now she approaches, disapproval carved into her face.

'Are you the abbot...for Ms Shah?'

'I am, yes,' he says getting up.

'You better come with me.'

'Is she all right?'

But sensing her power, matron won't be telling, walking briskly down one corridor and then another, her shoes clicking on the polished floor, until – until they both hear the screaming, a woman shouting, a nurse scurrying out of the room, looking flustered, as one who has had bad news and wondering what matron will think; while a male figure disappears in the opposite direction along the corridor, easing out of view. Peter pushes past the matron, runs along the corridor, enters the room and sees the terror.

'Oh my God!'

'He's been here,' says a woman who Peter doesn't recognise. 'Did you see him? He was here, just now – you must have seen him!'

'Can I have a word?' says the matron. She has caught up and she's insistent.

'If it's very quick.'

She takes him back into the corridor.

'We're concerned with her state of mind.'

'How do you mean?'

'She's talking nonsense, if you want the unvarnished truth. *Nonsense.* And sadly, it all sounds rather ungrateful – when Mr Fairburn as good as saved her. Well, he *did* save her, told us so himself!'

'I need a moment with her – alone,' says the abbot. 'We need to be alone.' He speaks with force, it seems to appear, like a hammer through the air and matron is taken aback.

'Don't be too long.'

Peter steps inside, shuts the door in her face and takes in the scene once again: the drips, the single hospital bed, the bed pan... and pale but sitting up, Tamsin, with eyes comprised of fear.

'He was here.'

'Who?'

'Fairburn. He came for me. He would have killed me but for a nurse turning up to take my temperature.'

'He "came for you"?'

'He was going to kill me.'

'OK. Well, he's not going to do that now.' *Is she all right?*

'If that nurse hadn't come in...I need to thank her; I really need to thank her.'

'Plenty of time for that; and you're quite safe now.'

'I'm not safe; I need to be out of here.'

'I'm not sure you can leave yet, Tamsin. You're still mending.'

'Then I want company, a guard on call outside my door.' Peter nods. 'It wasn't a dream.'

'What wasn't a dream?'

'I won't see that man again – not alone. Do you understand me? *Do you understand me, abbot?*'

Peter has never seen her like this. She is a shadow of someone, an occupant of some netherworld, reduced by weakness, diminished by fear. Has she truly lost her mind?

'Is this a dream?' she asks.

'No, this is not a dream. See?' He pinches her hand kindly. Tamsin smiles. 'But the nurse does say you're talking nonsense.'

The smile goes. 'The matron is an arse-licking acolyte of Fairburn, they all are, all of them. I needed a cleaner to give me my phone back. The bastard took it away from me.'

'Brave man.'

'I was *asleep*. And then he got his story in first. He said that I had lost it, that I needed to see a psychiatrist, that I was delusional, paranoid, whatever. Now, of course, everything I say is further proof of that.'

'Sow the seed...'

'Fairburn is a shit, abbot; and this is some kind of revenge – he's openly threatening me. Cardiac arrest.'

'I'm sorry?'

'Don't believe it.'

'Believe what?'

'I can't be left alone with him again, I really can't.' The desperation is there in her voice again.

'Has he tried to hurt you?'

'If the nurse hadn't come in just now, I'd be dead.'

'"Threaten his reputation, and he'll come for you." Cathy did say.'

And then he comes for them both. The door opens and Fairburn's face appears. Tamsin wilts; but the surgeon is all hail and hearty bonhomie.

'Oh, hello abbot! Come to see our lovely patient? Doing well, isn't she? And so sorry I had to rush off, Tamsin – another patient called and I forgot my stethoscope.' It's sitting on the chair. He collects it. 'A little loose in the head, obviously.' He talks in a conspiratorial manner; this is just for the abbot, a pastoral word in his ear – 'paranoid tendencies, seeing things, misreading things; but that happens sometimes after a big operation. Nothing to worry about – scars heal and delusions fade.' And now for the public. 'I'll check in later, Tamsin, when your guest has gone. I always have time for our Detective Inspector! Don't want you to be lonely!'

'I'll have him when this is over,' she says as the door closes.

'That's the spirit, Tamsin – revenge on your mind, you're clearly on the mend. But we will need allies, so I will let the Chief Inspector know.'

'Wonder?'

'We'll need him, with the hospital authorities lined up against us, as they will be. We bonded over Skegness.'

Skegness? She has no idea what he is talking about. 'It's still my word against his. The medical world's wagons are always drawn around their own.'

'They must have learned it from the police.'

'What was it? Testis unus...'

'*Testis unus, testis nullus*, yes.'

'And wasn't that where this all started?' She sighs, able at last to relax. Her breathing deepens.

'Seems a long time ago.' Maybe Peter can relax now too.

'Young Billy's note in his bedroom – and a dull evening at the Stormhaven Historical Society?'

'A very interesting evening, as I remember – and one you sadly missed. Feels like you've been playing catch-up ever since.' The abbot thinks back to the Crypt – the excellent heating and Melvyn Strutt in full flow, highlighting the difficulties of the single witness in court. 'It might be wise law, Tamsin – but it's poor truth. The single witness of Billy brought down a very nasty house – "a nest of vipers", as Wonder called them.'

'What happened?' She has almost forgotten the case. 'You need to fill me in. Who replaced me? Was it Sitwell?'

'There's time for all that.' *I replaced you.* She nods and they share a smile that draws on everything their relationship had come to be, without either of them noticing.

'We've had some adventures, haven't we?' she says, becoming tearful; in fact she can't stop the tears – though she would later deny the sense of joy in her words.

26

'I did say he'd come for you.'

Cathy has asked Tamsin to sit down and she has done, with due care. She is quite altered from her last visit to Cathy's home, still fragile in body and spirit.

'I heard about events at the hospital.' Tamsin nods cautiously. She cannot discuss those here. 'I have friends there; and the nurse who walked in on you when he was...and you were screaming accusations – well, it wasn't a story she could keep to herself. One coffee break is all it needs.'

'I can't comment, you understand. The matter is ongoing.'

'I understand. And whatever occurred or didn't occur, this is nothing to do with you. And I'll look a fool, no question – but I think it's the right thing to do... and as I say, done more for my sake than yours.' Cathy looks out on the golf course, her borrowed view. 'We spend so much time hiding what we were, don't we? To protect some image of ourselves, to keep people away from the less-than-impressive truth, when really, there's nothing to hide. What is there to hide?' Tamsin is tense; she has everything to hide. 'I mean, I'm a therapist now, competing in the market as some sort of wise person – but I *was* a woman who allowed a man to dominate me; a woman who allowed a man to feed me on baked beans for a week and said nothing, *nothing*, because I was afraid. I don't mention that in my advert.'

They sit in silence. Tamsin is wondering where this is leading. She's wishing she hadn't come.

'But I've said something now; I just wanted to let you know. It won't change anything – but who knows, perhaps someone said that to David when he was polishing his pebble before confronting Goliath? "I wouldn't bother with that, David! It won't change anything!"'

'Goliath?' *What or who is she talking about?*

Cathy smiles. Not every one has read the Old Testament, though that is one of the better stories. 'The local rag came and asked me my take on the hospital story – as his ex. They were just fishing really after the hospital rumours – but they seemed pleased with their catch when they left.'

Epilogue

He's almost ignores it. He's just too excited to read some e-mail from the worthy-but-dull John at the Stormhaven Historical Society.

Dear Melvyn,

I write to thank you for your wonderful talk the other night; it was much appreciated by all and sundry. Numbers disappointing, I know, but you certainly raised some very interesting issues!

I write also to apologise for the absence of payment so far. Unfortunately, the Crypt boiler has broken down again, and Maureen, the chair of the trustees, believes we may have been responsible when we left the building after your talk.

It seems I had misunderstood the instructions, so she is presently asking us to pay for the additional plumbing work necessary. Not an easy woman to deal with when it comes to money!

I'm sure the matter can be happily resolved, of course, but we presently have no funds for a rainy day, no secret stash, and so need to get this sorted first. We hope very much to pay you soon. We hope the agreed fee of £100 is still acceptable?

Though perhaps we will book you in the summer next time! And it may encourage more people to come and listen.

Yours historically,
John

And for once, Melvyn doesn't care, he really doesn't care – neither the disappointing turn-out nor absent cheque, they just don't matter anymore. And they don't matter because his life had changed this evening when he got in and opened the post.

The '*Royal Caribbean International*' logo on the crisp white envelope had set his heart a-racing. And once opened, it raced yet faster still. He'd got the cruise gig, next February! Oh my God! Two weeks touring the Caribbean islands with him as *Mr History* for the duration: a twelve lecture contract and he knows which one he'll start with, because even in paradise, everyone likes a brothel somewhere in the mix –

Testis unus, testis nullus.

An appalling night in Stormhaven is about to get so much better... though not for the surgeon, apparently. It's all very strange, but the reporter's on the news now, she's standing well-wrapped in a freezing Rodmell – and Melvyn hardly ever sees *News South-East*. They're showing a photo of him, it's up on the screen, and he knows him, the man from the Crypt, asking questions about underwear; yes, it is definitely him, because they spoke afterwards. So the surgeon lived in Rodmell, eh? Well, he would do, wouldn't he? And that's a bloody big house he had, so there's a lot of money coming to someone, because apparently this morning, early, the great surgeon did 'the Virginia Woolf walk' – his body found at lunch time in the Ouse by a dog walker. They find everything, don't they, those dog walkers? Good reason never to get a dog.

'There is a great sense of shock here in the village,' says the reporter, cold but clearly moved. '"A very decent man," was how one resident described him to me, while another commented on his "lovely garden. He always made sure that was looked after." A colleague from the hospital called him "a skilled surgeon and a man who ran countless marathons for charity. Our thoughts and prayers are with his family." James Fairburn has no history of mental illness and was a man with apparently everything to live for. So why this and why now? These are the questions the villagers are asking here in Rodmell tonight. And now back to the warm studio...'

  '*So no mention of the baked beans,*' notes Melvyn. He'd read the story just this morning in The Argus. The revelations of an angry ex – and seriously embarrassing for a high profile figure. But surely the two couldn't be connected?

  Who killed themselves for a can of beans, for God's sake?

The End